Behold, Darkness and Sorrow

Seven Cows, Ugly and Gaunt
Book One

Mark Goodwin

DEDICATION

This book is dedicated to the steadfast remnant in the Church, the true Bride of Christ, to my fellow brothers and sisters in the faith who have purposed in their hearts to stand for King Jesus, reject compromise, speak out against evil, and follow the Lamb, no matter the persecutions or consequences.

Who will rise up for me against the evildoers, or who will stand up for me against the workers of iniquity?

Psalm 94:16

ACKNOWLEDGMENTS

I would like to thank Dr. Peter Pry for his work with the EMP Commission in trying to convince federal and state governments to protect our country against the threat of EMP, and for educating the public on the nature of the threat.

I would like to express my gratitude to Rick Wiles and everyone at TruNews.com for their work in helping to spread the message of America's need for repentance and for providing accurate news presented in the light of prophecy.

Thank you to Nana, for all the love and fond memories down on the farm.

Thanks to my wonderful wife, best friend and editor-in-chief, Catherine Goodwin.

Thanks to Dutch Perry for his assistance with editing.

CHAPTER 1

And it shall come to pass in the last days, saith God, I will pour out of my Spirit upon all flesh: and your sons and your daughters shall prophesy, and your young men shall see visions, and your old men shall dream dreams. And on my servants and on my handmaidens I will pour out in those days of my Spirit; and they shall prophesy. And I will shew wonders in heaven above, and signs in the earth beneath; blood, and fire, and vapour of smoke.

Acts 2:17-19

Daniel Walker quickly tied his apron as he scurried to the point-of-sale system at the back of the restaurant to clock in.

"Danny, you're late again." Patricia Long, the night-shift manager of Lilly's, addressed his tardiness as she passed by with a stack of menus on her way to the hostess desk.

"Sorry, I had trouble finding a parking spot." Danny put on his best puppy-dog face and followed her to the front.

"As usual. You know parking is tight in Savannah, and you work on the river where there's no parking at all. You understood the conditions when you took the job. Plan accordingly."

"Yes ma'am. I'll be on time from here on out."

"I hope so. You're a good server, but I need people who can be on time. Lilly's operates like a machine. If one gear is missing, the whole operation goes off line. Get your section ready, I want to start seating you in ten minutes."

"Right away." Danny headed off to check his tables.

Lilly's was one of the busiest restaurants on the river. It served a fair-priced selection of fresh seafood and Southern cuisine. Much of the food was locally sourced, and every bit of it was prepared in-house. During peak season, all of the restaurants on the riverfront did well, but Lilly's stayed busy year round. That made it a good job for Danny who was working to pay his way through school. It was important for him to maintain his employment at this particular establishment. Sure, he'd have no trouble finding another restaurant gig in Savannah's historic district, but there were few others that could provide a steady stream of income like Lilly's. "I'll just have to start leaving earlier," he said in a low whisper as he shined the silverware laid out on the white tablecloth.

"Danny, you made it." Steven Lindsey, another waiter at Lilly's, patted him on the back.

"Yeah."

"What's wrong? Trish give you grief for being ten minutes late?" Steven picked up one of the water glasses on Danny's table and began to polish it.

"Yeah, I think her patience is wearing thin. I'm going to start coming in earlier. When classes start back, I'll come straight to work from school. I'll change clothes in the parking garage."

Steven laughed. "Just don't get arrested for indecent exposure. Then you'll be even later."

Danny cracked a smile and nodded. "I hate to pop this on you last minute, but you remember the days you were going to work for me Christmas week?"

"Yeah, what about it?"

"My sister's husband can't get off work that week, so she's coming down the week after Christmas. Is there any way you could switch out those shifts?"

Steven continued to help Danny shine his silver and glassware. "Then you'll be in Savannah for Christmas Eve? Why don't you and Alisa come to church with me?"

Danny got a sense that this was some sort of quid pro quo. While he didn't come out and say it, Steven seemed to be implying that his willingness to pick up those shifts were tied to Danny agreeing to attend church with him on Christmas Eve. "I would, but I'm not sure what Alisa will say. We'd already planned to spend Christmas Eve together. She's going to South Carolina with me to meet my sister and my grandmother."

Steven grinned brightly. "She's at table seventy-three taking an order. As soon as she's done, we'll ask her."

"Oh, sure." Danny had hoped he'd be able to cut Alisa off and cook up an excuse not to go to church before Steven got to her. He didn't want to offend him, both because he needed him to work those shifts, and because he genuinely saw Steven as a very close friend.

Danny followed Steven to the computer where Alisa had gone to ring in her order. He tried to catch her eye to deliver some type of sign, but she was focused on the screen.

Steven leaned against the service station. "Alisa, Danny said you guys are going to be in Savannah for Christmas, so we thought it would be nice if we all went to my church for Christmas Eve service. They'll have great Christmas music, candles; it's really pretty."

She glanced up from the screen for a second. "That's awesome! I'd love to. I love Christmas."

Steven looked over at Danny who was less elated. "Fantastic! It'll be fun. And just let me know which days you need me to pick up. Looks like I'm getting a table. Talk to you later."

"Thanks." Danny patted Steven on the shoulder as he walked away. It wasn't that he was afraid of church. Danny's grandmother had taken him and his sister to church when they were little, but he saw religion as a more personal matter, not something one did in front of others; not that he devoted much time to his "personal" pursuit of religion.

Trish walked up to Danny and handed him a bottle of champagne. "Table eighty-one is celebrating their twentieth wedding anniversary. The concierge at the Hyatt sent them. This is on the house. I gave them to you, because I know you'll take good care of them. You're one of our best servers, Danny. But you know it's not fair to the rest of the team when you're late."

"I know, Trish. I promise I'll do better." He took the bottle and smiled. Danny walked to the ice bin near the bar and filled a champagne bucket with ice and water.

Alisa walked up behind him and took down two champagne flutes from the glass rack overhead. "Are you still getting bawled out by Trish?"

"She just reiterated what she said earlier. But, it's her way of telling me to shape up or ship out."

Alisa filled the flutes with ice and water to chill them. "Two more years, and you'll have your degree. You'll be running some swanky old folks' home and raking in the cash. You'll be the one bawling people out for being late."

Danny was pursuing a Masters of Health Service Administration with a certificate in Gerontology from Armstrong State University. "I prefer the term 'upscale assisted living community' to 'swanky old folks' home,' but I hope you're right. And you'll be a famous artist."

Alisa chuckled. "SCAD was the most fun way I could get my parents to pay for me to get out of

Connecticut." Alisa's family had money, but they weren't about to pay for her to move away, get an apartment and live a life with no ambition. They had reluctantly agreed to put her through Savannah College of Art and Design. They paid for all of her necessities; tuition, books, supplies, housing, food and clothing, but she had taken the job at Lilly's to earn spending money, which they did not provide.

"You love to paint. I think you underestimate your potential."

Alisa poured the ice water from the chilled flutes into the sink and handed them to Danny. "I love art, but it's not a serious career, like old-peopletology."

"Gerontology. And thanks for chilling the glasses for me." Danny grinned. He really liked this girl.

"Whatever." Alisa fought back a blushing smile. It was obvious that she really liked him, too.

Danny took the champagne, the ice bucket and the glasses to his table. He wondered if some day, he and Alisa might be celebrating twenty years together. One thing was for sure, if they did, they wouldn't be staying at the Savannah Hyatt. Not that he had anything against the Hyatt. It was a very nice hotel, and he'd be happy to stay in one in most any other city in America. But in Savannah, there was a vast selection of beautiful Bed and Breakfasts available in the old homes built during the eighteenth and nineteenth century. Fine hotels were all over the world, but these one-of-a-kind homes were only in Savannah. Many of the luxurious homes, built in Federal, Georgian or Italianate architectural style, were situated on huge squares with towering monuments at their centers. In addition to providing green spaces throughout the historic district, the squares had a calming effect on traffic which had to proceed slowly around one-way streets laid out in round-about fashion to navigate the individual square parks.

Alisa's student housing was in one of the old homes on Bull Street which had been meticulously renovated by Savannah College of Art and Design. Danny loved the architecture, but he was putting himself through school and couldn't afford to live in the historic district. He lived in an apartment complex closer to work than school. It wasn't a great neighborhood, but several other students lived there, which made it safer. His commute to work from home was roughly ten minutes, but then he had to find parking and walk to River Street. His one-bedroom apartment was just off the Harry S. Truman Parkway, roughly twenty minutes from Armstrong State University.

The evening progressed and Danny's section filled up, as did the rest of the restaurant, but they never went on a wait. That was unusual for a Friday night. Danny returned to the service station to run a credit card for table eighty-three.

Alisa came behind him to close out a check from one of her tables. "I guess everyone is doing their last-minute Christmas shopping."

Danny replied, "Yeah, the restaurants around the mall are probably slammed right now. That's okay, I don't mind a couple of slower nights."

Alisa laughed, "I don't think anyone else would call this slow. But it looks like we might get out early. Do you want to head over to Moon River Brewing Company after work?"

Steven was waiting at the bar for two after-dinner drinks for his table. "We could head over to Leopold's. They're open 'til eleven."

Danny pulled the credit card receipt out of the printer and stepped aside to allow Alisa access to the computer too. "It's a little cold for ice cream tonight."

Steven put his drinks on the tray as they arrived. "Yes, but they have really good soup."

"And hot chocolate." Alisa pulled up the appropriate table's check on the computer screen and swiped the credit card.

"Leopold's it is then." Danny tucked the credit card receipt along with an ink pen into the check presenter and took it to his table to sign.

After work, Danny, Alisa and Steven walked the several short blocks to Leopold's. The air was cold and brisk, but it would have taken longer to retrieve Danny's car from the garage and find a new parking spot than to simply walk there from Lilly's.

As they walked, Danny looked around at the festive lights hung in the squares and the warm glow of the trimmed and lit trees in the windows of most every home. He held Alisa's hand inside his jacket pocket. "It feels ten degrees warmer once you get away from the river."

Steven walked on the other side of Danny. "Yeah, the buildings help to block the wind."

"It's a lot warmer here than it is back home in Connecticut at Christmas." Alisa followed Danny's lead and looked at the Christmas decorations on the old homes. "People don't have room for the big yard displays here like back home, but somehow, I like these decorations better. All the bows tied to the rails and the beautiful wreaths on the door; it's very classic."

They soon arrived at Leopold's. Once inside, Steven ordered the soup, which was crab chowder, and an egg-salad sandwich. Alisa ordered a hot chocolate, and Danny got a hot-fudge sundae.

Once at the table, Steven furrowed his brow. "I thought you said it was too cold for ice cream."

Danny looked confused by the comment. "Yeah, that's why I got hot fudge."

Alisa took a sip of her cocoa. "Ice cream is a staple for Danny."

Steven dunked a corner of his sandwich into his soup. "So, where does your sister's husband work?"

"Washington, D.C., the Department of Defense. Actually they both do, but her husband has a slightly more critical role. She just compiles budget reports for the DOD accounting office, so she can take off any time she wants, but if he's not there, other people with his clearance level have to cover for him." Danny scooped up some fudge from the side of the dish where it had mixed with the melting ice cream and spooned it into his mouth.

"Wow. So he's a big wig at the Pentagon? What does he do?" Steven tasted his soup.

"I don't know actually. He says it's something to do with budgeting and approving out-sourced private contractors, but he's always so evasive when

I try to talk to him about work that I suspect it's more than that."

Steven turned to Alisa. "So why didn't you go home for Christmas?"

She rolled her eyes at Danny. "I was supposed to be going to South Carolina to meet Danny's family. Besides, my parents have parties to go to during the holidays. I'd just be in the way. I was pawned off on babysitters and nannies growing up. When I opened presents, my parents were as surprised as I was to see what I got. They paid the nanny to do the Christmas shopping too. Now that we're going to South Carolina for New Year's, I'll be out of their hair for the whole season. Why didn't you go back to Iowa?"

Steven laughed. "I was supposed to be working for Danny. Plus, I usually go home for most of the summer. Anyway, I didn't want to tell my parents that I dropped out of SCAD."

"Wait! What did you just say?" Alisa demanded.

"I dropped out."

"Why?" Danny quizzed.

"The program I was in required me to take a human figure drawing class. The models are nude. I'm not willing to make that compromise."

Alisa lightly slapped his arm. "Steven! It's art. It's not porn."

Steven sighed. "Jesus said that if you look at a woman lustfully, you've already committed adultery with her in your heart. I want to live a life that pleases God."

Danny continued to eat his sundae. "Doesn't Savannah College of Art and Design have other programs that don't require you to take that class?"

"Yeah, but I wanted to study fine arts. I'm not going to sign up for another program that I'm not interested in. And, I think God might be calling me to full-time ministry."

"So you're going to be a preacher now?" Alisa sounded annoyed.

"There are other ways to be in full-time ministry besides preaching. But maybe. I'm not sure." Steven continued eating his sandwich.

Danny slid his sundae toward Alisa, who had been sneaking a few bites. "Let's all have Christmas dinner at my house."

"Great! What time?" Alisa completely took over the sundae.

"How is one o'clock?"

"Isn't that too early for dinner?" Alisa asked.

Danny shrugged. "What else are we going to do all day?"

"You're right. One o'clock is fine with me. What do you think, Steven?" Alisa turned to face him.

"One is perfect. What should I bring?"

Danny said, "I'll make a turkey, gravy and cornbread stuffing. You can bring a dessert and a side dish if you want."

Steven smiled. "I'll make homemade Christmas cookies; the cut-out kind with icing."

Alisa clapped her hands. "This will be great! I'll bring eggnog; from the store, though. I have no idea how to make it. No one ever taught me how to cook."

Danny ran his hand through her hair. "You can help me with the turkey. I'll show you how to cook if you want to learn."

"Your grandmother taught you to cook?" She took his hand and held it.

"She taught me the basics. I picked up a lot from being in the restaurant business as well."

Alisa shot Steven a look. "I could invite Dana from work."

"Please don't do that." Steven shook his head.

She protested. "Why? What's wrong with Dana? She's cute."

"Nothing is wrong with Dana, but you've got some kind of match-maker strategy going on here. I appreciate the thought, but I'm quite content. I don't need a girlfriend to feel complete."

Alisa crossed her arms and pouted. "Fine. Be lonely for Christmas."

"He's not lonely. He'll be with us." Danny sighed.

Alisa let her arms drop to her side. "I know. I just want everyone to be as happy as we are. I spent a lot of lonely Christmases growing up."

Danny gave her a hug. "Well, none of us will be lonely this year."

The three friends finished making plans to spend Christmas together. They had two more days of work, and then Lilly's would be closed for Christmas Eve and Christmas Day.

CHAPTER 2

Thy words were found, and I did eat them; and thy word was unto me the joy and rejoicing of mine heart: for I am called by thy name, O LORD God of hosts.

Jeremiah 15:16

Danny pulled up to the curve near Steven's apartment on Christmas Eve. He hit the button to unlock the car door.

Steven stepped out of the front door of an old row house built in the late 1800s which had been converted into several one-bedroom apartments. It wasn't as meticulously renovated as the house where Alisa lived, but it was no less charming. Steven opened the back door of Danny's car and got in. "Thanks for picking me up."

"You can sit up front."

"I'll let Alisa sit up front. Besides, it's probably as close to a chauffeur and Limo as I'll ever have."

Danny glanced in the rearview. "It's a '98 Camry that still smells like pizza from my delivery days. I hope you get a little closer to a Limo than this."

Alisa's apartment was only a few blocks northeast of Steven's. They were there in a matter of minutes. Danny picked up his phone and texted her to let her know he was downstairs waiting.

Seconds later, Danny's phone buzzed. He turned toward the back of the car and read the text aloud to Steven. "Ten more minutes, please."

"Rats." Steven checked the time on his phone. "Does ten minutes mean ten minutes?"

"Probably fifteen. Why? Are we going to be super late?"

Steven pursed his lips. "We might still make it on time, but there won't be any seats left. It's not a very big church, which is okay the rest of the year, but everyone shows up on Christmas and Easter. It's my fault, I should have sandbagged the time so we could get there earlier."

"Don't blame yourself. Alisa is usually on time. I think she just wants to get all dolled up for Christmas."

"I wasn't talking about Alisa." Steven winked.

"Hey! I was on time!" Danny protested.

"Yeah, but if I'd planned on you being late, it would have made a buffer for Alisa and we'd still be on schedule."

Danny sighed. "Well, I can't argue against that logic."

Fifteen minutes later, Alisa dashed down the stairs of her building and jumped in the car. "Sorry, I'm running late."

"Go! Go! Go!" Steven slapped the side of the car door with each successive command.

Alisa turned around as she put her seat belt on. "Steven! It's church! We're not robbing a bank! Settle down!"

Danny laughed as he drove off. He'd been worried that the evening was going to be boring. How could he ever have thought such a thing when he knew he'd be with these two?

When they arrived, the parking lot was full, so they had to drive around and find a spot on the street. The closest parking space was three blocks away from the church.

Steven sprinted ahead.

Alisa called out, "Wait up! I'm wearing heels!"

Steven paused and looked at Danny. "You grab her arms and I'll grab her feet. We can carry her and run!"

"NO! Steven!" Alisa pointed at him.

Danny wasn't sure if either or both were joking or serious. He didn't care, it was providing his entertainment. As they approached the church, they could hear the choir singing *Come All Ye Faithful*.

"See, they just started." Alisa scolded Steven.

"Or, it's the last song," he retorted.

When they finally entered the doors, the usher informed them that the only remaining seats were in the balcony, so that's where they went. Danny was mesmerized by the ornate ceiling and beautiful glass windows. The architectural details had been very well maintained since the facility was built in 1891. The candelabras, wreaths and bows made it even more gorgeous.

The congregation joined with the choir as they sang four more classic Christmas hymns; *What Child is This, O Holy Night, Hark The Herald Angels Sing*, and finally, Danny's favorite childhood Christmas carol, *The Little Drummer Boy*.

The pastor stepped to the podium to pray, and then everyone was seated. He began his message.

"If you will, please turn to Isaiah 55 with me as I read verses 1 through 7.

"Ho, every one that thirsteth, come ye to the waters, and he that hath no money; come ye, buy, and eat; yea, come, buy wine and milk without money and without price. Wherefore do ye spend money for that which is not bread? And your labour for that which satisfieth not? Hearken diligently unto me, and eat ye that which is good, and let your soul delight itself in fatness. Incline your ear, and come unto me: hear, and your soul shall live; and I will make an everlasting covenant with you, even the sure mercies of David. Behold, I have given him for a witness to the people, a leader and commander to the people. Behold, thou shalt call a nation that thou knowest not, and nations that knew not thee shall run unto thee because of the LORD thy God, and for the Holy One of Israel; for he hath glorified thee. Seek ye the LORD while he may be found, call ye upon him while he is near: Let the wicked forsake his way, and the unrighteous man his thoughts: and let him return unto the LORD, and he will have mercy upon him; and to our God, for he will abundantly pardon.

"I know this wasn't the passage most of you were expecting for Christmas. We usually read the Christmas story from the Gospel of Luke, but I felt called to do something a little different this year.

"This passage from Isaiah sums up the Gospel message about as well as any other section of Scriptures. And I find it utterly appropriate for this time of year.

"The last carol we sang was *The Little Drummer Boy*. In the song, the young boy comes to Jesus and sees the finest gifts being laid before the Messiah. The wise men present Christ with frankincense, myrrh and gold. He feels inadequate because he is impoverished and has no means to purchase such gifts. He asks Mary if he can play for Jesus, an act of pure worship. Of course, she consents and he plays his best for the newborn King. Then something miraculous happens. Jesus smiles at him. That approval we all seek; the little drummer boy gets. He came without money but he placed his gifts and talents before the King. That's all that Jesus expects of you."

The pastor looked back down to the Bible and read again. "Every one that thirsteth, come ye to the waters, and he that hath no money; come ye, buy, and eat; yea, come, buy wine and milk without money and without price. Wherefore do ye spend money for that which is not bread? And your labour for that which satisfieth not?"

He looked back up. "How much do we labour and toil, how much do we expend our resources for stuff? Not only at Christmas, but all year round. We work and slave away for a better car, a bigger house, newer clothes, and the latest i-gadget. But we're never satisfied."

Once more, the pastor read from the text. "Hearken diligently unto me, and eat ye that which is good, and let your soul delight itself in fatness. Incline your ear, and come unto me: hear, and your soul shall live."

The pastor paused for a moment, then said, "In our busy world, it sounds like such a sacrifice to give up your way of life, to take time to read the Bible or come to church and hear God's Word, especially if you're not used to that sort of thing. But once you do, you find that it is the only thing that will really satisfy you. All of that emptiness that you try to fill with stuff; suddenly that simple smile of approval from your King fills it up, when you come to Him and dedicate a few moments of your time for true worship.

"Seek ye the LORD while he may be found, call ye upon him while he is near: Let the wicked forsake his way, and the unrighteous man his thoughts: and let him return unto the LORD, and he will have mercy upon him; and to our God, for he will abundantly pardon.

"If you feel the LORD near to you right now, if you hear that still small voice calling you to forsake your way and to return to Jesus, come down front and pray with one of our prayer counselors. God can't wait to show you mercy and abundantly pardon you."

The choir began softly singing *The Little*

Drummer Boy once more.

Tears were streaming down Danny's eyes. He wiped them with his shirt sleeve.

Steven put his arm around Danny's shoulder. "Do you feel like you need to go down there?"

Danny nodded.

Steven smiled. "I'll walk down there with you. Alisa, are you coming?"

"I'll wait for you guys here or meet you by the door."

Steven nodded. "Okay."

Once down front, the prayer counselor asked Danny if he would like to dedicate his life to Christ.

Danny dried his eyes. "Yes."

"Then just ask him to forgive you, invite him into your heart and confess that Jesus is God."

Danny lowered his head. "Jesus, forgive me; for running in the other direction from you. I've heard you calling me through so much of my life. I know that you are God and I invite you inside."

"Amen." The prayer counselor hugged Danny. "Welcome to the kingdom of God."

"Thanks." Danny felt a warm glow deep inside.

"Congratulations." Steven gave Danny a big hug.

They began walking back to the balcony. Danny said, "I feel so light."

Steven patted him on the back. "I bet."

Alisa gave Danny a warm hug when he got back to their seats.

He kissed her on the cheek, but he felt awkward because she hadn't walked down front with him.

Shortly after they'd returned to the balcony, the service was dismissed and the three friends went home.

CHAPTER 3

Suddenly there came up out of the river seven cows, fine-looking and fat; and they fed in the meadow. Then behold, seven other cows came up after them out of the river, ugly and gaunt, and stood by the other cows on the bank of the river. And the ugly and gaunt cows ate up the seven fine-looking and fat cows.

Genesis 41: 2-4 NKJV

Danny couldn't remember such thick fog. Savannah was subjected to it from time to time, but this looked more like the fog he remembered from Nana's house, where it hung low in the valleys of the Appalachian foothills, soft and musty like a velour comforter from a cheap hotel. However, something about the moss hanging from the Southern live oaks in the Bonaventure Cemetery seemed to trap the fog and hold it. It was as if the graveyard wanted to keep the fog as a veil of obscurity. He had often driven out to Bonaventure to walk and clear his thoughts. The occupants were quiet and didn't seem to mind his presence. These days, it was rare that he would come out here by himself. Alisa had been hypnotized by the serenity of the place and usually insisted that she tag along.

Danny drank in the solitude and tranquility, but for the first time ever, he felt a certain uneasiness about being amongst the tombs alone. Perhaps it was the opacity of the thick fog. Even someone as familiar with the cemetery grounds as himself could get lost if he didn't keep a firm grip on his bearings. He sat down on a bench for a moment and told himself there was nothing to worry about, but it helped little.

Danny glanced to his left and noticed a tombstone he didn't remember seeing before. He bent down to look at the name. "'Amerigo Vespucci, 1776 to' . . . huh, never put the death date." Danny started to walk around to the other side and nearly stepped into the freshly dug, open grave. He stumbled and fell backwards with one foot dangling over the side of the abyss. His heart pounded as he looked over the side. The heavy fog was spilling over the sides and pouring down into the excavated earth, thereby creating the effect of a bottomless pit. "You're kidding me! These idiots dug a grave and didn't put anything around it to keep people from stepping in it? I could have broken my neck!"

Danny's heart rate normalized; he stood and brushed off the dirt. Something wasn't right about all of this, and it added to his feeling of disquietude. He quickly assessed his location and decided to head home. What had been intended as a therapeutic stroll was becoming a source for serious anxiety.

He wanted to forget about the incident, but it haunted his thoughts. "That headstone looked old. I wonder why it had a freshly dug grave. Could have been grave robbers; they might still be around. These ghost tours around the city attract a lot of kooks and people that are into the occult. Amerigo Vespucci; wasn't he the explorer who died in the 1500s? Maybe it's someone else named after him."

Danny chuckled as his history lessons from college came back to him. "America was named after him. 1776 . . . fresh grave, no death date. Probably a hoax with some political message."

The reasoning seemed sound enough and quelled his apprehensiveness to some degree. Nevertheless, he'd had enough for one day and was ready to go. He stopped short as he saw a large, luminous form just ahead which was shrouded by the dense fog. Once again his heartbeat quickened.

"What the heck is that?" he said in a low whisper.

Whatever it was, it was big, it was moving, and it stood between Danny and the front gate. He cautiously stepped backwards hoping for a window in the fog, just enough to make out the ghostly form. None came. He considered his options. *I can't navigate through the fog to get around it. I'll end up lost if I even try. I could back up and wait for the fog to clear, but who knows how long that will take?*

I wish I had a better weapon. He ran his hand across his front pants pocket to feel the contour of his knife. If the form belonged to someone or something with hostile intent, the knife might not be of much use.

He sighed deeply, wishing he weren't in such a predicament. "Hello." There was nothing else to do but confront the spectral form. He called out again, just a bit louder. "Hello, who's there?"

He took small, calculated steps toward the dim glow of the figure in front of him. It didn't move toward him or away from him. He retrieved his knife from his pocket, opened the blade, and continued in the direction of the vague image. "Hey, did you hear me? What are you doing here?"

Still no answer. *Maybe I just got spooked by the grave. Maybe my mind, my eyes, and this fog are all conspiring to prank me. It's probably nothing. I'll laugh when I see what it really is.*

Danny took a deep breath and walked a little closer. "It's an animal. Get out of here!" he yelled. But whatever the animal was, it just kept grazing. "Is it a deer? Whatever it is, I'm sure it isn't dangerous." Danny spoke aloud to comfort himself. "It still has that weird glow, must be the way the light is filtering through the moss in the oaks and down into the surrounding fog."

He waved his hands and yelled again as he got closer. "Get! Go! Move out!" The animal, which

Danny could now see was a cow, was undeterred by his shouts. "Wow, that thing is skinny. No wonder it won't stop eating. It must have been trapped somewhere and just broke free. I can't believe it's still alive, being so thin."

He kept walking to get a better view of the strange sight of a cow grazing in the cemetery. It was ghastly and emaciated. The rib bones looked as though they might rip right through the paper-thin skin of the sickly creature. Its hip bones and shoulders also protruded outward as there was not enough flesh nor fat to conceal them.

He slowly approached the lean beast. It stopped eating for one moment and looked up to stare at Danny. Its eyes were empty and soulless, grey and set back in the hollow sockets. A swarm of flies circled over its head and around to its body. The cow flipped its tail to shoo them away. The effort was in vain as the insects continued to molest the frail creature. It lowered its head and resumed eating.

Danny looked at the ground to see the vegetation that the animal was grazing on. "Money?"

The ground beneath the cow was covered with U.S. currency: singles, fives, tens, twenties, and hundreds.

"What is going on here?" Danny was getting really freaked out now. He looked around; the fog was growing thicker. It obscured his view of the cow, which was only a few feet away at this point. He was stricken by an overwhelming sense of doom and fear. He turned to run back the way he had come, but the fog was too dense. He couldn't even see his feet. Danny began to scream for help, but no sound came out. He was paralyzed by terror. He strained even harder to scream. He could force out only a slight whimper. He tried and tried, but a slight, squeaky moan was all he could manage.

"Danny! Danny!" Alisa's voice pierced the fog.

What is she doing here? It isn't safe for her, he thought. "Alisa! Alisa!" The dream faded and he looked up at Alisa as she shook him.

"Are you okay? You're soaking wet with sweat."

Danny caught his breath and looked around the room. "Yeah."

"You were having a nightmare." She stroked his sweaty hair back from his forehead.

He continued to look around. Oddly, the dream had felt more real than being awake. He sat quietly and concentrated on his breath for several seconds. "I've never had a dream that intense before, at least not that I can remember."

"You're white as a ghost, and you're trembling. Maybe I should call Steven."

Danny glanced at the clock, which read a quarter 'til six. Calling Steven sounded like a good idea for a moment. Maybe he would have an answer. Perhaps he'd had similar dreams after committing his life to Jesus. "No, it's too early. I'll talk to him later. I'll be okay."

"Do you think you can go back to sleep?" She kept stroking his hair.

"I don't know."

"I'll make you some chamomile. That will help. You can sleep in tomorrow and you'll forget all about it." Alisa got up to make the tea.

"Yeah, thanks." But somehow, Danny knew he would never forget that dream.

He felt the area of the bed where he'd been lying. It was drenched with sweat, as was his pillow. He exhaled deeply. "I can't go back to sleep in a puddle."

Danny actually felt more tired from the dream than if he'd never went to sleep at all. He put his feet on the floor and went into his drawer to get a clean tee-shirt. Alisa had assigned him a drawer to keep a few things at her apartment for when he stayed over. After the Christmas Eve service, he had intended to drop her off and go home, but that didn't really work out.

Danny put on a pair of socks as well. The tall ceilings in Alisa's apartment were beautiful, but they allowed all of the heat to go straight up, and it was always a bit chilly. Next, he walked groggily into the kitchen and sat at the table.

"Merry Christmas!" Alisa kissed him on the forehead.

He forced a smile. "Merry Christmas."

She stood by the stove waiting for the water to boil. "It's almost morning. Would you rather cancel the tea order and just go straight to coffee? I don't think I can go back to sleep at this point."

Danny sighed. "As tired as I am, I doubt I'll be able to go back to sleep either."

She turned off the burner under the teapot and filled the coffee maker. "What about breakfast? Are you hungry?"

Danny had been worried that his decision to follow Christ the night before might create a schism in their relationship, but it was obvious that Alisa still felt the same way about him. "Sure. Thanks."

"How about waffles?"

"You know how to make waffles?"

"Yes. Take them out of the freezer, put them in the toaster, and push the button."

Danny laughed as he thought about how much he loved this girl. "It's Christmas. Let's go to my house and I'll make a real Christmas breakfast."

"You're going to be cooking all day."

"I don't mind."

"Okay, I'll get ready. We can have a cup of coffee then go to your house."

Danny got dressed and poured a cup of coffee while he waited for Alisa. His head was haunted by the dream. Normally, a bad dream would have all but faded away by now, but not this one. It was still more vivid in his mind's eye than most of his real memories.

Alisa was soon ready to leave. She wore a cute red sweater with a snowman, and she held several large shopping bags in each hand. "Can you help me carry some of these presents?"

Danny was quickly distracted from his thoughts of the eerie nightmare. "Wow! Who are those for?"

"You, silly. Well, one is for Steven, but the rest are yours."

"I bought you like one present. I feel horrible."

"Good. No, just kidding. You're doing all of the cooking. That takes more thought and effort than shopping."

Danny grabbed his coat, finished his coffee, and they headed to his house.

The faintest glimmer of sunlight was peeking over the horizon as they arrived. Once inside, Danny started making French toast, bacon, and another pot of coffee while Alisa stacked the presents in one corner of Danny's living room. Danny hadn't put up a tree, so she arranged the gifts as festively as possible.

They ate breakfast in the living room while watching *Rudolph the Red-Nosed Reindeer*.

After they'd eaten, Alisa drifted off to sleep. Danny covered her with the comforter on the couch and went to start cooking the turkey for lunch. His hands were busy preparing the Christmas feast, but his mind was on other things. "I wonder if that dream is some kind of message. I had it right after I prayed that prayer. Of course it is." He continued preparing the meal and thinking about the dream. "I don't know, maybe I'm making too much of it."

At ten o'clock, Danny called Steven. "Hey, man. Are you awake?"

"Yeah. What's up?"

"We got an early start today, so if you want to come earlier, you can. But if you've got other stuff to do, we can stick to the original time."

"Thanks. Sure, I can come on over in a while. Do you need me to pick anything up?"

"Alisa was going to get eggnog, but didn't. Can you grab a half gallon?"

"I doubt anyone is open except Parkers. I'm not sure gas station eggnog is the best."

"Yeah, but we have to take what we can get."

"Okay, see you in a bit."

Danny pulled the turkey off the bones so he

could use the bones and drippings to make a stock. He crumbled the cornbread and leftover bread that he'd been saving for stuffing.

Alisa awoke and came into the kitchen. "I slept through Christmas! You were supposed to teach me how to cook! No one will ever want me for a wife now."

Danny knew she was fishing for a hint, but he refused to feed into it. Still, his heart quickened at the thought of marrying Alisa. "You never know. A lot of guys are looking for a girl that can toast a frozen waffle."

She rolled her eyes. "You drank all the coffee? I'm going to make another pot."

"Sure, I'll have some too."

She scooped the grounds into the filter. "Oh, no! I forgot to get eggnog!"

"Relax. Steven is bringing some. He's coming early; he should be here in a bit."

"I can't even buy eggnog. I'll never be a good wife."

Danny hugged her. "There's more to being a good wife than buying eggnog."

He thought about the ring hidden in his sock drawer, wrapped in Christmas paper. This supposed to be the day he'd pop the question. He was confident he would get the answer he was looking for, but now he was having second thoughts. Not that he doubted his feeling for Alisa, but he remembered that his grandmother, Nana he called her, had told him some Scriptures that said Christians shouldn't marry non-Christians. It had gone in one ear and out the other when she said it;

after all, he had just become one less than a day before.

But would it be right to leave Alisa when they loved each other so much? He was sure he wouldn't be able to do that. And if they stayed together, there was no way they could avoid intimacy. He knew that sex outside of marriage was considered a sin. Quickly enough, he had reasoned, in his own mind, that while marrying Alisa might not be the best thing to do biblically, he wasn't likely to maintain a sexually pure relationship with her either. Proceeding with his plan to give her the ring tonight seemed to be the lesser of the two evils.

Steven knocked before entering but had long since abandoned the notion that he should wait for Danny to open the door for him to come in. "Merry Christmas!"

"Merry Christmas!" Danny took the plastic bag with the eggnog and plastic food-storage container filled with homemade cookies from Steven and set them on the counter.

"Presents? We didn't get you anything." Alisa took the presents from Steven.

"That's okay. I didn't expect anything."

"I'm kidding. We got you something, too." Alisa winked.

"So why did you guys get such an early start?"

Alisa walked back into the kitchen after putting the gifts with the others. "Danny had a nightmare and couldn't go back to sleep."

"That's terrible. Do you have bad dreams often?"

"No. I've actually never had a dream like this one." Danny proceeded to give Steven a quick synopsis of the dream.

"Weird. Kind of sounds like it might be prophetic. Pharaoh had a dream about seven skinny cows in Genesis. It was a revelation that a seven-year famine was coming upon the land. Each cow represented a year."

"Well, I only saw one cow, so I guess that's good news."

Steven raised his eyebrows. "If it's even remotely prophetic, the term 'good news' would be hard to pair with your dream. The part about the empty grave is particularly spooky."

"Why would his cow be eating money? How could that be prophetic? It just sounds like a bad dream to me." Alisa looked confused.

Steven shrugged his shoulders. "I don't know. Maybe we're going to have to spend all of our money to survive the one-year famine. I think we should go talk to Pastor David tomorrow."

"Yeah, okay. This thing really has me freaked out. I think that might help."

Lunch was soon ready and the three friends had a delectable Christmas feast. They didn't talk anymore about the dream, but it was in the back of Danny's mind the entire day.

After lunch, they exchanged gifts.

Danny opened his gift from Steven. "A King James Bible! How did you know I was going to need that?"

Steven smiled. "I guess I'm a bit of an optimist. That's calfskin leather. Very high quality."

Alisa opened her gift from Steven next. "A New King James Study Bible. You are an optimist, aren't you? Why does Danny get King James and I get New King James?"

Steven began opening the gift Alisa had given him. "I think the King James is the most accurate, but some people can't get past the *thees* and the *thous*."

"I'm not smart enough to read seventeenth-century English. Is that what you're saying?

Steven shook his head and pursed his lips. "No. I was hoping you two would read one of the Bibles together. I just thought if you guys wouldn't read it in the King's English, you'd maybe read the New King James, which is probably the closest of the modern translations. It wasn't meant to be a commentary on anyone being smarter than anyone else."

Steven continued opening his present from Alisa. "A new brush set. Wow! Thank you!"

"Yeah, I bought that before I knew you'd dropped out of SCAD, but you can't stop painting. Going to school for art doesn't make you an artist. You just are or you aren't."

Danny continued to open the stack of gifts from Alisa. She'd bought him cologne, a new watch, two pairs of jeans, and three shirts.

She opened the single gift from Danny. "A sweater. How nice."

Danny could see the disappointment in her eyes. He wished he could give her the ring right now, but he wasn't going to propose in front of Steven. He glanced over at Steven who knew about the ring. Steven winked as if to say he knew how Danny was feeling and that it would all be okay once she got her other gift.

The three of them enjoyed the rest of the afternoon, watching Christmas cartoons and Christmas movies.

Steven got up to leave. "Danny, I'll call the church office first thing in the morning and we'll go speak to Pastor David. Alisa, you can come if you want."

Alisa looked surprised to be invited. "Oh, I thought it would be top secret. But If I'm allowed, I want to be the first one to hear if America is going to die."

Danny stood to walk Steven to the door. "Thanks, man. See you in the morning. Merry Christmas."

Steven waved. "Merry Christmas."

Danny turned to Alisa. "Want some more eggnog and another cookie?"

"Sure." She wrapped herself in the comforter and clicked through the channels.

Danny retrieved the refreshments and sat them on the coffee table. "Mind if we listen to a little Christmas music?"

She sat the remote on the table and took the eggnog. "Sure."

Danny turned off the TV and went to his room to play the music. He selected "Have Yourself a Merry Little Christmas" and took the ring out of his top drawer. "You have one more present, I forgot."

"I do?"

He walked back into the living room with his hands behind his back. He presented the box to her.

She took the box and began pulling the ribbon

off. Her expression was one of overwhelming emotion. It was as if she knew what was in the box but wouldn't dare let herself get excited until it was confirmed. Her lip quivered as she tore through the paper.

Danny watched in anticipation. He was confident that he knew what her answer would be, but he also wouldn't let himself get excited until he had heard it from her lips.

"Danny Walker! It's beautiful!" She took the small white gold band with the quarter-carat round diamond and placed it on her finger.

He knelt down and took her hand. "Will you marry me?"

She began to cry as she nodded and put her arms around his neck. Through the sobs of joy, she said, "Yes, I'll marry you."

They held each other for a while, then she kissed him. "I thought you were going to ask me. Then when we opened presents, I thought you weren't. I tried not to look disappointed. Then, when you came in the room with the little box, I knew. Danny I love you so much. I'll love you forever."

"I love you, too. That's why you only got a sweater. With school and rent and everything, it was the most I could afford, but I'll get you a bigger one someday."

She grabbed him and kissed him again. "I don't care. It could be plastic. I'm just so happy that we're getting married!"

The rest of the evening was spent speculating about the wedding, and the rest of their lives.

CHAPTER 4

I say unto you, that likewise joy shall be in heaven over one sinner that repenteth, more than over ninety and nine just persons, which need no repentance.

Luke 15:7

The next morning, Danny came downstairs and got into the car with Steven. "She'll be down in a second."

"What did she say?"

"She said yes." Danny was glowing.

"Awesome! Congratulations!"

"Will you be my best man? You better hurry up and say yes. She's going to ask you to be the maid of honor."

"That ain't happening anyway, but yes, I'll be

your best man. So, did she stay over?"

"Yeah. Why?"

"I'm only saying this out of love, but if you want God to bless your marriage, you two really shouldn't be sleeping together. You'll be married soon enough and you'll have the rest of your lives to be together."

Steven was only telling him what he already knew. "You're right."

Alisa came down the stairs, got in the car, slammed the door, and stuck the ring right up to Steven's nose. "Look!"

Steven pushed her hand back to where he could see it. "Beautiful! Congratulations."

She took her hand back and examined the ring herself. "Thanks."

They were at the church by 9:30, and in the pastor's office shortly thereafter. Danny gave Pastor David his account of the dream, covering every detail as best as he could remember it.

The pastor listened patiently until Danny finished. "Danny, we have a lady who attends here; she's a psychiatrist and sees some of our congregants free of charge. It's her ministry in the church. She may be able to schedule you for a few sessions and try to find the underlying issues. In the meantime, she may be able to prescribe something to help you with anxiety or depression or something to help you sleep better. If you need it, that is."

Danny wasn't expecting that response, but he wasn't sure what he was expecting. "Uh, okay."

Steven wasn't quite as docile. "Wait a minute. You're going to pawn him off on a shrink who you expect to dope him up? He's not depressed, or anxious, or having trouble sleeping. He came to you to see if you thought his dream might have some prophetic significance."

"Settle down Steven." Pastor David put one hand in the air. "We don't believe in prophetic dreams. Danny's nightmare sounds very disturbing. I've done my share of counseling and sometimes it's a physiological issue, chemical imbalance, or sometimes it's a traumatic event from a person's past, but that's not a normal dream. If he is waking up pale, shaking and sweating, he needs to get some professional help."

"Why don't you believe in prophetic dreams?" Steven lowered his voice, but was still visually upset.

"Well, we don't see the need for that manifestation." The pastor opened his Bible for the first time since they had arrived. "In First Corinthians 13, Paul writes, 'whether there be prophecies, they shall fail; whether there be tongues, they shall cease; whether there be knowledge, it shall vanish away. For we know in part, and we prophesy in part. But when that which is perfect is come, then that which is in part shall be done away.' Paul was talking about the canonization of the Scriptures. Now that we have the complete Holy Bible, that which was in part was done away with. That includes prophetic dreams."

Steven opened his Bible and turned to that section of Scriptures. He continued reading where the pastor left off. "'For now we see through a glass, darkly; but then face to face: now I know in part; but then shall I know even as also I am known. And now abideth faith, hope, charity, these three; but the greatest of these is charity.' Paul is talking about when he gets to heaven. That is so obvious to me. How can you not see that? Why does he say the greatest of these is charity, which can also be translated as love? I'll tell you why. Because he was talking about life in heaven, where we won't need faith nor hope, because our faith and hope will have been fulfilled. How in the world could you possibly twist that Scripture to mean prophetic dreams don't exist? I'm sorry we wasted your time. Danny, Alisa, let's go."

Danny wasn't sure what just happened, but he followed Steven out the door, as did Alisa. Once they were back in the car, Danny asked, "So that guy doesn't believe the Bible? I got saved listening to his sermon. Does that mean I'm not really saved?"

Steven's voice was filled with disappointment. "No, that has nothing to do with your salvation whatsoever. Isaiah 55 says 'God's Word doesn't return void.' You can hear God's Word from the devil himself and be saved. It's all about the message, not the messenger."

"You think he was of the devil?" Danny was still confused.

"No. Pastor David is a good man. He's deceived, like many pastors in America, but he's a good man. I'm sure he's saved and all that, but they are so quick to believe a bunch of garbage and throw their lot in with Egypt?"

"Egypt? What are you talking about?" Alisa

asked.

"Don't mind me. Egypt is a type of the world in Scriptures. It has to do with handling things the world's way rather than God's way. Biblical counseling is great, but too many churches are quick to rubber stamp the modern psychiatric solution of doping everybody up, rather than trying to find a spiritual method of solving problems. I feel bad because I brought you here."

"Bro, don't blame yourself. You didn't know. If you hadn't been there, I would've probably let them pump me full of Thorazine."

Steven fought back a smile. "No, you wouldn't have."

They were soon back at Danny's apartment. Danny and Alisa got out of the car. "Are you coming in?" Danny asked.

"No. I'm going home to do some research. I have to find a better church; one that believes the whole Bible. I'm going to get you some good answers and wise council."

"Okay, call me when you find something. Thanks." Danny waved as his friend drove away.

Once they reached the top of the stairs, Danny opened the door for Alisa. "What do you think?"

Alisa shrugged as she walked into Danny's apartment. "This is all new to me. The guy had me going with chemical imbalance and all of that. It seems more logical than messages from God. People do some kooky stuff and claim they had a message from God telling them to do it. Promise me that you'll at least talk to a professional if it gets worse. I saw what you looked like when you woke up. It wasn't just a bad dream."

Danny tossed his keys on the kitchen counter. "If it gets worse, and Steven can't find a church that can help, I'll talk to somebody. But, I'm not going to let them get me hopped up on antidepressants until I've exhausted every other possible solution."

She kissed him. "Fair enough. And always remember that I love you, no matter what."

Later that afternoon, Steven called Danny on the phone. "Hey man, I found a little church out on Abercorn, near your school. It's called Savannah Christian Chapel and claims to be a non-denominational, Spirit-filled congregation. Some of these places can get a little extreme."

Danny furrowed his brow. "What do you mean?"

"Everyone speaking in tongues at once, dancing around, that sort of thing."

"Whoa! That sounds nuts."

"Well, the apostle Paul gave a prescription of how speaking in tongues should be handled during a church service. In First Corinthians 14, he said no more than two or three people should speak in tongues at a time, and only if there is an interpreter. If there's no interpreter, they shouldn't speak in tongues out loud. Unfortunately, it's tough to find a church that can follow directions. They either go to one extreme, dismissing spiritual gifts altogether, or they go to the other extreme and create a worship environment based on emotion and filled with disorder. I hope we can find a church that can keep it in the middle, but if not, you may have to err on the side of too charismatic. We already know that the cessationist want to throw you in a padded room."

"Cessationist?"

"Yeah, that's a fancy term for folks who think the gifts of the Spirit aren't for today."

Danny sighed. "Sounds like I've got a lot to learn."

"You just focus on praying and reading the Bible yourself. Don't get caught up in all of the divisive arguments between the factions. They're all saved, but Satan tries to get us too far to the left or the right to make us less fruitful."

"Okay, so when are we going to check this place out?"

"They have a service tonight, but I have to work. You and Alisa can go. Otherwise we can all go Sunday morning."

"I think I'll go ahead and check it out. We were planning to leave for South Carolina early on Sunday."

"Sounds good. Give me a call later tonight and let me know how it went. If it gets too weird, just get up and leave. There are plenty of other places to check out. We'll find something."

"Okay, I'll call you later." Danny put the phone down and told Alisa the plan.

She squinted as if she was hesitant to go along. "I'll go, but if they start passing snakes around or flopping on the floor, I'm out!"

"If I see a snake, you'll have to race me to the door."

At 6:30 that evening, they pulled into the parking lot of a strip mall.

"I don't see any churches around here. Are you

sure you have the right address?" Alisa surveyed the surrounding areas.

Danny looked at the addresses on the stores in the strip mall. "Look, it's there. Between the pizza place and the pre-paid phone store."

"That's not a church. Where are the steeple and stained glass?"

"Come on. We're here already. We might as well check it out."

Alisa huffed as she closed the door. "I'm going to kill Steven for sending us here. It looks like a cult recruitment center."

Danny snickered. "Maybe it won't be as bad as all that."

When they came inside, Danny was surprised at how nice it looked. There was a small stage with a podium, good lighting, and clean, comfortable-looking chairs. Approximately twenty other people were milling about near the back, at a table with coffee and donuts.

"Hi, I'm Chuck and this is my wife Lois. Welcome to Savannah Christian Chapel."

"I'm Danny and this is my girlfriend, Alisa." Danny shook hands with them.

"Actually, I'm his fiancé. We just got engaged last night, so he's still acclimating. Nice to meet you both." Alisa also shook hands with Chuck and Lois.

Chuck motioned toward the box of donuts. "We've still got a few more minutes before service starts, so help yourself to a donut."

Alisa sighed as if she'd been defeated in a great athletic contest. "Chocolate iced, glazed? I'm going to be so fat by the time the holidays are over!"

Danny took a donut with Christmas sprinkles. "You're not fat! But you might be by the time Nana gets done with you. Everything she makes contains pork fat, sugar, butter or some combination thereof."

Alisa spoke through her teeth as she bit into her donut. "Great."

They found seats near the back, just in case they had to escape in a hurry. A drummer, guitarist and keyboard player walked onto the stage and began playing.

"This is kicky. I like it!" Alisa gave Danny's hand a squeeze as she smiled and nodded her head to the music.

"I like it too. Steven plays Christian radio in his car, but most of it sounds like benign pop music. This really gets in your soul."

The female keyboard player sang along to a sweet, rhythmic worship song as the other congregants sang along with their hands lifted toward heaven. Danny and Alisa sang along from the words which were displayed on a projection screen over the stage.

After the music stopped, the pastor walked out. He was slightly overweight, in his late seventies, with thin white hair, and a warm smile that may have been stolen from Santa Claus himself. He prayed, then looked up. "I'd like to welcome our visitors. I'm Pastor Earl, and we're honored to have you worshiping with us tonight."

He proceeded to give a short message from Romans chapter 3. Danny mostly listened, but he was also sizing up the other attendees. A couple of them looked like they've had hard lives. One of them looked familiar. He resembled one of the panhandlers who worked with the tourists on River Street. They were usually high, hungover, or somewhere in between. But this man looked sober, alert, freshly shaven, and clean. Everyone else seemed to be well-adjusted members of society.

After the message, Pastor Earl put his Bible down and prayed. The worship team came back to the stage and played softly. Next, the pastor asked if anyone had a word from the Lord.

Alisa gently nudged her elbow into Danny's rib. "Here comes the horse-and-pony show."

Danny looked around to see if anyone would say something, but no one did.

Pastor Earl said, "We can wait as long as we need to." Still, no one spoke.

The worship team played two more songs, then Pastor Earl said, "To whom much is given, much is expected. Anyone who has ever read the story of Jonah, can tell you it's much easier to obey God from the start. Danny, has God given you something to share with us?"

Danny felt his face turn white as he looked at Alisa.

She grinned at his pasty appearance. "It's someone else with the same name silly."

Danny took comfort in her explanation and turned back toward the front.

Pastor Earl dismissed the service and cut around to the back door before the final song finished. He shook hands with Danny when he made it to the back. "I didn't mean to put you on the spot, but did God give you a vision, a dream perhaps?"

Danny's mouth went dry as a desert breeze. He looked at Alisa as if he expected her to confess that she'd told the pastor about the dream. "I . . . I . . . had a nightmare the other night."

"Would you like to hang around for a while after everyone leaves and tell me about it?"

"Yes." Once again, Danny wasn't sure what he was expecting, but this certainly wasn't it.

When the other people were gone, Danny, Alisa and Pastor Earl sat in the seats near the back. Danny started with their trip to church on Christmas Eve, then gave the pastor as many details as he could about the dream.

Danny was surprised when Pastor Earl turned his attention to Alisa.

"Why didn't you go up front with Danny at the church on Christmas Eve? Don't you think you need Jesus?"

Alisa looked down at her feet which were pressed tightly together. "I can't be saved."

"Why not?" the pastor asked.

She shook her head and began to cry. "I can't be forgiven."

"Everyone can be forgiven, child. You just have to ask."

"Not me. I've done something too terrible." She kept her face hidden as she sobbed.

Danny put his hand on her back, but he had no idea what to say or what to do.

"The only thing that is too terrible, is to think you are righteous by your own works and that you have no need of the precious blood of Jesus. I can tell you right now, that's not you. What do you think was so bad that God can't forgive you?"

She sobbed louder. "When I was in high school, I got pregnant. My mom . . ."

Pastor Earl held her hand. "It's okay, you can tell me."

Danny got up to retrieve a box of tissues from the front row of chairs and brought it to Alisa.

"My mom took me to get an abortion. A lot of my friends in school had them. I thought it was just a blob." Alisa continued sobbing. "Until the second I walked out the door of that clinic. At that moment, I knew I'd done something for which there was no forgiveness."

By this time Pastor Earl was sobbing as well. "Oh child, that liar called the devil is the one who told you it was just a blob of flesh. And ever since, the devil has been lying, telling you that God won't forgive you. Lies, lies, lies. Yes, you broke God's heart when you took that child's life. Just like I've done things that break His heart, but he wants to forgive you.

"Jesus paid the price for that sin and every other sin you've ever committed or ever will commit. His blood is the perfect sacrifice. Satan is lying to you when he tells you the blood of Christ isn't powerful enough to pay for your sin. No matter how great or how small the offense, by His stripes, we are healed."

Alisa lifted her face. Her makeup was running down her cheeks and her eyes were red from the tears. "God, I'm so sorry! Please forgive me. If you will, I'll live for you. I'm so sorry." Her voice trailed off into the sobs.

Pastor Earl continued to hold her hand and pray softly with his head bowed.

Danny kept his hand on her back and prayed silently. He also listened to the pastor. He couldn't make out what he was praying. He wondered if the man might be praying in tongues. He couldn't tell. Danny had been certain that hearing tongues would frighten him before, but not now. This was surely a man of God.

Minutes later, Alisa regained her composure and dried her face.

"Welcome to the family. The two of you are going to be mighty warriors for the Lord." Pastor Earl lowered his brow. "But, you need to stay pure until you're married. You might think I'm getting in your business, and you might be right. Nevertheless, I don't want to see the enemy making you ineffective, stealing your blessings and jeopardizing your souls."

Danny and Alisa looked at each other and nodded as they smiled.

"Now, about that dream. What do you think it means?"

Danny sat up straight. "Well, my friend Steven reminded me of Pharaoh's dream with the skinny, ugly cows. Each one of the seven cows represented one year of famine in the land. Of course, in my dream, there was just the one cow and it wasn't preceded by any fat cows. If I thought it was indeed a prophetic dream, I suppose it would mean that one year of famine is coming, since there were no fat cows indicating years of prosperity. My guess is that it's less than a year away. What do you think?"

"I would agree with your analysis. What do you think the grave means?"

"Well, it's empty, so I suppose America is still alive, but it seems to indicate that her death is imminent."

Pastor Earl rubbed his chin. "And what about the money?"

"No idea. What do you think?" Danny shrugged.

"In biblical times, famines were caused by either droughts or pestilence. Either the crops didn't grow or hordes of insects destroyed field after field. Hail and floods can also wipe out crops, but that was typically a localized event. In modern times, famine is usually either economic or political.

"Communism attempts to do the work of the free market and control the production and distribution of goods. It ends up creating famines either by accidentally misallocating resources, or by intentionally restricting goods to control the population."

"It sounds like your dream is about an economic famine. Every final good produced in our modern economy has several levels of credit transactions. For example, let's look at these donuts. First, someone had to grow the wheat. Most likely, they had to purchase the land and the farm equipment to plant, maintain and harvest the wheat on credit. Once produced, the wheat had to be transported. The trucker or logistics company also had to purchase their trucks and trailers on credit. Next is the wholesaler, who likewise purchased his delivery trucks and warehouses on credit. Finally, the donut shop purchased the ovens, fryers, buildings and franchise rights on credit. All along that process are goods supplied by other producers who used credit. Think about the separate components in the delivery truck, the tires, battery, radio, and engine are all produced by separate companies who are dependent on credit. If credit freezes up, that entire process goes down. Our way of life is absolutely dependent upon credit."

Danny listened closely. "I had to take some financial management and economics courses for my degree, but they were all related to health care. I can see how it all carries over though."

The pastor continued, "The cow in your dream was eating money, lots and lots of money, but he was still thin. It was as if the money had no nutritional value, which is on par with our current monetary system. The U.S. dollar is backed by absolutely nothing. Well that's not completely true; it is backed by a very big military and the remnants of the petro-dollar system. I won't bore you with the details, but since the seventies, the Saudis have used their influence in OPEC to ensure that oil is traded in U.S. dollars, in exchange for military support from the U.S.. Fewer and fewer countries have been going along with that program, and our recent support of Iran has even jeopardized our relationship with the Saudis. On top of all that, we doubled the supply of dollars since the crisis we had ten years ago. More dollars competing for the same amount of goods and services eventually means what?"

Danny applied this to what he'd learned about supply and demand in economics. "Higher prices?"

"Exactly! As a direct result of the dollar having no value, or in reference to your dream, no nutritional value to stem off the economic famine."

Alisa looked unconvinced. "But they fixed the problem last time. Credit didn't freeze up."

Pastor Earl grinned. "Not really. They kept us from going over the cliff by cutting interest rates to zero and doubling the money supply. It would be tough to cut interest rates this time. If you give people a negative rate of return, they'll just stick the money under their mattress, which will also work to restrict funds available for credit. The Fed could theoretically double the money supply again, but the economy is like an addict. It requires an ever-higher dose of the drug to get a decreasingly lower level of intoxication. Doubling the money supply last time didn't save the job market. It only served to re-inflate the bubble in financial assets and put in a temporary bottom for the crisis. Even after the Fed's best efforts, just over half of working-age Americans have jobs. Many of those are in the service industry, which is very volatile. Restaurants, retail stores, and bars are the first to feel the pinch in an economic downturn."

Alisa interjected. "We work in a restaurant, but it stays busy, even when the other places around us are slow."

Pastor Earl glanced at her, then at Danny. "That might buy you a little time, but in an economic famine, very few restaurants will be able to stay open. You should save as much money as you can.

"Back to what I was saying. Doubling the money supply last time meant creating ten trillion new dollars. This time it would mean twenty trillion. There is no way bond holders would sit still for that. We would see dramatic price increases for food and housing. And in the end, it wouldn't do much to stop the crisis. But that doesn't mean the government won't do it. When a desperate person only has one choice of action, he'll usually take it."

Danny considered how everything the pastor was telling him fit in with his dream. "Sounds like you've been following all of this pretty close. I guess you aren't surprised by the dream."

"First Chronicles 12 talks about the sons of Issachar who understood the times and knew what Israel should do. Unfortunately, not enough pastors pay attention to the times and therefore have little advice for their flocks as to what they should do. If the church was more involved in politics, economics and culture, we wouldn't be in the mess we're in."

"The American church at large has held a much-distorted gauge for success. Most have looked for filled seats or a large income to be their measure of achievement. Even the high-minded, perhaps the best of the bunch, have looked for conversions to prove they've discharged their duties faithfully. While it is a far better thing to win souls than to fill seats and coffers, it wasn't the great commission. In Matthew 28, Jesus instructs his disciples to go teach all nations to observe everything he'd taught them. It wasn't about getting someone to say the magic prayer, but to live lives committed to the teachings of Christ."

Danny was unsettled by that comment. "Wait. I prayed a prayer on Christmas Eve, Alisa just prayed a prayer asking for forgiveness. Are you saying we're not saved?"

Pastor Earl put his hand on Danny's shoulder to comfort him. "I'm not implying that at all. That is a very important first step. Look at that beautiful ring on Alisa's finger. I expect that eventually, she'll have another one, as will you. You'll have a ceremony and publicly declare your devotion to one another. But is it the ring or the wedding that makes you husband and wife, or the commitment?"

"The commitment, I suppose." Danny was beginning to understand.

"If after the wedding, Danny runs off with another woman, and you never hear from him again, do you think that ring and that ceremony means anything?"

"I'd kill him, but no. None of it means anything without the commitment." Alisa patted Danny firmly on the knee.

The pastor chuckled. "It's the same concept. There's nothing mysterious about salvation. The enemy just likes to keep folks confused."

"Pastor Earl," Danny asked, "How could the church have stopped the death of America, if that's what my dream means?"

"Over sixty-five million children have been murdered in abortion clinics since Roe vs. Wade. According to the Pew Research Center, over ninety percent of the country called themselves Christian, whether Protestant or Catholic, when the ruling was passed down. And while that number has declined rapidly, even today those who call themselves Christians are still near seventy percent. How could the politicians who uphold abortion continue to be elected for over four decades if pastors were involved in the political process and teaching the truth to their congregants? Every pastor in America who has been derelict in their duty will have the blood of those murdered children on their hands on judgment day. Every so-called Christian who has either not voted, or cast their ballot for a pro-choice candidate will have to answer to God for their action or inaction."

"But they can be forgiven, right?" It was obvious that Alisa was still worried about her own salvation.

"Of course, if they repent." The pastor took her hand.

"I understand how that's a sin morally, but what does it have to do with economics?" Danny inquired.

"Pastors have also sat idly by while our country has abused our monetary system. Not that it was a sustainable system in the first place, but that's another rabbit trail that we won't go down tonight. But, ancient Israel's prosperity was directly linked to their obedience to God, throughout the Hebrew Scriptures."

"What does that have to do with America? We're not Israel." Alisa put her chin on her hand and her elbow on her knee as she leaned in for the pastor's response.

The pastor explained. "No, but in the book of Isaiah, God calls all the nations of the known world to account for their disobedience to him. Isaiah specifically has prophecies against the two major empires at the time, Babylon and Assyria. He also calls out Egypt, Cush, Moab, Damascus, and Tyre. Isaiah 34 is a blanket judgment to all nations. If God's curses for disobedience are applicable to all nations, we might assume that his blessings for obedience could also be incurred. Does that make sense?"

Danny nodded. "Yeah, it's a lot to take in."

"Why don't we wrap it up for tonight? If you don't mind, I'd like to share your dream with the congregation on Sunday. Will you be here?"

"No, Alisa is going to South Carolina with me to meet my family. Our friend Steven will probably be here though. And we'll be here the following week. Any suggestions on what we should be doing to get ready for all of this?''

Pastor Earl stood up. "That's a big question. For now, make sure you are spending time in prayer and reading the Bible; and watch your spending habits. Don't spend money on anything you don't need. Of course, it wouldn't hurt to have a few staples around. If it's a famine, food resources will get tight."

"What should we read in the Bible? Should we start at the beginning?"

The pastor walked them to the door. "Start with Romans. Then read the New Testament, beginning in Matthew, front to back. When you get to Romans, read it again. It's worth understanding. We'll see where you are after your visit with your folks and talk more about it."

Danny shook the pastor's hand, then he and Alisa left.

On the ride home Alisa took Danny's hand. "I'm so glad we came tonight. I feel free. Like I have never felt in my life."

"Me, too."

"So you're going to drop me off at my place?"

"Yeah. I'll miss you, but it's the right thing to do."

"I know. I'll call you to say good night."

He pulled her hand to his lips to kiss it. "Okay."

CHAPTER 5

I charge thee therefore before God, and the Lord Jesus Christ, who shall judge the quick and the dead at his appearing and his kingdom; preach the word; be instant in season, out of season; reprove, rebuke, exhort with all long suffering and doctrine. For the time will come when they will not endure sound doctrine; but after their own lusts shall they heap to themselves teachers, having itching ears; and they shall turn away their ears from the truth, and shall be turned unto fables.

2 Timothy 4:1-4

Danny was at work fifteen minutes early the next day. He grabbed a stack of clean cloth napkins from the laundry room, took them to a table near the back of the restaurant and began making the intricate folds before placing them on the table.

Steven walked in shortly thereafter. "Hey, you're early. I'm going to order some shrimp and grits before my shift. Do you want anything?"

"No thanks."

"Okay, I'll be right back." Steven walked to the computer, rang in his food and returned to the table where Danny was folding napkins. "How did it go last night?"

"Alisa committed her life to Jesus."

"Praise God!" Steven looked very excited.

The two of them folded napkins together, silently for a while.

Danny broke the silence. "The pastor over there, Earl, he's a smart guy. I can't understand why it's such a small church."

Steven smirked. "People don't want to hear all that; even Christians. They want to go to church on Sunday so they can check it off their to-do list. They like to hear a warm, fuzzy message that makes them feel good. Very few want to be instructed on how to live a life that pleases God. If Pastor Earl is challenging them with sound doctrine, most folks will go to another church where a pastor will tell them what their itchy ears want to hear."

"Wow. That's sad. I guess I don't understand why they would bother going in the first place. But you're right, Pastor Earl wasted no time getting up in our business."

"Let me guess, he told you the same thing I told you."

"Yep. Alisa slept at her house last night."

"Good job. Is she working tonight?"

Trish came out of the kitchen with a plate in her hand. "Steven, here is your shift meal, enjoy. Danny, nice to see you here early."

"Thanks." Steven bowed his head to pray silently before eating.

Danny smiled at Trish. "I told you I would be."

"Keep it up." Trish continued walking to the front.

Danny continued to fold the napkins. "Alisa will be here at six."

"Tell me what the pastor said about your dream." Steven ate his shrimp and grits while Danny told him all that Pastor Earl had told him about the dream and the economy.

As the evening progressed, the restaurant filled up with people that were lined out the door waiting for tables. Danny poured all of his focus into keeping up with his tables. The kitchen got backed up with orders around eight o' clock, but the service staff intentionally began stalling tables to give them a chance to get caught up. By 8:45, the kitchen had cleared the ticket board and the food was coming out smoothly once again. Danny was so busy he didn't get a chance to say much to Alisa until the end of the night. It was after 10:30 by the time his last table paid. He walked to the rear service station to close out the last check.

Alisa was there. "What a crazy night! Do you think you'll walk away with 200 dollars?"

"Easily. What about you?"

"I think so, but it will be close. Of course, I didn't come in until six, so you got a head start on me." Alisa reached in her pocket and took out her closed checks, credit card statements and cash to organize it into separate piles.

Two hundred in tips represented a mile marker for a good night at Lilly's. It was rare that anyone would exceed that amount by more than twenty or thirty dollars.

Steven walked into the service area. "I was slammed tonight."

"You did good?" Alisa asked.

"Oh yeah, I think I'm close to 250. I had some big spenders. I hope it stays like this for a while before Danny's dream comes true."

Danny smiled out of one side of his mouth. "Make it while you can and save as much as possible."

"So you're really buying into this." Alisa got a drink of water.

"Aren't you?" Steven looked surprised by the comment.

"Yeah. I guess, but who knows how far out in the future it could be." Everyone had been too busy to stop for breaks all night, so she chugged the rest of her water.

Steven leaned against the counter. "Danny is right. Save all you can while you can. As Pastor Earl pointed out, there was no fat cow in his dream, so it sounds like an imminent event to me."

"Did you tell your parents that you two got engaged?"

Alisa threw her head back in mock disgust. "Ahh! Don't make me think about that! Yes, I told them."

Steven held both hands out. "And?"

"And they want me to have the wedding up there."

"Is that so bad?" Danny asked.

"Yes! All of our friends are here. I don't even speak to the girls I went to high school with. They, well we, were like piranhas. Our clique was more about a status symbol than companionship. I'm not like that anymore and I want nothing to do with them."

"Your parents will understand if you want to have the wedding here," Steven said.

Alisa pursed her lips and shook her head. "Their circle of friends operates just like mine did in high school. While it exists on a more complex playing field, it's a status symbol as well. Weddings are all about showing everyone else up."

"But it's our wedding. We can have it wherever we want. We don't have to play into that. You're not a pawn in their chess game." Danny hated that Alisa's own parents would make her feel like that.

She sighed. "True, but we've got our own chess game to play. Especially if we really believe that an economic famine is coming."

Danny was confused. "What do you mean?"

"I mean, if we force them to come down here, they'll be very stingy about gifts and such. If we go up there, they'll have to impress their friends. Not to mention, all of their friends will be obligated to give big gifts."

"Where are we going to put a bunch of fancy gifts?"

"We take them back and get the cash. That's how it works. That's what everybody does."

Steven crossed his arms. "Then why don't they just give cash in the first place."

Alisa turned to him. "Because nobody sees the cash when we're opening presents."

"What a sick world." Danny shook his head. "But whatever you decide, I'll be okay with it."

"Good answer." Steven winked at Danny. "Let's get this place cleaned up and get out of here. I'm beat."

Alisa hugged Danny. "We'll decide together."

CHAPTER 6

How is the faithful city become a harlot! It was full of judgment; righteousness lodged in it; but now murderers. Thy silver is become dross, thy wine mixed with water: Thy princes are rebellious, and companions of thieves: every one loveth gifts, and followeth after rewards: they judge not the fatherless, neither doth the cause of the widow come unto them. Therefore saith the Lord, the LORD of hosts, the mighty One of Israel, Ah, I will ease me of mine adversaries, and avenge me of mine enemies: And I will turn my hand upon thee, and purely purge away thy dross, and take away all thy tin.

Isaiah 1: 21-25

Danny was still sleeping when his phone rang Friday morning. He picked it up without looking at the number. "Good morning sweetheart."

"Bro, please don't ever call me that again."

Steven's voice was not what he had been expecting. "Alisa calls me right before she goes to sleep and as soon as she wakes up."

"Turn on the financial channel."

Danny groggily got out of bed. "Last night wore me out. That's no way to make a living. What's happening?"

"The S&P dropped seven percent in the first hour of trading and triggered the circuit breaker which shut the market down for fifteen minutes. When it reopened, the market rebounded several hundred points, but it looks like it's headed back down."

Danny found his remote and clicked on the television. "Sounds like a lot."

"Yeah, it's a record-point plunge. The Dow was down 1,300 points when the circuit breaker popped. This could be the fulfillment of your dream."

Danny looked at the red numbers scrolling across the bottom of the screen. "The reporters don't look that upset. Are you sure it's such a big deal?"

"These guys are shills, man. Their job is to talk investors off the ledge; stem the panic. My uncle is a day trader. He taught me a thing or two about how all of this stuff works. The big financial reporters get fed inside information by the government which they can use to trade for mega money, and in exchange, they have to report whatever they're told."

"Isn't that illegal?"

"As Nixon said, it's not illegal if the government does it."

Danny paused for a second to process everything. "What are you doing right now? Can you come by? Maybe we should start trying to think of a game plan."

"I can do that."

"Great. Would you mind picking up Alisa and bringing her when you come?"

"I can swing by and get her."

"Thanks, I'll call her and tell her to be ready." Danny hung up and quickly called Alisa.

"Hello?"

"Hey, Steven is on his way to pick you up. The market is crashing. He thinks this is what my dream was about."

"Oh, okay. What should we do?"

"I'm not sure. We'll talk about it when you get here. I love you."

"Love you, too. Bye."

Danny made some coffee and had a bowl of cereal as he watched the financial news. Steven and Alisa arrived within the hour.

Steven helped himself to a cup of coffee. "What has happened since we last spoke?"

Danny shrugged, "They said it's now down more than nine percent. If the S&P plunges to thirteen percent, they halt trading again for fifteen minutes. The reporters said people were selling today because Monday is the last trading day of the year.

Then the market is closed Tuesday for New Year's and buyers will probably step in on Wednesday."

Steven shook his head. "That's hogwash. They don't believe it for a second. If that happens, it's only because the plunge protection team steps in and starts buying unprecedented amounts of equities."

Alisa made herself a bowl of cereal. "But markets crash all the time. They're up one day and down the next."

"Not like this. This is a record one-day point decline and besides the crash in the eighties, the S&P has only been down nine percent, one other time."

"How much was it down in the eighties?" Danny asked.

"I think they said twenty percent." Steven furrowed his brow.

"And the world didn't end." Alisa continued eating her cereal.

"Danny's dream wasn't about the end of the world. It was about the death of America."

"Good point. So what should we do?" Alisa took another bite.

Danny stood up to get a notepad and an ink pen. "Pastor Earl explained that if credit markets freeze up, everything comes to a halt. Maybe we should stock up on some extra food; can goods, stuff that will keep for a long time."

Alisa took her bowl to the sink and washed it. "We all have to go to work in a couple of hours. Then, we're supposed to leave for South Carolina on Sunday. I guess we could go tomorrow morning, but I haven't even packed yet."

Steven sipped his coffee. "Why don't we go ahead and make a run right now? I'm not even sure what kinds of things to buy. If we go buy some stuff now, we can get an idea of how much all of this is going to cost."

"We could do that." Danny jotted down some ideas on the notepad. "If I have cereal and coffee, I can make it through the first half of the day."

Alisa poured a cup of coffee. "Write down pop tarts, candy bars, cookies, hard candy . . ."

"What, are you an elf?" Steven smirked.

Alisa put her hands on her hips. "For your information, sugar is a natural preservative."

Steven rolled his eyes. "Tell that to a dentist. Canned soup is good. And you better get powdered milk unless you're going to eat cereal with water."

Danny wrote down all the ideas. "And canned pasta, chicken, tuna, vegetables."

"Don't you think regular pasta will keep?" Alisa asked. "It's cheaper than canned pasta."

"Good idea." Danny kept writing.

Steven walked over to look at what Danny was writing. "Leave some space next to each item on your notepad. We need to write down the prices and figure out how much we can spend."

Alisa lifted her brow. "If we have another busy night, we can all pitch in whatever we make tonight."

Steven pointed at her. "Good plan. In fact, can we all put in tonight's and tomorrow night's tips?"

Danny nodded. "I think so. I've got rent set aside for a couple of months, plus my trip to South

Carolina is covered."

Alisa said, "I'm fine, too. Two night's worth of tips for all three of us; that should be well over a thousand dollars. We can buy a lot of food if we budget it right. Plus, we can look for sales."

"And coupons!" Danny wrote down every idea as it was tossed out.

"Where will we store everything?" Alisa asked.

"I can put some shelves on my bedroom wall." Danny said.

"So can I," Steven added.

Alisa bit her fingernail. "Sorry, I can't live in a warehouse. Maybe I can clean out some junk from under my bed."

Danny sat his notepad on the coffee table. "Let's not count our chickens before they hatch. Let's go to the store, see what we can get, then worry about where to keep it all."

"The S&P is down eleven percent. I think we should get a move on." Steven grabbed his jacket and stood by the door.

Danny put on his jacket. "Let me grab my shoes and I'm ready to go."

Alisa put her boots on. "Whole Foods is right up the street, on Victory."

"No way, much too expensive. Kroger is just up the road from Whole Foods." Danny said as he opened the door.

Steven led the way out the door. "BI-LO is on Victory also, and they're even cheaper if you get the off brands."

"BI-LO it is then." Danny closed the door behind him and they headed out.

"Who's driving?" Alisa asked.

Steven looked at Danny. "Maybe we should both drive so we'll have more cargo space."

"Yeah, let's do it. See you there." Danny held Alisa's hand as they split ways with Steven to go to Danny's car.

Once at the grocery, Danny and Alisa grabbed a cart.

"No one else seems to be worried about anything. Maybe we are overreacting." Alisa surveyed the aisles as they waited for Steven.

"I don't think a one-day stock market crash, in and of itself, is necessarily such a catastrophic event. But, perhaps if we panic early, we can avoid the rush. Besides, we're just getting a few things today. Then we can think about what else to get later. Come on, Steven will find us."

Steven found them in the soup aisle. "These soups are buy one, get one free."

Danny compared them to the store brand condensed soups he was looking at. "These are still cheaper. And being condensed, they'll take up less room."

Alisa took a can of the condensed soup. "Is there any chance we could lose municipal water? If so, condensed soup might not be the best choice."

Danny nodded. "I doubt that could happen from an economic collapse, but other disasters could certainly disrupt the water supply. It's a really good point."

Steven put several cans of the ready-to-eat soup

in his cart. "These look like higher quality soups anyway. I'm going to splurge."

Danny and Alisa put a few cans of each type in their basket.

"Look, pasta is buy one, get one!" Alisa was excited.

"Great. Too bad the pasta sauce isn't on sale as well." Danny put some of the pasta in his cart and looked at the prices of the sauce.

Steven also took some pasta. "I'm going to hold off on the sauce. We can look online and see if Kroger has a deal on it."

"Or, we might find coupons." Alisa added.

"Dried fruit, apples, bananas, pineapples; it's a little pricey, but it has a high-calorie content," Steven said.

"You say that like it's a good thing." Alisa furrowed her brow.

Steven retorted, "It is. If there are no grocery stores open, you won't have to count calories unless it's to make sure you are getting enough of them. It's tough for us to imagine in this country; we're the fattest nation on the planet. In the majority of the world, people are looking for foods with the highest amounts of fat, calories and carbs so they can stay alive. If what Pastor Earl told you guys about Danny's dream turns out to be true, we may soon have the opportunity to find out what that's like."

The three friends spent the next half hour collecting an assortment of low-priced items that they could eat in an emergency.

Danny made a quick estimate of the cost in his

head. "That's pretty close to what I can spend for now. Why don't we haul this stuff home and assess how much we have. We can look at the calorie count, nutritional content and cost. That will let us know how long we can survive on what we have and give us an idea of how to spend the rest of our money."

Steven and Alisa agreed and they headed to the checkout.

Friday night at the restaurant was even busier than Thursday had been. On Saturday morning, the three of them met up at Steven's apartment.

Danny handed Alisa and Steven copies of a spreadsheet he'd made with the items they'd bought, prices, calories, and a price-per-one-hundred-calorie ratio.

"What the heck is this?" Alisa looked up from the paper with an expression of confusion.

Danny explained. "It shows how much stuff we bought, what it cost us and how long it would keep us alive, based on 2,000 calories a day."

Steven chuckled. "I eat 2,000 calories by lunch and I'm still skinny."

Danny pursed his lips. "We may have to make some adjustments. I would just need to change the numbers in the formulas. I have everything saved in Excel."

Alisa scanned the document. "I could never study business or administration. What am I looking at here?"

Danny pointed to the price-calorie ratio column. "This shows how much one hundred calories of each item costs. As you can see, the high carb items are the cheapest. The proteins are the most expensive. Obviously, we need proteins, but we'll have to make the majority of our food storage plan with carbohydrates. That's okay because most nutritional pyramids have carbs as the base anyway."

"We spent about a hundred and fifty dollars yesterday and bought enough for the three of us to stay alive for three weeks, of course that was assuming 2,000 calories a day. If I bump that up to 2,500 calories, it will knock a few days off our survival time."

Alisa handed the paper back to Danny. "How about I let you guys figure all of this out, and you just tell me what to buy."

Steven looked more closely at the paper. "Beans have protein, and they're cheap. Did you look at the price of the dried beans?"

"No. Do you know how to cook them?" Danny asked.

Alisa plopped down on Steven's couch. "We can ask Chef Eric from work. The kitchen uses dried black beans and dried red beans. They can't be too hard to cook."

"Good idea. And rice is cheap. I looked at the big twenty-pound bags yesterday. It's a lot of food for not much money." Danny took out his notepad and jotted down some notes.

"And rice goes great with beans." Steven walked out of the living room and soon returned with his jacket.

"Lets' go stock up. Alisa and I are leaving to

Nana's in the morning so this will be our last haul until we get back." Danny took Alisa's hand and helped her up from the couch.

"Then let's make it count. I suppose we should take both cars again." Steven held the door open for Alisa and Danny.

The first stop was Kroger. Alisa waved a handful of coupons in the air. "I've got coupons for pasta sauce, and they have it buy one, get one free!"

Steven grabbed a cart. "They won't let you use a coupon on a BOGO deal."

"Oh yes they will. I looked up the store coupon policy online this morning. They even let you use a coupon on the item you're buying and the free item."

"I'll believe it when I see it." Steven led the way to the beans and rice aisle.

Danny grabbed another cart and followed him. "Alisa, you better get a second cart. The rice is going to take up a lot of room."

Steven grabbed a twenty-pound bag of rice and set it in his cart "Wow. There's a big difference in price between the cheapest twenty-pound bag of rice and the most expensive. Nine bucks for these, but those are twenty dollars; more than double."

Danny grabbed one also. "And they only have three of the cheap ones. It would be worth the drive to hit some other grocery stores and see if they have some more of the lower-priced rice."

"We've got time. We can check out Publix and Walmart. I just wish I had known ahead of time so I could have looked for coupons." Alisa flipped through the sales paper she'd grabbed from the front of the store. "Look, the two-pound bags of red beans are on sale for three dollars."

Danny grabbed the last nine-dollar bag of rice. "I'll check with the clerk. They may have more in the back."

Steven and Alisa cleared out the bags of red beans while Danny went to find a stock clerk. He found one in the next aisle over. "Excuse me, do you have any more rice in the back? You only had three of the big bags for nine dollars."

The clerk was polite. "Sorry, we don't have much of anything in the back. When we run out of an item, it gets ordered and comes in on the next truck."

"Wow! So if there is a run on the store, the shelves get cleared out, and stay that way until the next truck comes?"

The clerk nodded. "It happens every time we get a scare from a hurricane. It's called just-in-time inventory. All grocery stores run on that system now."

"Thanks for your help." Danny smiled, then walked back over to find Alisa and Steven.

"There's no such thing as a back room with boxes and boxes of food. What you see is what you get. I never realized that." Danny's face showed his enlightened concern.

"Then it's a good thing that we're stocking up now before panic sets in." Steven pushed his cart to the next aisle.

Alisa found a few other sale items that everyone liked, then they headed for the checkout. Their next stop was Walmart where they headed straight for the beans and rice.

"Same story here. Only a few of the low-priced bags of rice." Steven began loading his cart.

"But the beans are a lot cheaper." Alisa began picking up several bags of the Great Value brand beans.

Danny looked at the variety of dried beans available. "Did you ask Chef Eric how to cook them?"

Alisa picked up several more bags. "Soak them overnight in water with a tablespoon of baking soda and then simmer them for an hour or until they are tender."

"What is the baking soda for?" Steven asked.

"It reduces the cooking time by nearly half. And it makes them more digestible so they don't give you gas."

"Then we better get some baking soda. What about salt?" Danny led the way to the baked goods aisle.

Alisa answered, "Chef said not to add salt until they were almost finished. It can make your beans hard and require a longer cooking time."

Steven held up some large boxes. "Pancake mix. It's cheap and full of carbs."

"Yeah, but what do you have to add to it?" Danny inspected the boxes. "You need eggs and milk for this one."

"This one says just add water. I'm going with it." Steven placed four family sized boxes in his cart.

They hit the next aisle where Steven located the dried fruit. "The Great Value brand dried fruit is much cheaper as well. And they're fairly well stocked with it."

The team soon had three carts quite full of staples and headed home.

That night was extremely busy at Lilly's. After the rush, the three friends congregated in the back service station.

Danny grabbed a glass of water for the first time that evening. "Steven, you were running through the restaurant."

"Yeah. I was weeded." Steven made himself a Coke at the beverage station.

Alisa organized her cash into stacks of ones, fives, tens, twenties, fifties and hundreds. "How much did you guys make?

Danny shrugged. "225 dollars."

Steven gulped down his soda. "Same here. Maybe 250 dollars. If so, that will be a record for me."

Alisa counted. "I'm way over 200 dollars. That's good. We'll have a nice chunk of change to buy supplies when we get back from South Carolina."

Danny finished his water. "Are you going to Savannah Christian Chapel in the morning?"

"Yeah." Steven made himself yet another Coke.

Alisa scowled at Steven. "If you don't oversleep because you had too much pop tonight."

"Doesn't affect me." Steven shook his head. "We've still got at least three more hours before we get this place cleaned up and get out of here. This sugar rush will be long gone."

Danny smiled. "Tell Pastor Earl that we'll see him when we get back."

"Sure. Think I should tell him that we're buying supplies for the famine?"

Danny thought for a second. "It was his idea. I guess that would be okay."

It was late by the time they'd cleaned up their sections and checked out.

Alisa hugged Steven. "We won't see you, so happy New Year."

"You, too."

Danny gave him a hug next. "Thanks again for working those shifts for me."

Steven patted him on the back. "If it stays this busy, I'll be thanking you."

Danny dropped Alisa off at her house. The next morning would come early and he was exhausted.

CHAPTER 7

Go to the ant, thou sluggard; consider her ways, and be wise: Which having no guide, overseer, or ruler, provideth her meat in the summer, and gathereth her food in the harvest.

Proverbs 6:6-8

Sunday morning, Danny climbed the stairs of the old house and rang the bell to Alisa's apartment. The buzzer sounded and he opened the front door. He walked down the hall to her apartment. "Good morning."

"I'm running late. Sorry. I set my alarm. I should have gotten up the second it went off." Alisa scurried back and forth, drinking her coffee, packing her suitcase and nibbling on a muffin.

"Don't worry about it. I told Nana we would be there before dark. We have plenty of time. I didn't want to get up either. I feel like I've been hit by a truck after the last three nights at work. The money is great, but the stress of trying to keep up with so many tables, being on your feet for so long, and rushing to get everyone taken care of takes a lot out of you."

"Yeah, poor Steven has to do it every night this week. So what time would we have to leave to get there before dark?"

"It's a four-hour drive. Why? How much longer is it going to take you to get ready?"

"An hour, tops. Is that okay?"

"Sure. That should get us there an hour before dark, even with breaks. Is there anything I can do to help you?"

"No, I was going to get up early and pack, so that's the big thing. Between the grocery shopping the last two days and working, I didn't get a chance. I don't want Nana to hate me."

Danny laughed. "Why would she hate you?"

Alisa buzzed through the kitchen, refilled her coffee cup then left the room again. "For making us late. She's already not going to like the fact that I'm a Yankee."

Danny rolled his eyes. "She's going to love you. She might not understand your Yankee talk, but she'll love you."

"Ha. I hope I can understand her." Alisa called out from the bathroom as she put on her makeup.

By 12:30, Alisa was packed and Danny was carrying her suitcase to the car.

Ten minutes later, Alisa said, "Rats! I forgot my Bible. I was hoping I'd have a little time to read it."

"I brought mine, I'll share. There's no shortage of Bibles at Nana's anyway."

"What time is your sister getting there?"

"I talked to her yesterday morning. She said around 9:00 or 10:00 tonight. It's about an eight-hour drive for them. She's coming in an RV."

Alisa cocked her head to one side. "Are they going somewhere else besides Nana's?"

"Not that I know of, why?"

"Isn't it strange that they would come in an RV?"

Danny shrugged. "Maybe they are sleeping in it so we can each have one of the guest rooms."

"You said she has a pull out couch. It seems that would be better. The temperature is going to be in the low thirties. Your sister and her husband will have to run a heater if they sleep in the RV."

"You're right. I didn't think to ask why they were coming in the RV. I'm sure we'll find out soon enough."

They were silent for the next several miles. Danny relaxed as he took in the rural winter scenery along State Road 21.

"Have you had any more dreams?" Alisa broke the silence.

"Thankfully, no."

"You'll tell me if you do, right?"

"Of course."

"Even if they're bad? Even if you think it might scare me? You'll still tell me?"

"Even if they're horrible dreams, you'll be the

first to know. I promise."

Alisa looked out her window. "What about premonitions? What do you think will happen to the stock market tomorrow?"

"I don't have any premonitions. I have no idea."

"Logically speaking, what would you expect to happen?"

Danny sighed. "Logically speaking? I don't know. I guess if Steven's uncle is right, the government will pull strings to prop up the markets. But if the financial news blamed the crash on year-end selling, maybe they will let it fall tomorrow and wait until Wednesday to put it on life support. What's your theory?"

"Looking at a spreadsheet makes me dizzy. I don't have a theory. If the market keeps going down, do you think it will affect business at the restaurant?"

"Absolutely. My Health Care Economics professor was a pretty sharp guy. It wasn't part of the curriculum, but he taught us a thing or two about retirees spending habits as it relates to the market. Historically, most retirees have tried to invest in fixed income investments, things like CDs and government bonds. Since the interest rates have been so low, more retirees have had to invest in more speculative stocks to try to make up for the returns lost by low-interest rates. When the market goes up, they see higher account values and feel more comfortable spending money. When it goes down, the opposite happens."

"That makes sense. But all of our customers aren't retired."

"Yeah, but I suspect that same principle would spill over into other sectors of the economy. However, even if it was only retired folks, they probably make up close to twenty percent of our customers. Think about it; if we suddenly had twenty percent fewer tables that would be a big hit."

"That's true. I hope it doesn't happen for a while. Should we stop to eat somewhere?"

"I made ham sandwiches. I also have chips and some sodas in the trunk. Remember what Pastor Earl said, we shouldn't spend any money that we don't have to. We can pull over at the state park, just ahead. The sun is out, so it's not too cold. We can eat at a picnic table if that's okay."

Alisa smiled at him. "Yes, it's fine with me. I'm glad you're disciplined. When it comes to cutting back on my spending, I'm going to have a rougher time than you."

They made a quick stop for lunch at Magnolia Springs State Park. Danny retrieved the cooler out of the trunk and took it to the picnic table. He grabbed a sandwich and handed one to Alisa.

"This place is so pretty. You have to bring me back here sometime."

"It is nice. We'll come back." They finished their lunch and got straight back on the road. Danny wanted to get to Nana's before sundown.

They arrived shortly after five o'clock. An older, mixed-breed farm dog ran up to the car and barked with his tail wagging.

"Rusty, how you doin', boy?" Danny greeted him with a scratch under the chin and a firm pat on the back.

Alisa got out and petted the animal. "I bet you're a good dog, aren't you?"

Nana opened the door, stepped onto the porch and called out in a thick Southern accent. "How y'all doin'?"

"We're good. Nana, this is Alisa."

"Why, you're prettier than a speckled pup in a little red wagon."

Alisa was obviously caught off guard by the odd compliment. "Uh, nice to meet you."

"Come on in here and get something to eat. Y'all must be hungry." Nana disappeared back into the house.

"Not really, we just . . ." Alisa tried to respond, but Nana was already out of earshot.

Danny opened his eyes wide and shook his head. He whispered to Alisa. "Never say no when she offers you food."

Alisa looked very confused. "Okay."

Danny led the way into the house. "Nana, Camille, and her husband won't be in until later tonight. I'm sure they'll be hungry. We can eat a little snack now and have dinner with them when they get here."

"Alright, I'll make you a plate of butter beans, ham and cornbread. Does she eat butter beans?"

"What's a butter bean?" Alisa sounded worried as she whispered the question.

"It's like a dark colored lima bean, but much better." Danny whispered his response to Alisa then called back to Nana who was in the kitchen. "She'll try a few. Thanks, Nana."

Alisa and Danny sat down at the table and

waited.

Minutes later, Nana came in with two plates, generously filled with butter beans, ham, cornbread, turnip greens, and macaroni and cheese. "Danny, you want to say grace?"

Danny bowed his head. "Lord, we thank you for a safe trip and this time to visit with my family. We pray that you'll watch over Cami and Nick as they drive here. We ask you to bless this food and we are so grateful for the sacrifice that you made so we might be saved. Amen."

Nana had a big smile on her face. "You invited Jesus into your heart, did you?"

"Yes." Danny grinned.

"Thank you, Lord. I've been praying that you would since you were a little boy. Guess I'll have to find something else to pray for. Y'all want tea?"

"Please." Danny took a bite of the macaroni.

"Unsweet for me, please." Alisa took a bite of the cornbread.

Nana went back in the kitchen to make drinks. "Unsweet? Where're you from?"

Alisa looked at Danny as if she'd just stepped in dog poop. "Connecticut. But sweet tea is fine."

"Bless your heart. You're a long way from home."

Alisa whispered. "Is that the polite way to say 'Yankee go home'?"

Danny snickered. "No, that's just Nana."

"I thought we were having a snack? This looks like a plate from Mrs. Wilkes' Dining Room."

"Wait 'til dinner. You ain't seen nothing yet."

Nana came back with two glasses of sweet tea.

"Daniel, when did you get saved?"

"Christmas Eve."

"Did you get saved at the same time, Lisa?"

"It's Alisa, but no. I got saved two days later."

"Hallelujah! Daniel, what has God been showing you?"

Danny looked at Alisa then back at Nana. "Uh, well, we started reading Romans. It's helping us understand how all of this works and how we should live."

Nana smiled and patted Danny on the hand. "You just got here. You can tell me whenever you get ready."

Danny's heartbeat quickened. Could she possibly know about the dream? Obviously, God had found some way to communicate it to Pastor Earl. Was it possible that Nana also had some sort of inside line? He grinned somewhat nervously and said, "Okay."

Alisa stopped chewing for a moment and looked at Danny. She evidently found the exchange to be peculiar as well.

After they finished eating, Danny and Alisa went to the car to retrieve their luggage.

Nana held the door for them when they came back in. "Danny, you can sleep on the pull-out couch and I'll put Lisa upstairs, in the small guest room. Remember, this old house is made out of wood planks, so I hear everything squeaking up and down those stairs. If I hear any sneaking around in the middle of the night, Danny will sleep in the barn the rest of the week. And I ain't got no heater in the barn."

Danny winked at Alisa. "Yes, ma'am."

Camille and Nick arrived just after nine o'clock. Danny introduced Alisa.

Alisa shook hands with them and rolled her eyes toward Nana. "I answer to Lisa, also."

Cami seemed to have picked up on the joke right away and laughed. "But she's a really good cook. And she'll always be there if you need her."

Alisa smiled out of one side of her mouth. "Yeah, we had a *snack* earlier. It was fantastic. It reminded me of my favorite place in Savannah, Mrs. Wilkes."

Cami chuckled. "We love that place. We go there every time we visit Savannah. Probably because it reminds me of Nana's."

As soon as Camille and Nick had brought their things in, Nana had dinner on the table and it was time to eat; again.

Alisa grabbed Danny's arm and whispered. "There's no way I can eat anything else. I'll pop."

"Just have a couple of bites." He whispered and kissed her on the head.

After Nick said grace, they began eating.

"So, Nick, are you guys going on a trip when you leave here?" Danny asked.

"No. Why?" Nick spooned some green beans onto his plate and passed the bowl.

"Because you brought the RV."

"No, Nana said it would be okay to park it on the other side of the barn. Our homeowners association won't let us park it on our property in D.C. and storage lot fees are outrageous." Nick cut into the ham on his plate.

That answer made sense to Danny. "Oh, that's

cool."

Alisa pried further. "But you have an eight-hour drive both ways every time you want to take it somewhere. Won't that eat into your vacation time?"

Nick looked at Cami as if he were letting her take that one.

Cami caught the look and said, "Yes, but we usually visit Nana anyway, so it actually works out to be more convenient."

Danny nodded as he ate. Sure, Cami visited Nana regularly, but while it might be the economic thing to do, an added sixteen-hour drive was hard to sell as convenient. He sensed there was something they didn't want to discuss. He'll talk to Cami tomorrow after breakfast to get the whole scoop.

Nana generally woke up with the chickens and wasn't careful about not making noise so others could sleep in. Danny knew if he wanted to get any sleep, he had best get everyone headed toward bed. "It's getting late. I guess we should all hit the hay soon."

Nick and Cami were familiar with the early mornings and didn't need much of a hint to go to bed.

"Yeah, we had a long trip. I could go to sleep right now," Cami said.

Alisa, however, didn't know what to expect. Danny wished he'd prepped her for the experience a bit more thoroughly, but he'd been worried that she might get scared and not want to come at all. "So breakfast is probably around 7:30."

"Oh, I should have brought an alarm clock,"

Alisa said.

"Nana will make sure you're up." He kissed her on the head and sent her upstairs. She survived the initial impact, and while there would always be surprises with Nana, it would get easier from here.

After breakfast the next morning, Cami said, "Nick has to make some calls for work. Alisa, do you and Danny want to walk down to the creek with me?"

"I need to call my parents. Can I take a rain check?" Alisa smiled.

"Sure. Danny, how about you?"

"Yeah, I'm sure Rusty will come along also." Danny grabbed his coat and a toboggan and followed Cami out the door. They walked out the gate and down the hill toward the creek.

"Alisa seems to be adapting well. Remember the first time I brought Nick here?"

Danny chuckled, "Yeah, he always sat as close to the door as possible; like he might have to make a run for it at some point. He's an old Army guy. Imagine how intimidating it can be for a little girl like Alisa."

"She's got fire, though. She can take it."

Danny smiled. "Yeah. She's sharp too. Plus, working in the restaurant, you learn to deal with peculiar folks."

"So when is the wedding?"

Danny sighed. "Soon, I hope, but her parents are kind of taking over all of that."

"Yeah, that stinks."

"What's the deal with the RV?"

"What do you mean?"

"I don't know. It seemed like I wasn't getting the full story. Is everything okay with you and Nick?"

"Oh yeah. We're making some contingencies."

That provided no clarification to Danny whatsoever. "Contingencies? For what?"

"Did you see the big market move on Friday?"

"Yes. It was frightening."

"It's actually something the Pentagon has been watching for a while. A lot of the top people at DOD are apprehensive. They've been bringing in experts to access the vulnerabilities to our monetary system and economy for several years."

"What does the economy have to do with the Pentagon?"

"A lot. For starters, you can't keep a trillion-dollar-a-year industry that produces no products going without a serious tax base. A bad economy eventually leads to deep cuts in the defense budget.

"On the next level of concerns, historically, when a nation's monetary system fails or the economy implodes, the entire governmental system is at risk. You're probably too young to remember when Argentina's president, de la Rua, fled the country in a helicopter back in 2001. Their economy had collapsed, the currency was garbage and the president had to bug out. Can you imagine something like that happening in America?"

"Wouldn't that be great if the socialist in office right now would run away?"

Cami laughed. "That part might be, but not the aftermath. Hitler came to power because of the dramatic political instabilities following the economic collapse of the Weimar Republic. You don't hear about it on the news, because no one wants to incite a panic, but everyone in Washington is worried."

"And you guys brought the RV here in case you have to get out of Washington? Couldn't you have driven it down whenever it was time to leave?"

Cami took a deep breath. "Maybe, or maybe not. Who knows what the conditions might be when and if something like that happens. There could be massive riots, roads could be blocked, and gangs could be stealing everything. We have a few provisions stocked up in the RV. We figure if we ever need to come here, the RV would give us a place to stay so we could have our own space. And, in the meantime, we can keep our supplies in there."

"Supplies? Are you talking about dry storage food?"

"That's part of it, yeah."

Danny considered what to tell Cami. He wanted to give her a clue that he'd been thinking along the same lines, but he wasn't ready to reveal the dream to her. "Alisa and I went to the store and bought a few extra things after we saw the market crash on Friday."

"That's smart, but Savannah might not be a very safe place to be if the world starts coming unglued."

Danny hadn't considered that. "Oh. You think we would have riots? Don't you think that type of stuff would be limited to places like DC?"

"If people don't have food, they'll get very desperate, very fast."

Danny remembered the chain reaction that Pastor

Earl had explained if credit began to disappear. Now he was hearing a similar scenario being suggested by his older sister. He had considered what the outcome might be, but Cami was forcing him to take a closer look. "Couldn't the government provide food in that type of situation?"

Cami pursed her lips. "The government can't do anything. You were really young when Katrina came through New Orleans, but I remember it. FEMA couldn't even get water to those people and it was only one city. Imagine an economic catastrophe thousands of times bigger than Katrina. It's an opportunity for a colossal failure of government. Washington doesn't know what to do when times are good, they have zero aptitude for solving problems. In fact, they're the ones who have created this debacle.

"It's good that you're stocking up on a few extra items for your apartment, but if things get really bad, you need to have a plan to come out to the farm. And don't wait until everything fails. The second you see conditions begin to deteriorate, drop everything and leave.

"Do you think Alisa will understand and follow your lead if the worst happens?"

"Yes. She is all in on everything we're doing. We have a friend in Savannah, Steven. He's been helping us with putting together a plan. I'd hate to abandon him."

Cami stuck her hands in her pocket to keep warm. "Talk to Nana about it. We'll need more people around here. If he's a hard worker, there will always be a place for people like that."

"Yeah, right! Do you think Nana is going to buy into the idea that the world is about to come unglued?"

"You should give her a little more credit. Nana keeps up with things and she lived through the depression. She was young, but she can remember what tough times are like."

Danny took his phone out. "Do you have an internet connection? I'd like to see what's happening with the markets."

Cami checked her phone. "Nothing. I barely have cell service. Let's walk across the bridge and up the hill. We might get something if we're a little higher. If worse comes to worse, we've got satellite service for the RV. Nick has to have access to the internet at all times for work."

The two of them reached the top of the hill.

"Still nothing, let's go to the RV." Cami led the way back down the hill toward the bridge that crossed the creek.

Danny paused to look for the dog. "Where did Rusty go?"

"Probably off to chase a rabbit. He gets bored and runs off to do his own thing."

When they reached the house, Alisa was sitting on the porch. She ran out to meet them. "Hey, that was a quick walk."

"We're going to the RV. Tag along if you'd like." Danny took her hand as they continued toward the barn.

When they reached the RV, Cami unlocked the door, went inside and turned on the laptop.

"Wow, this is very nice." Danny was impressed.

"It's two years old, but the guy we bought it from used it maybe three times. Unless you're a real connoisseur, most people wouldn't know the difference between this one and a brand new RV on the showroom floor. Until they saw the price. We paid about half what a new one would cost." Cami logged into the computer and opened a browser.

Alisa looked over the living area and the kitchenette. "This is almost as big as my apartment."

"We like it." Cami quickly navigated to the financial news. "Check this out. Due to Friday's extremely volatile behavior and the historically low volume of traders on New Year's Eve, the SEC has elected to suspend trading for the day. The chairman said that a market which lacks a sufficient number of buyers and sellers can create an environment that is inherently susceptible to wild swings. Markets will reopen at their normal time on Wednesday morning."

Danny pursed his lips. "Do you buy that excuse?"

Cami sighed. "I don't know. If panic selling sets in, then low volume can cause prices to accelerate toward the downside."

Danny looked at the computer over her shoulder. "Our friend said the government steps in as a buyer when the markets start crashing. I think he called it the plunge protection team. Do you think that's true?"

Cami nodded. "The official name is the President's Working Group on Financial Markets. Yes, they really exist. But it seems like it would be easier to control a market with low trading volume. I don't know why they would rather deal with it on Wednesday than today."

Danny scratched his head. "What about the people who wanted to sell now so they could take the tax loss for this year?"

"I guess they'll get the write-off next year. If the government would have stepped in today, they would likely have to do more buying on Wednesday."

Alisa seemed to be more interested in the RV than the markets. "Is that the bedroom through this door?"

"Yeah, but it's filled with boxes. We'll check it out some other time." Cami shut the computer and led the way out the door.

Alisa looked the barn over once they were out of the RV. "Can we have a look inside the barn? I've never been in one."

"Sure. Cami, do you want to look around the barn with us?"

"No, it stirs up my allergies. I'll see you back at the house."

"Okay, tell Nana we'll be there after a while. We might trek back through the woods. I want to show Alisa all the places where we used to run and play when we were kids."

Cami waved and headed back to the house.

Danny opened the door for Alisa.

"Wow, a real barn. This looks like something out of a movie."

Danny grinned. He thought she was so cute with her child-like amazement over such a simple thing.

He couldn't help but feel a little bit sorry for her, having never been exposed to a rural lifestyle. *At least she gets to see it now*, he thought.

"Where does this ladder go to?" Alisa didn't wait for the answer before she began ascending the steps of the ladder.

"The hayloft." Danny waited for her to reach the top before he started up. The ladder had been made by his grandfather. It was very well made, but the wood, itself, had seen better days and he didn't want to take an unnecessary risk by putting the weight of two people on it at a time.

Once in the loft, Alisa climbed around on the hay. "Look, there are some plastic totes up here. What are they for?"

Danny was curious and came over for a closer look. "I'm not sure. I've never known Nana to keep anything up here except hay."

Alisa checked the lid of one of the tubs. "They have holes drilled in the sides of the lids with zip ties holding them on. Whatever it is, I guess Nana doesn't want us snooping through them."

"It could be to keep the critters out of the totes." Danny checked the zip ties. They were on snugly.

Alisa lay back on one of the bales of hay. "I feel like I'm in a country music video. Kiss me."

Danny wasn't about to deny her the opportunity of feeling like a country girl. He knelt down and kissed her. "Did you get to talk to your parents on the phone?"

"Shhh. Just kiss me."

Two minutes later, Alisa sat up. "Stop, stop, stop. We can't."

Danny sat up. His heart was racing. "I know. Come on, let's get out of here."

He stood up but she held his hand as if she didn't want to go. "My parents want to have the wedding in May."

Danny took a deep breath and quickly did the math. "Five months. We can make it."

Alisa looked down at the straw on the boards. "They couldn't get the venue they want for the reception this year. It has to be next May."

"Next year?" Danny felt his stomach drop. He wasn't worried about losing Alisa, but he wanted to honor God by living according to his statutes, and he had just been reminded of how difficult that would be. Nevertheless, he would do whatever it took. He loved Alisa with all of his heart, and he was committed to pleasing Christ. "Okay, next year." The tone of his voice betrayed his deep disappointment.

Alisa looked up with pouty eyes. "I don't know if we can wait that long. I don't know if I can wait that long."

Danny pulled her hand. "Well, let's get out of the hay loft so we can at least make it through today."

They climbed down the ladder and left the barn. Danny held her hand as they walked back through the woods.

"What if we eloped?" Alisa asked.

Danny looked at her to see if she was joking, but he couldn't really tell. "Are you serious?"

She pulled his hand and stepped in front of him. "Yes! I'm serious!"

"So, no big wedding? Your parents will hate me

until the day I die . . . or they die; whichever comes first."

"No, we'll still have the big wedding in a year, ... or two . . . or three, or whenever the stars align for their big production, but that has nothing to do with us. But, we can have our own secret little wedding."

Danny liked the idea. "Who do we tell?"

"Steven, obviously. What about Nana and your sister?"

"I don't know. I would hate to make them come to the real wedding, then have them come to the sham wedding in Connecticut also. But Steven, definitely. He won't mind coming to both weddings; as long as they both have cake."

"Then have Nana and Cami come to the secret wedding. Tell them the sham production is optional."

Danny laughed. "But then I wouldn't have any family at the one in Connecticut. Wouldn't your parents think that was odd?"

Alisa rolled her eyes. "Not at all. I could almost get away with not being there. Nana doesn't even speak the same language."

"I don't know about Nana and Cami. I'll think about it. When do you want to do it; the secret wedding?"

"Soon." She put her arms around him and kissed him. "Really, really soon."

They walked toward the back pasture. Alisa stopped short when she saw the cows. "Are they dangerous?"

Danny grinned. "No, they won't bother you. The

bull might get after you if he feels like you're threatening him."

"Are you messing with me?" Alisa's voice was less than calm.

Danny chuckled. "No. Just don't stare him down."

Alisa positioned herself to have Danny between her and the cattle. "How does Nana take care of these cows?"

"Rocky Cook, the farmer that lives up the hill, on the other side of the creek, he feeds them in the winter and keeps an eye on them. Whenever she sells one of them, they split the proceeds. If any fences need mending, he does all of that and takes the cost of the materials off the top, whenever they take a cow to market. My grandfather, Pop we called him, used to do most everything himself. Nana took care of the house and the garden; she'd help Pop on the farm when he needed it. After Pop died, obviously she couldn't keep raising tobacco and corn, but having the cattle grazing, keeps the farm somewhat productive and provides a small income on top of her Social Security. I'm glad she has Rocky to help out and look in on her from time to time."

Alisa held his hand firmly. "It sounds like it works out for everyone."

Danny nodded. "Rocky goes to her home Bible study. Her church is all the way in Anderson, so a few people from this area meet at her house on Wednesday nights. It saves them all the drive into town."

"Cool, is she having Bible study this

Wednesday?"

"No. It would be too much on her to have it when she already has a house full of company."

"That's too bad. I'd love to have a Bible study with Nana."

"Maybe we will."

"Would Cami and Nick like that? Nick seems a little standoffish."

"They go to church, but I know they had a rough time finding a good church in DC. Nick used to be real personable. He's a great guy. Ever since he got this new gig at the Pentagon, he acts like he has the weight of the world on his shoulders. He did two combat tours in the Middle East, and it didn't seem to affect him. I can't imagine how tough his job is now, that it has him so aloof."

"You don't really know what he does?"

"I know it isn't budgeting like he claims. No one in Washington gets stressed out over spending money. If I had to guess, I'd say it has something to do with threat analysis. Something has him and Cami seriously spooked if they are buying an RV and stocking it full of survival supplies."

"So that's why they came in an RV. What did Cami tell you?"

"Not much, but she said we should have a plan to come out to Nana's if we see cracks in the veneer of society."

"She's talking about economic stuff, like your dream, right?"

Danny gave Alisa the short version of everything Cami had told him. "I get the sense that she knows more than she's saying."

"I wonder what they know."

Danny shrugged. "Ignorance is bliss, I guess."

"Until it isn't."

Danny laughed. Alisa was very perceptive, especially for an art student. Of course, so was Steven. Both of them were classic right-brained people. That didn't make them ditzy. It was the liberal infiltration of the collegiate school system and culture that made artist types seem so disconnected from reality.

Danny was very left brained. Logic, order, and organization ruled his world, yet he had to stay on guard to keep the infestation of the left from clouding his own sound judgment through the education system and culture. Thanks to well-rooted conservative people like Cami and Nana in his life, he'd been able to resist most of the nonsense that was force fed to the general public.

Later that evening, Nana got up from the couch and headed toward the kitchen as she announced, "I'm just going to make some snacks for dinner since it is New Year's Eve."

"That'll be fine, Nana," Alisa said.

"Wait 'til you see what her definition of *snacks* is." Danny winked.

Alisa asked, "Does that mean Nana is going to stay up to watch the ball drop?"

"Ask her," Danny replied.

Alisa gave him a distrustful look but followed through with the suggestion anyway. "Nana, are you going to watch Dick Clark's New Year's Rockin' Eve and ring it in with us?"

Nana hollered back from the kitchen. "I don't have no concern for what them heathens in New York City do. Besides, I thought Dick Clark was dead. But y'all suit yourselves. Just don't play the TV too loud."

Alisa snickered. "You knew what she was going to say."

Danny gave a mischievous grin. "Yeah, but I could have never conveyed the delivery quite the same way that she would say it."

Cami and Nick walked into the living room. Cami held up a deck of cards in a green box. "Want to play Blitz?"

"Never played. What is it?" Alisa asked.

Danny answered for both of them. "Sure, we'll play. It's Dutch Blitz; basically, you try to get rid of all of your cards before anyone else. Once someone goes out, everyone else stops. You get points for the cards you get rid of and you lose points for the cards left in your hand."

Alisa listened closely. "Sort of like Uno?"

Cami tilted her head to one side. "It's a little more..."

"Fast paced?" Danny tried to help her finish the thought.

Cami nodded. "Violent was the word I was looking for. I've never had to get a Band-Aid from playing Uno."

"There's blood involved? Bring it!" Alisa clapped her hands together.

The four of them went to the dining room to play on the table. Danny explained the rules to Alisa. They played two hands slowly, going in turns so

Alisa could get the hang of the game, then the chaos commenced.

The swift-moving card game even seemed to distract Nick from his worries. Soon, they were all laughing and having a grand time.

In between hands, Cami counted up her points. "Nick, I had suggested to Danny that it might be a good idea for him and Alisa to have a plan, to get out here in case things turn south. Can you give them some pointers?"

Nick organized his cards. "Sure. You both look like you're in good shape. That's probably the biggest thing most people have to worry about."

Alisa smiled. "Thanks, I don't get to the gym much, but our job requires us to walk a lot and we have to move fast when it's busy."

"Being able to move fast is important. It would be a good idea for both of you to keep some clothes here at Nana's. If she doesn't have anywhere to put them, you can keep some things in the RV. In fact, any of the clothes you brought with you, that you think you can live without, you should leave them."

Danny shuffled his deck. "I usually bring older clothes out here, so I don't have to worry about getting them messed up. I can probably leave all of them when we go home, except for my coat and whatever I wear back to Savannah."

Nana brought a plate of fried apple pies into the dining room. "Ya'll eat. Danny, you and Lisa can keep some things in the closet of the bedroom where she's sleeping if you want. Just leave your clothes in the hamper. I'll wash them and put them away. Then they'll be here next time you come."

Danny hadn't had a conversation with Nana about bringing Alisa in the case of an emergency, but that sounded like an open invitation. "Thanks, Nana."

"Thank you, Nana." Alisa picked up one of the fried apple pies. "I guess I can leave all the clothes I brought also. By the time we leave, I'll be too fat to fit in any of them anyway."

Nick took a pie as well. "Cami said you guys already bought some extra food items."

Danny looked at Alisa. "Yeah, we bought enough to keep us fed for several weeks."

"That was smart. It's a good idea to have a few extra supplies around anyway. You never know when you're going to be stuck somewhere and have to shelter in place. Knowing when to bug out and when to stay where you are, is critical. In any type of emergency, you only leave when you're absolutely sure it will increase your odds of survival. You could wake up one morning, turn on the television and find that the world went to heck overnight. Savannah could be in a state of complete social collapse. Your first instinct might be to evacuate, but if the streets aren't safe due to rioting, you might be better off to stay situated until it dies down. Then again, if you can smell the smoke and hear the yelling, it might be getting close. You don't want to get stuck in a position where you have no options because you waited too long. If you see a window to get out, take it. It's better to go too early, miss a couple classes or have to call in sick to work than to lose your life. Worst case scenario, you miss a test or lose a night's worth of tips, then go back home when things settle down. When you're talking about a potential life or death situation, there's no comparison in the trade off.

"Do you have a detailed map of Savannah?"

"No, but I'm very familiar with the area." Danny took a bite of his pie.

"You might know the area, but a map will help you find alternate routes if your planned evacuation path gets cut off. Also, your ability to recognize your location can be compromised during social chaos. If you're used to taking a right at Wendy's, you might miss your turn if Wendy's has been burnt down and the signage is no longer recognizable.

"Walking instead of driving can also throw you off. A map is a very worthwhile investment. Once you get it, map out at least two good evacuation routes that keep you away from problem areas. One should be a direct route out of town and one should focus on getting you away from areas with high population densities as fast as possible, even if it takes you out of the way.

"You should both put together a bug-out bag, in case you need to leave in a hurry."

"I'm not sure what that is." Alisa said.

Nick grinned. "It's a bag, preferably a large backpack that won't draw too much attention, filled with the essentials you'd need to keep you alive for seventy-two hours."

Alisa nodded slowly. "Still not sure I know what that is."

"Well, for starters, you know you need water to stay alive. You need a minimum of a half-gallon a day just to stay hydrated. That's if it's not super-hot and you're not sweating a lot."

Alisa looked at Nick. "So, I need to keep a gallon and a half of water in my buck-out bag?"

"It's bug out, like get out of town. Not necessarily. You could, but a gallon weighs eight pounds, so your bag would be twelve pounds before you put anything else in it. I'd recommend keeping a half-gallon in your bag and getting a good light-weight water filter. Then, you can reuse your containers and refill them whenever you came across another water source. Streams, lakes, ponds and creeks are pretty common in this part of the country. If you lived in the desert, that would be a different story. You'd have no other choice but to keep the full three days of water in your pack."

Danny listened closely to what Nick was saying. "How much does a good filter cost?"

"You can get a good one for under a hundred dollars. Katadyn and MSR both make high-quality portable filters."

"Since we would be traveling together, could Alisa and I share one?"

Nick nodded. "Yes, but whichever one of you isn't carrying the filter should at least be carrying water purification tablets. You can buy them online for five or ten bucks. Water is too important. You don't want something to happen to one of your backpacks, then you'd both be up a creek. You also need some type of shelter. You can find a small emergency tent for around twenty-five dollars. Just make sure it weighs less than five pounds and try to find something in an earth tone color. If the worst happens, you might not want to advertise your position with a bright-colored tent."

Alisa asked, "Should we have sleeping bags?"

"You'll need something to keep you warm, but a sleeping bag is heavy and bulky. Space blankets are a great alternative; not the thin little aluminum foil blankets. A real Space blanket will run you around fifteen to twenty bucks."

Danny tore off a sheet of the notepad they had been using to keep score, and began writing everything down. "What else should we have in the bag?"

"Three days' worth of food, a small flashlight, a radio; Ambient Weather makes a great little AM/FM Weather band radio that weighs next to nothing and takes up very little room in your bag. I think it even has a flashlight, but you should still have another flashlight. I'd also want a good multi-tool with the basics; screwdrivers, pliers, knife. Make sure you have a decent fixed blade knife as well. Nothing expensive, but you want a good cutting tool. You should have a couple different ways to make fire. Maybe a couple of lighters in each pack and a magnesium fire starter." Nick paused to give Danny a chance to get everything written down.

Danny glanced up from his paper. "Any suggestions on what type of food we should pack?"

"Yeah. Pack things that are ready to eat. Canned soups are great. If you have the opportunity to stop and build a fire, you can warm them right in the can. Otherwise, you can eat them cold. You want to always have the option of eating your food cold. You might not have time to stop, or you might not want to send up smoke signals by building a fire to cook over. Granola bars and canned pasta also fit into that category."

Cami rubbed Nick on the back. "Should they buy MREs?"

Nick looked sideways at Danny's notes. "That's a good option, but if they are trying to do everything on a budget, it will be cheaper to pack canned foods."

Danny kept writing. "What else?"

"Do you have a gun?"

Alisa raised her voice. "Whoa! Why would we need a gun?"

Nick pursed his lips. "The bad guys are going to have guns. If they have them and you don't, you'll do whatever they tell you, or you'll die. Especially for a girl, that can get pretty ugly. And unfortunately, when society breaks down, that sort of thing happens quite a lot. When you turn off the lights, the roaches tend to come out of the cracks."

A horrific image ran through Danny's head. He couldn't stand the thought of something like that happening to Alisa. "What kind of gun should I get?"

"If you're trying to get by on a budget, you should probably think about a revolver. Something like a .38. You don't have to worry about a revolver jamming. If you want to up the ante and look at a semi-auto, you'll be looking at five or six hundred for a Glock. Although, you can always buy a decent used Glock from a reputable gun store."

"How much for a revolver?"

Nick shrugged. "You can probably find one for

around three hundred; maybe a little less."

Danny jotted down the ball-park prices Nick had given him and added them up. He was close to $500 and he still hadn't figured in batteries or ammunition.

Nick smiled. "I've got several cases of MREs and some dehydrated long-term-storage food in the RV. I'll set you guys up with a couple weeks' worth. That will get you started. Check out some of the thrift stores around Savannah. You might find some deals on good backpacks."

Danny folded up the paper and stuck it in his shirt pocket. "Thanks."

Cami shuffled her deck of cards. "Let's finish up this game before Nana fills the table up with food."

Danny dealt out his three piles of cards which he would play from when the game began. "I guess we have a lot of things to buy when we get home."

Nick dealt out his cards as well. "The good thing about a bug-out bag is that you also have three days' worth of essentials and emergency supplies in the event that you can't leave. A bug-out bag can also be a bug-in bag."

Alisa counted out her cards. "And I suppose we should have some basic hygiene items; toilet paper, soap, a towel."

Nick snapped his fingers. "Yes, and some basic first aid supplies as well. Band-Aids, Neosporin, tweezers, alcohol pads at the very least."

The game began and all talk of bug-out bags ceased. Everyone's focus was on the action at the table.

Nana came in at the end of the hand. "Here are

some pimento cheese sandwiches, fried taters and Hello-Dolly cookies. Y'all eat up."

"Thanks, Nana." Alisa went straight for the cookies.

Cami tallied up the final hand. "Alisa won. Good job!"

They all ate and put the cards away. At ten o'clock, Nana announced that she was going to bed.

Danny walked into her room to give her a goodnight hug.

She handed him a box.

"What's this?" It was heavy.

"It's Pop's old .32 revolver. I want you to take it. There's a box of bullets on the dresser. Take them too. Maybe Nicholas can take you out to the woods tomorrow and show you how to shoot it."

"I can't take this, Nana. You need it."

She gestured to the gun leaning in the corner near the bed. "I've got my shotgun. Anyone fool enough to come in on me will wish they hadn't."

Danny kissed her on the cheek. "Okay, thanks, Nana. Good night."

Danny took the box and the bullets and closed the door behind him. He fought the urge to look the weapon over right away and placed it by his bag. He would inspect it first thing in the morning.

Danny, Alisa, Cami and Nick stayed up to watch the ball drop in Times Square, then Cami and Nick turned in for the night.

Alisa gave Danny one last kiss to ring in the New Year. "What did Nana give you?"

"A gun."

"No way! Let's see it."

Danny opened the box to find a very old, nickel-plated revolver. "Looks like an antique."

"As long as it shoots."

"I'm going to ask Nick if he will give me some pointers tomorrow. I'll find out if it still works then."

"You've never shot it?"

"Pop taught me to shoot the shotgun when I was younger, but we never shot the pistol."

"I want to shoot it, too!"

"You looked like you were going to freak out when Nick said we needed a gun. Why the sudden change in attitude?"

Alisa shrugged. "Nick's reasoning was very convincing."

"If it works, that will be a big chunk of the budget that we won't have to spend."

My parents sent me a gift card. We can use it to buy all the stuff for our bug-out bags."

"You don't have to spend all of your Christmas money on survival gear."

"It's our money now. And besides, once we buy it, we'll always have it. It's a one-time investment."

Danny gave her one more kiss. "You better get to bed before Nana wakes up and I end up sleeping in the barn."

Alisa laughed, hugged him tight and headed upstairs to sleep.

Danny was apprehensive about the coming year because of his dream, but he was also excited to see what else God had in store.

The next morning came early, as Nana made it

clear that it was time to get up by banging around in the kitchen as she prepared breakfast. Danny had learned not to fight it long ago, so he got up and helped himself to a strong cup of coffee from the old blue-speckled enamel percolator. The others joined him shortly thereafter.

Once breakfast was finished, Danny asked, "Nick, Nana gave me Pop's old .32 revolver. Would you mind giving Alisa and me some pointers on shooting?"

"Sure. Let me see what I can find for targets."

Nana sipped her coffee. "Take some of them milk jugs on the back porch. They ain't doin' nothing but clutterin' up the place. Y'all take my shotgun too. Lisa might see a squirrel she wants to shoot."

Alisa giggled. "Thanks, Nana."

The three of them got dressed and headed to the back field. When they arrived, Nick went over the basics of firearms safety, such as never pointing the muzzle toward a person you didn't intend to shoot, being aware of what was beyond your target, and keeping your finger away from the trigger until you were ready to fire.

Danny took right to shooting the pistol and was easily hitting the milk jugs from ten yards away.

Nick patted him on the back. "Not bad for someone who's never shot before. A person is a much larger target than a jug. If you have to defend yourself, you'll be able to hit 'em. Of course, people tend to not stand still when you're shooting at them, but that's a lesson for another day."

Alisa wasn't quite as proficient with the pistol at

first. She fired five shots and missed every time. "I think the aim is off."

Nick took the pistol and emptied the spent rounds. "Let's try something different. I think you are anticipating the round going off and closing your eyes." He closed the cylinder and handed the empty gun back to Alisa. "Practice keeping the gun steady as you pull the trigger and make sure you keep your eyes open."

She frowned as she took the pistol from him. "But it's empty."

"Yep. Get used to dry firing it without anticipating the noise. Then, you'll be able to do the same thing when it's loaded."

Alisa drilled with the pistol several times, then Nick reloaded it. Her next shot hit dead center on the jug, sending it flying backwards.

"Look at that!" She squealed. "I hit it!"

"Good job!" Danny clapped his hands.

She fired the pistol four more times, missing only once.

After each of them shot the pistol several more times, they moved on to the shotgun. Nick started Alisa off by dry firing the old single-shot, break-action shotgun. Once she was comfortable, he loaded a shell for her.

She practiced getting a good cheek weld, just as Nick had showed her and holding it firmly against her shoulder. Then, she pulled the trigger. BOOM! Her shoulder kicked back and the muzzle rose, but she annihilated the milk jug.

"Wow!" She lowered the gun and looked at it intensely. She looked up at Danny. "We need one of these!"

When Danny picked up the shotgun, he had fond memories of shooting it with Pop. After firing several shells he asked, "What would a good shotgun like this cost?"

Nick stroked his chin. "Not much, but for a few dollars more, you could get a good pump-action shotgun that would hold several rounds at a time. If you're in a firefight, you don't want to be breaking the action every time to reload. You could pick up an eighteen-and-a-half-inch-barrel Maverick 88, which is Mossberg's entry-level shotgun for around two hundred. You could buy a pistol grip for another twenty bucks. That would allow you to put it in a large backpack in case you have to bug out on foot and you needed to keep it concealed. Just make sure you get the total length of the shotgun before you buy your pack."

Alisa sized up the length of the shotgun with her hands. "You think you can get a pack that will hold a shotgun?"

Nick nodded. "If it has a pistol grip, sure. The barrel is just over eighteen inches. Add another ten or eleven inches for the rest of the gun. I know you can find a good hiking pack that's thirty inches long. The good thing about a shotgun is that it would be great protection, and you can add a longer barrel for hunting."

Danny considered everything Nick was telling him. "Since Nana gave us the pistol, I guess we could fit it into the budget."

"Just make sure you're leaving a little cushion in your budget for ammo. And make sure you buy the exact same ammo for the revolver; it's .32 H&R, not .32 auto."

Danny nodded. "Thanks."

Nick motioned for them to follow him. "Come on, let's go to the RV and we'll get these both cleaned up and oiled. If you treat your guns good, they'll return the favor."

When they finally made it back to the front yard, there was an old rusted out pickup truck in the drive. The mid-seventies vehicle had seen better days and many moons since its last wash. Beneath the grime, was faded red paint and a wide band running down the side that was once white.

Nana called out the door. "Ya'll get in here. Lunch is getting cold."

Danny rapidly led the way in the house. He washed his hands and hurried to the table with Alisa and Nick close behind.

"Daniel, Nicholas, Lisa, this here is Catfish. He lives up the road a piece. Comes to our Bible study when the Spirit moves him."

"Nice to meet you." Danny didn't have to wonder how the man had earned the moniker. The wild hairs sticking out of his wiry grey beard closely resembled the stringy barbels extending outward from a catfish's face. His faded, dingy overalls were only slightly cleaner than the truck outside, giving him the impression of a true bottom feeder.

Alisa offered her hand to Catfish. "I'm Alisa. It's a pleasure to meet you."

Catfish shook her hand. "Much obliged."

Danny was very impressed with Alisa's ability to *correct* Nana, without *correcting* Nana.

Nana invited Catfish to say grace, which he did with expedience.

Nana passed a bowl of collard greens to Danny. "Catfish brought greens and black-eyed-peas. He thinks you won't have a prosperous year if you don't eat them on New Year's Day."

"Miss Jennie don't keep with the traditions, so I come by every year with a big pot of peas and collards to protect her from herself." Catfish grinned revealing teeth that were badly stained from chewing tobacco.

Nana protested, "I feel sorry for you, after all the work you do cookin' everything. That's the only reason I put up with it. I don't pay no mind to your silly superstitions."

Catfish chuckled. "But Miss Jennie puts a right smart faith in them old injun cures."

"The Indians knew more about medicine than most of these high falutin' doctors. They can't no more cure a body than they can stop the sun from a settin'." Nana forked a slice of ham onto her plate.

Catfish winked at Danny. "Just you watch if I don't come next year. Miss Jennie'll be ringin' me on the telephone a hollerin', Catfish, where you at with them vittles!"

"Hush up, you old coot. I won't do no such a thing!"

Nana's dissent seemed a bit exaggerated. Danny wondered if Catfish might be right. No matter, the verbal sparring between the two certainly kept lunch interesting.

Alisa exclaimed, "There's a penny in my peas!"

Nana pointed the prongs of her fork at Catfish. "I told you not to be a puttin' no penny in them peas!"

Catfish shielded himself from the utensil with a piece of cornbread. "Now Miss Jennie, you know the luck won't take if you don't put a new penny in the pot. Besides, that little girl will have extra luck all year."

Alisa rolled her eyes and pushed the penny off of the plate and onto her napkin with her fork.

Danny snickered. He considered the dream he'd had and the imminent collapse of America's finances. Penny or no penny, he seriously doubted anyone would call the coming year prosperous and he wondered what excuse Catfish would find when his theory ran awry. Still, Catfish seemed to be a good-natured person and he was glad that he kept Nana company from time to time. With Cami and himself living so far away, she didn't have any family to check in on her.

For dessert, Nana served coffee and the remaining fried apple pies from the night before. They all sat around the table and enjoyed the conversation about this, that, and the other thing for the remainder of the day.

Danny and Alisa followed Cami to the RV after breakfast Wednesday morning to check out the opening action in the markets.

Cami opened the financial news website at 8:30. "Futures are up. It looks like we could be in for a major rebound at this point. Why don't we take a walk and come back once regular trading starts?

Pre-market action is easily controlled because trading is thin. We'll see if they can keep the green arrows going once the bell sounds."

"Sounds good." Alisa was the first back out the door. "If they can get through the day, does that mean the crisis has been evaded?"

Cami closed the door after she and Danny exited the RV. "It will certainly help, but the plunge protection team will have to keep the ball in the air at least 'til Friday to really quell the sense of uneasiness after the SEC kept the market closed on Monday. They can't print enough money or buy enough stocks to completely prop up the markets without some level of confidence. Confidence is the lifeblood of markets, and what they did Monday spooked a lot of people."

Alisa patted her leg. "Come on Rusty, let's go to the woods."

Rusty had been lying in the grass just outside of the RV. He quickly got up and ran over to Alisa. He wagged his tail in such a way that it flapped up against her leg. He had taken a liking to Alisa and stayed close to her whenever she left the house. He gave her just enough space to walk without tripping over him. Alisa didn't seem to mind. She petted him and hugged his neck every time she saw him.

They took a long slow walk around the farm and arrived back at the RV around ten. Cami pushed the door open. "Hey, Nick. We just wanted to check the markets if you're not too busy on the computer."

Danny, Alisa and Rusty waited outside.

Cami came back out a minute later. "Still up, the Dow has gained about 150 points. We'll see how long that lasts."

"Maybe everything will be okay." Alisa tilted her head as a signal to Rusty that they were heading back to the house. He took the cue and followed along.

Cami sighed. "We're well past the point of everything being okay. It's just a matter of time. Everyone in Nick's department at work knows it. We're all just postponing the inevitable. I'm sure you both understand that you can't tell anyone about any of this, right?"

"Nick would have to kill me, right?" Danny cracked a smile.

"Right!" Cami tussled his hair.

Alisa said, "We kind of already knew."

"What do you mean?" Cami's face showed her extreme interest in Alisa's statement.

Danny exhaled. "Long story. If you can wait 'til we get back to the house, I'll explain. I have to tell Nana also, so I'll tell you both at once."

Cami looked at him curiously. "Hmm. This sounds interesting."

Once back in the house, Danny called Nana to come sit down at the table with Alisa and Cami. "Remember when you asked me what God had been showing me?"

Nana smiled. "You ready to tell me?"

Danny grinned with a nod. "Yeah."

As Danny gave his account of the dream, he saw that Nana found it less surprising than Cami.

Nana got up to make a pot of coffee. "I reckon we ought to do what we can to get ready. If folks had known the great depression was coming, they could've been a lot more prepared for it."

"You're in a pretty good spot, Nana. What else do you think you'll need?" Cami asked.

"Couldn't hardly get no sugar in the depression. I'll probably get a bunch of that; coffee, too. I'll have Catfish put me up some rabbit hutches and mend that old chicken coop out back. Ain't neither one of them animals too much work. Sure ain't as hard as starvin'."

"We can try to come out here and help when we can, Nana. We're both off on Sundays," Danny said.

Nana shook her head. "By the time you get here, it'd be time to turn around and go home unless you have a Monday off from school. You just keep working and saving what you can. When it gets to be time for y'all to come out, you'll know. Then we'll do whatever need's doin'."

The next two days added a little more than 300 points to the Dow. It was a small percentage of the nearly 2,000 points it had lost the previous Friday, but the fact that it hadn't plunged further was cause for celebration. For the rest of the week, Danny and Alisa enjoyed the remainder of their visit with Nana, Cami and Nick, then headed back to Savannah, early Sunday morning.

CHAPTER 8

But he that received the seed into stony places, the same is he that heareth the word, and anon with joy receiveth it; Yet hath he not root in himself, but dureth for a while: for when tribulation or persecution ariseth because of the word, by and by he is offended. He also that received seed among the thorns is he that heareth the word; and the care of this world, and the deceitfulness of riches, choke the word, and he becometh unfruitful. But he that received seed into the good ground is he that heareth the word, and understandeth it; which also beareth fruit, and bringeth forth, some an hundredfold, some sixty, some thirty.

Matthew 13:20-23

Danny arrived at work early Tuesday night, as was becoming his new habit. It was the first night that he, Alisa and Steven were all scheduled to work together again since his trip to South Carolina. He clocked in and began preparing the tables in his station by polishing the silverware and glassware.

Steven arrived five minutes later. "Hey. Did you have a good visit?"

"Yeah, we did. Thanks again for working for me. Was the restaurant busy?"

"Pretty busy. How was last night?"

"It was dead. I walked with about seventy-five bucks."

"I guess that's not bad for a Monday night after the holidays. People always cut back after Christmas. Tonight will probably be about the same. How did Alisa like your family?"

"She fit right in. They all seemed to like each other. I told my sister about the dream."

"Did she think you're crazy?"

"Not at all. They've actually been getting ready for some type of an event. Evidently, everyone that works in my brother-in-law's department at the Pentagon is a little concerned."

"About the markets?"

"That's one of the things they've had their eyes on. He thinks some event could bring society to a screeching halt. He wasn't very forthcoming on the exact nature of the threats, but he did give me a laundry list of things I need to buy to start getting prepared."

"Oh yeah? Like what?"

"I'll make you a copy and we can talk about it tonight after work. Can you come by Leopold's?"

"Sure. Can you give me a little preview?"

"He said we need bug-out bags; basically backpacks with essential survival gear, in case we have to go to my grandmother's farm in a hurry."

"So that's your new plan, to go to Nana's?"

"Yes, but you're invited."

"Thanks, but if society collapses, I'll be going back to Iowa."

"If you can get back. It could be that you have to hunker down for a while to let things cool off, then head back to Iowa. Keep your options open. Either way, you need a plan if things get too dicey to stay in Savannah."

"You're right. Thanks for the invitation. Did you clear it with Nana?"

"Of course." Danny looked up at Steven, but kept polishing the glass in his hand. "Did you see what happened with the stock market today?"

"The Dow closed down 400 points. But it was up 200 yesterday, so I don't know if it's that big of a deal. The financial reporters said it's an unusual level of volatility."

Alisa walked in and took off her coat. "Hey. Did you tell Steven?"

"He told me."

"What do you think? Are you excited" Alisa tied her apron.

"Frightened might be a better word than excited."

Alisa slapped his arm. "Frightened! Why the heck would you be frightened?"

Danny chuckled. "I don't think you two are talking about the same thing. I told Steven about the bug-out bags and the new plan. But not the other thing."

"Oh." Alisa seemed to quickly get past the misunderstanding. She put her arm around Danny. "We're going to elope!"

"Shut up!" Steven exclaimed.

Danny grinned from ear to ear. "You're the only person who knows so far."

"When?"

"Valentine's Day." Alisa said.

"Busy day in the restaurant. You'll probably have to tell Trish why you need the day off."

"If we have to tell her, we have to tell her. But you've got to be there, so you need to take the night off also," Danny said.

Steven shook his head. "I really doubt all three of us can take off. The wedding will be in the daytime. If you have it early, we can go to lunch afterwards, then I can go to work. In fact, you guys probably won't want me around after the sun goes down."

"Oh yeah. He's got a point." Alisa looked over at Danny. "Okay then, we'll have it early."

Steven's section was next to Danny's. He began getting his tables ready for the evening. "Are you going to get married at the courthouse?"

Danny was finished with his section so he picked up a glass from the table Steven was working on.

"We were thinking to ask Pastor Earl. Did you

meet him Sunday?"

"Yes, he's a really nice man. I liked that church a lot. Everyone was very friendly, and you could feel the Spirit."

Alisa chipped in to help with Steven's table. "But if he says no, we'll go to the courthouse. One way or the other, we're getting married on Valentine's Day."

The evening progressed and, indeed, turned out to be slow which gave the three friends plenty of time to talk about the wedding and the new plan to go to Nana's if Savannah became too dangerous and they couldn't stay.

The next evening, Danny and Alisa went to church, but Steven had to work. After the service, they said hello to a couple of the folks that they'd met the first time they visited Savannah Christian Chapel.

Pastor Earl quickly made his way over to them. "I'm so glad to see you again. How was your trip?"

Danny shook his hand. "It was good. Alisa hit it off really well with my grandmother. My sister and her husband were there, so Alisa met them also."

Alisa chuckled. "You sounded like you didn't know if we'd be back."

Pastor Earl furrowed his brow. "If I had a nickel for every new believer that said they'd be back next week, it's what we, in the ministry, call the fall-away rate. Folks get excited about the prospects of going to heaven, but when church threatens their way of life, lots of them never come back. They'd rather keep their weekends open, or their friends ridicule them, or sometimes, they have a favorite sin that they'd prefer to hang on to. Jesus said you can't have two masters. He had quite a bit more to say about folks falling away, but we'll talk about that another time."

Danny pursed his lips. "If they'd had the dream I had, they wouldn't let anything get in the way."

Pastor Earl sighed. "I wish that were true. You'd be surprised at the number of pastors who are blessed with exploding ministries, they've seen God work in miraculous ways, yet they throw it all away for a few moments of pleasure in an adulterous affair. Paul tells us in Galatians 5 that the flesh and the spirit always want something contrary to each other. It's a constant battle."

"But the spirit eventually wins, right?" Alisa seemed sure of her answer.

The pastor shrugged. "It depends on which one you feed the most. If you feed your spirit, through Bible reading, prayer, worship music, fasting; it will win. But if you consistently give in to the flesh, it grows stronger and stronger."

"Kind of sounds like the light side and the dark side of the force." Danny smiled.

"That's a fair analogy." Pastor Earl nodded. "Speaking of spiritual discipline, have you two had a chance to start a daily Bible-reading plan?"

Danny held Alisa's hand tight. "Yes. We were reading while we were in South Carolina. We finished Romans and are almost done with Matthew."

"Fantastic. What are you learning?"

"Some of it is sort of confusing, especially

considering Danny's dream," Alisa said.

"Like what?"

She opened her Bible to Romans chapter 1. "Like this. It says God is pouring out his wrath because people aren't grateful to him and won't worship him. It sounds like he just gives up on these people and they become worse and worse. Is that talking about now, or back in the day? I guess I'm trying to find clues to help me understand Danny's dream in the Bible, but I don't know what I'm looking for."

Pastor Earl rocked to and fro in his chair. "There's no better place to look for clues than the Bible. What you're talking about in Romans 1 is a basic biblical principle. Paul explains that we don't have an excuse for not believing in, worshiping, and being thankful to God. He claims that the creation, itself, is evidence that there must be a creator. And, since the Bible and prayer were taken out of our schools, they've been replaced with the religion of atheism, propagated through Darwinism.

"When we say the Bible is wrong and the world didn't come to be the way it says, we create our own gods. Either ones that fit our imagination, or we make ourselves out to be gods. In verse 22, he says, 'professing to be wise, they became fools.' So, to answer your question, that section of Scriptures was true in the time when Paul wrote it, and is very relevant today. I also believe it fits in with Danny's dream."

Alisa still looked unsettled. "In the next few verses, it sounds like God just gives up on them."

"Hmm." Pastor Earl took her Bible from her and read starting with verse 28. "'God gave them over to a debased mind, to do those things which are not fitting; being filled with all unrighteousness, sexual immorality, wickedness, covetousness, maliciousness; full of envy, murder, strife, deceit, evil-mindedness.'

"At some point, if people want nothing to do with God, he won't force himself upon them. When asked to leave, God will be a perfect gentleman, but he is the only force that keeps the wickedness of our sin nature in check. Once he is out of the way, all manner of evil from inside ourselves is free to express itself. This is what some people call God's abandonment wrath. The theory is that God doesn't have to do anything to punish us. Rather, if he simply quits actively blessing us or protecting us, natural forces will destroy us."

"And is that what you think my dream was about? God's abandonment of the United States?" Danny was trying to fit everything Pastor Earl was telling him into the vivid memories of his nightmare.

Pastor Earl flipped to Isaiah. "In Isaiah chapter 5, God uses an allegory about a grapevine to describe rebellious Israel. Beginning with verse 5, he says, 'I will take away its hedge, and it shall be burned; and break down its wall, and it shall be trampled down. I will lay it waste; it shall not be pruned or dug, but there shall come up briers and thorns. I will also command the clouds that they rain no rain on it.'

"By taking away the hedge and breaking down the wall, he is removing his protection so that it can be destroyed by its enemies. But he says he will lay it waste, which sounds like he plans to be an active participant in the disciplinary actions against the nations. I believe your dreams speaks to both God's abandonment wrath as well as his direct judgment upon America; sort of a double whammy."

Alisa squinted her eyes. "But that's about Israel, what does that have to do with Danny's dream about the death of America?"

"Again, it's a Biblical principle. All through the Bible, we read about the blessings for obedience and the curses for disobedience." Pastor Earl handed the Bible back to her.

Alisa marked the page Pastor Earl had been reading from with the ribbon attached to the Bible. "Is all of Isaiah about that kind of stuff?"

"Yes. So is Jeremiah and most of the books of prophecy from that point forward. But, if you are going to start reading that section of Scriptures, I ask that you do it in addition to your current reading plan. Read a couple chapters from the New Testament first, then read what you like from the prophecy books. Otherwise, it's going to be like trying to do algebra when you haven't developed basic math skills."

Danny smiled. "Okay, that makes sense. But I have to admit, you really sparked my curiosity with that last passage."

"Well, there's no better book to be curious about. And you have my number on the back of the church bulletin. Call me any time you have questions. It's no bother at all.

"On another matter, I spoke to a friend down in Florida, Ricky Willis. He runs a radio program that covers news events, particularly those that pertain to biblical prophecy. He often has guests on his show who've had prophetic dreams. He'd like you to come on his show and share your vision."

Danny was taken completely off guard. "I don't know. It's on the radio in Florida?"

"It's all over America. It's a fairly popular show."

"I don't think I'd be a very good radio guest. I kind of stammer when I get nervous."

"God didn't give you that dream just so you could take cover yourself. It was meant to share. There are other people who need the information God has given you so they can prepare for the coming storm as well."

Danny was not at all comfortable with this request. "I'm not even sure it was from God. The market looked like it was going to crash the Friday before last, but it has pretty much leveled off ever since."

"I know what the market has done. It took the largest one-day point dive in history four days after you had your dream. You'd have to be pretty thick headed to not believe that came from God. I know you're not slow, you know where it came from. I can understand that you're apprehensive about putting your dream out there to the public. It's intimidating. What if you tell everyone and nothing happens? But, what if you don't tell anyone, and the economic system comes crashing down? You'll feel guilty, because you saw it coming and you didn't warn them."

"I'll be there beside you for the interview if it will help you. You're brave. You can do it." Alisa gave his arm a squeeze.

Danny looked at her and took a deep breath. "When does he want to do the interview?"

"I told him you work nights and go to school in the daytime. How is Saturday afternoon, around 2:00 ?"

"Yeah, I guess I could do that." Danny held Alisa's hand tightly for security.

"Great. I'll let him know."

Alisa smiled at the pastor. "And we have a favor to ask you."

"Oh? What is it?"

She held up her ring. "Will you perform the service on Valentine's Day?"

Pastor Earl took her hand and inspected the ring. "What a beautiful ring. Of course I will. But isn't that a little fast? Will your folks have time to prepare?"

Alisa explained their quandary; how her parents were planning a grand spectacle that would force them to wait more than a year. "Honestly, Pastor, we are committed to honoring God by staying pure, but I don't think we can make it that long. My parents aren't Christians, so that's not even part of the equation for them."

Pastor Earl wrinkled his brow. "I really hate to be a part of sneaking behind your parents' back, but I understand your dilemma."

Danny made sure his tone was polite. "Either way, we're getting married on Valentine's. We'll respect your decision, but we'll go to the courthouse otherwise."

The pastor sighed. "I hate to see the government doing God's job of making the two, one flesh, so I guess you've backed me into a corner. If I agree to officiate your wedding, will you two watch a DVD series?"

Alisa was elated. "Sure. What is it about?"

"It's a premarital class. It gives you some very valuable biblical information on marriage. It might also bring up some issues you weren't expecting, like how the money is going to be handled between the two of you, how many kids you want, stuff that can get in the way of a good marriage. If there are serious incompatibilities, it's much better to find out now than after you've tied the knot."

Danny felt a pang of worry. He hoped they didn't find anything out that would be an issue. But, the pastor was right. It was much wiser to make sure they were on the same page, before they made the big commitment. "Thank you, Pastor."

"It's in my office. I'll go get it and be right back." Pastor Earl left them near the door as he went to retrieve the series.

"You're not worried are you?" Alisa held both of Danny's hands and looked him in the eyes.

Danny did his best to shake off his concern. "No. I'm sure we're a good fit."

Alisa kissed his lips. "I'll be a good wife to you, Danny Walker, I promise."

He pulled her toward himself. "And with God's help, I'll be the best husband I can be."

Pastor Earl returned with the video series. They thanked him for it, then headed home for the night.

CHAPTER 9

Let the high praises of God be in their mouth, and a two-edged sword in their hand.

Psalm 149:6

Friday night at the restaurant was somewhat busier than the rest of the week had been but nowhere near as busy as before the holidays. Toward the end of the shift, Danny counted his credit card tips and made a rough estimate of his cash tips.

Steven cleaned up the beverage station, wiping it down, emptying out the tea urn, and washing the overflow tray of the soda dispenser. "How did you do?"

"If I break a hundred, I'll be surprised. That's not so bad, but the rest of the week has been really slow."

"I didn't even come close to that; probably around eighty bucks. The gun show is at the civic center this weekend. Do you want to go tomorrow before work? It might be a good place to find some things for our bug-out bags. And guns, of course."

"I have that radio interview tomorrow. Maybe Sunday after church."

Alisa walked into the station with a tray of glasses for the bar. "What are we doing after church?"

Steven rinsed out his bar towel in the sink. "Danny and I were talking about going to the gun show on Sunday at the civic center. You don't have to go."

"That's right by my house. Why wouldn't I want to go?"

"Well, it's mostly guns."

"Don't underestimate her. She's a pretty good shot." Danny chuckled.

Steven paused from his work. "Wait a minute. You used to rail against guns, hunting, all that stuff."

Alisa pursed her lips. "That was before the countdown to doomsday started."

Danny winked at Steven. "My brother-in-law made a pretty convincing argument for gun ownership."

Steven resumed his task. "Fantastic. We can grab lunch after church, then head straight to the show. Have you guys already bought everything for your bags?"

"Not everything, but we found most of it online.

We bought a good AM/FM radio with Weather band, a water filter, a lightweight dome tent, flashlights, and two large backpacks." Alisa wiped down her tray, then sat it on top of the other clean trays to dry. "What have you found so far?"

Steven shook his head. "I've been searching online, but I really like to touch stuff so I can feel how it's made before I buy it. That's why I'm hoping I can find some things for my bag at the gun show."

Danny pulled a box of straws from the top shelf to restock the straw dispenser at the beverage station. "If you want to wait 'til we get our order; you can check out our supplies. I hear what you're saying about wanting to get a feel for how things are made, but you can't beat the customer reviews to see what the quality is and why one particular item works better than another."

"Sure, Steven. We'll be your guinea pigs and buy all the garbage so you won't have to waste your money on junk that doesn't work." Alisa's voice was sarcastic.

Danny looked over at Steven, who'd known Alisa long enough to not take her seriously. "At least, the apocalypse won't be boring as long as we have Alisa to provide the drama."

The three friends finished their chores and left for the evening.

After the Sunday service, Danny, Alisa, and Steven walked to Danny's car since they all rode to church together. Danny unlocked the doors. "Where do you guys want to eat?"

Alisa was quick with an answer. "Clary's. It's just a few blocks from the gun show."

"Clary's is fine with me. I could live off of their burgers." Steven got in the back seat.

Danny stuck the keys in the ignition. "I love their French toast. I wonder how late they serve breakfast."

"All day. That's all I get there; either the eggs benny or the waffle. I might get both today. I'm starving!" Alisa buckled her seat belt and stuck a thumb drive into the USB port of Danny's stereo. "Steven, did you get to hear Danny's interview on Real News?"

"No. Is this it?" Steven looked attentive as the intro to the news program played.

"Yep."

Danny shook his head. "Listening to the sound of my voice gives me the creeps."

The interview began, and Alisa giggled. "We have to listen to your voice all the time. You can handle it for twenty minutes."

When they arrived at the café, all the tables were full, so they sat at the bar. They ordered, and the food came out quickly, considering how busy it was. Steven had a burger, Alisa had Eggs Benedict and a waffle, and Danny had ham and eggs since he knew he'd be helping Alisa with the last half of that waffle. This wasn't his first experience watching her order more than she could ever hope to eat.

Alisa slid most of the waffle toward Danny. "I'm stuffed. Steven, what did you think about Danny's show?"

"Amazing. If I hadn't been motivated to get prepared before, I would be now. That's so cool that this guy has a show which covers alternative news from a biblical perspective. Even more cool that it covers prophetic dreams."

Danny poured more syrup on the now cold waffle. "I was a nervous wreck."

"You didn't sound it," Steven said.

"Alisa was literally holding my hand to get me through it."

She rolled her eyes. "He would have been fine even if I hadn't been there."

After eating, they paid their tab and headed to the show.

Once inside, Alisa covered her mouth. "No way! Look at all these guns!"

"Cool huh?" Steven surveyed the floor.

"Let's stay focused. We need to look for survival gear." Danny tried to be the voice of reason, but like Steven and Alisa, he was mesmerized by his first visit to a gun show.

Alisa walked straight to the nearest table full of pistols. "What's that?"

The man behind the table handed her the pistol to look at. "Beretta, 9 millimeter."

She held it in her hand, then passed it to Danny. "Nice"

Danny took the pistol and tried to remember the lessons Nick had taught him. Treat every gun like it's loaded, don't point it at anyone you don't intend to shoot, keep your finger away from the trigger until you are ready to fire it. "Very nice. Thanks."

He handed back to the man at the table who was being bombarded by Alisa with questions about every gun on the table.

"Didn't you guys say you wanted a shotgun? Here are some over at this table." Steven led the way to the next booth where he inspected a pump-action shotgun.

Alisa quickly gained the attention of the attendant and began quizzing him on his selection of shotguns. "Do you have a Maverick 88 that comes with a regular stock and a pistol grip?"

The man chuckled. "Sounds like you know what you're looking for."

Danny put his arm around her. "My brother-in-law gave us some suggestions."

The man picked up a black, pump-action shotgun from the end of the table. "The fellow in the next aisle sells pistol grips for it. They're the same grips as for a Mossberg 500."

"How much is it?" Steven asked.

"235 dollars. Includes the background check."

"Is there a waiting period?" Steven looked very interested in the shotgun.

"Nope. Your background check should come back in a few minutes; then it's all yours. You can take it home today."

"What about pistols? Is there a wait for those?" Alisa asked.

"Not in Georgia. Same thing, pass the background check and take it home today. But you do have to be twenty-one."

"I'm twenty-one!" Alisa sounded moderately offended.

Steven commented, "Barely."

Danny shook his head. "Are you buying it?"

Steven ran his fingers through his hair. "Maybe. I'm going to look around and think about it. Seems like a good form of defense for the money."

The man behind the table handed Steven a clipboard and a pen. "Take it right now and I'll give it to you for 225 dollars, including the background check, and I'll throw in a box of buckshot."

"Done!" Steven took the clipboard and began filling out the information. "Can I leave it with you, so I don't have to pack it around all day?"

"No problem at all."

Once Steven had filled out the form, he paid the man, and they continued browsing the aisles.

"Here's your pistol grip." Danny pulled the package from a rack and handed it to Steven.

Steven asked the man, "How hard is this to change?"

"You just need a really long screwdriver to take off the stock. If you can change a light bulb, you can install a pistol grip."

Steven took out his wallet. "I can change a light bulb."

Once that purchase was made, Alisa found a table full of battle rifles. "Wow! Check this out."

Danny examined the all-black AK-47 with the under folding stock. "That is insane!"

Alisa held up the price tag. "Six hundred. Look, it's shorter than the shotgun with the pistol grip. It will fit in our bug-out bags. Do you want it?"

"We don't have money for that. I thought we were buying a shotgun."

"Steven already bought a shotgun. I'll put it on my dad's card."

"You said they won't give you spending money."

"I told them Savannah was getting more dangerous, and I need a gun. Since I'm making them work to have the wedding in Connecticut, they didn't argue."

"So they'll be okay with you buying an AK-47 for personal protection?"

"The receipt will just have the name of the gun dealer. It won't say what I bought."

Danny couldn't help but imagining himself shooting the rifle. "How dependable are these?"

The man at the table picked it up and handed it to him. "Russia, Eastern Europe, and most militaries in Africa use em'. In tough battle conditions, it's the thing to have. That's why they like em' so much in the deserts and the jungles."

"And it comes with one clip?"

"I'll throw in an extra magazine. Technically, a clip is a strip of metal that holds several rounds of ammunition together for fast loading into a magazine. A magazine is the ammunition container made to be inserted into the firearm. But most people will know what you're talking about if you say clip."

"How do I fold out the stock?"

The man depressed a button at the base of the stock. "There you go."

"Do I need to take out the clip, I mean magazine to unfold it?"

"No, not with a standard 30-round mag."

Danny liked the way the weapon felt in his

hands. "How much are bullets for this?"

"Little under fifty cents a round for steel. Little more than fifty cents for brass."

Danny looked the gun over. "I guess brass is better."

"Brass is always better, but AKs are made to shoot anything."

"But if it were you, you'd buy brass?"

The man nodded.

"And how much for extra magazines?"

"I've got steel mags for twenty-five dollars. Fellow over on the back wall with all the cheap ammo has plastic mags for fifteen dollars, but you won't find a better deal or a better rifle at this show."

Danny was sold, but he didn't want to show it. "Okay, we'll be back."

Alisa looked at him. "You don't want it?"

Danny waited until they were out of earshot. "Yes, but I want to get a better deal. Let's walk around and come back. Besides, I don't want to pack it around for the whole day. By the time I buy a couple of extra mags and some ammo, we'll be out, at least, 700 dollars."

"But we'll be the toughest kids in the apocalypse." Alisa gripped his hand tightly.

"I guess you can't put a price on security. Maybe I should buy the rifle and let you put the other survival stuff on your dad's card."

She shook her head. "It won't work. I have clearance to buy a gun, but not a bunch of junk."

"Won't they want to see the gun you bought?"

"I'll show them Pop's old gun."

Danny grimaced. "But now we're lying."

"Technically, I'd be buying the AK, and you'll be trading me for the revolver. So, I'd be buying the revolver with the AK, which is what my dad will see on the credit card."

"I don't like it. It sounds sneaky." Danny looked over at Steven for advice.

Steven put his hands in the air. "I'm not touching that one. You're on your own."

Danny smiled at him. "But it is a cool gun."

Steven fought back a grin and looked away rather than respond.

Alisa pulled on his arm. "Danny, trust me. If they ask, I'll tell them the whole story, but they don't want the details. This is all a chess game to get me to have the wedding in Connecticut. You'll wish you got more than an AK out of this deal by the time that wedding is finished."

"I'm getting *you*, out of this deal. I'm pretty happy with that."

She smiled and kissed him on the lips. "You've already got me."

The three of them wandered the aisles until they came upon a booth called Prepper Depot. The table had a wide assortment of water filters, first aid supplies, fire starters, and backpacks.

Steven began examining the gear. "Here's a nice multi-tool. What do you think about it?"

Alisa pulled out her phone and quickly pulled up the same brand online. "It's cheaper from this website."

Steven grimaced and moved on to a survival

blanket. "What about this?"

Alisa typed in the keywords. "Yeah, that looks like a good deal. Get it."

Danny picked up a camping stove and inspected it. "Check this out. It folds flat and weighs almost nothing."

The man at the table handed Danny a can of Sterno. "It works with a variety of fuel sources. You can use Sterno, twigs, or charcoal."

"Wow. I'll take one." Danny paid the man.

Steven continued browsing the table. He picked up some water purification tablets and a metal canteen. He browsed the selection of backpacks but didn't see any that would be long enough to hold the shotgun.

Danny picked up a small camouflage pup tent. "This is light. Check it out."

Steven took the box, looked it over and sat it back on the table. "I wish I had a shopping cart. We still have to get ammo."

Alisa inspected the packs. "These are really cool, with all of the compartments. Let's get one of these and give our other long one to Steven."

Danny liked the look of the military-style packs. "Sure. How about the tan-colored one?"

Alisa held up the tag. "It's coyote, not tan. Danny, if you can't get the lingo right, there's no hope of you surviving the apocalypse."

Danny laughed and shook his head. He picked up a small clam shell pouch. "These strap on to the loops on the pack."

The man at the table said, "It's called MOLLE which stands for Modular Lightweight Load-carrying Equipment. You can put any MOLLE pouch on any other MOLLE pack or vest. I have some good medical kits over here that attach right to the back of this pack. Take the kit and the pack and I'll throw in 200 feet of paracord."

"Sounds like a good deal, but what is paracord?" Alisa crossed her arms.

"It's the cord the military uses for parachutes. It holds up to 550 pounds. Each strand has seven inner strands that can be used for constructing shelters, fishing lines, snares, trip wire or restraining hostiles." The man handed a package of the cord to Danny.

Danny handed it to Alisa to check out. "What do you think?"

She shrugged. "What's in the medical pouch?"

"Suture kit, EMT shears, tourniquet, Quickclot, which stops bleeding and a compression bandage. There's some other stuff in there as well, like aspirin, gauze pads, and Band-Aids." He handed Alisa one of the medical kits.

"Do you have magazine pouches that attach to the MOLLE pack?" Danny asked.

"I don't because most of the other dealers carry gun-related items exclusively, but the fellow near the back, with all of the tactical vests, he has those."

Danny looked at Alisa. "That would be convenient, to have the magazines on the outside of the pack so we could get to them fast if we needed to."

Alisa took her money out of her purse. "We'll take it."

Danny took out his wallet. "I'll get everything

else. You're paying for the gun."

Alisa quickly thrust the cash toward the dealer. "My dad is buying the gun. And you still have to buy ammo."

Danny knew it was no use fighting, so he put his wallet back in his pocket.

Steven paid for his items next. "Mind if I put some of this in your backpack? I'll wear it around while we get everything else."

Danny placed his camping stove and paracord in the pack and handed it to Steven. "Go ahead, but save some room. I might have to put some ammo in there."

"No problem." Steve placed his emergency blanket, pistol grip, canteen and water purification tablets in the pack while Alisa attached the medical kit to the loops on the side of the pack.

The next stop was the ammo table. Steven bought 100 rounds of shotgun shells in assorted shot sizes.

Danny picked up 400 rounds of ammo for the AK-47 but couldn't find any .32 H&R. He asked the attendant if he might have any behind the table.

"That's sort of an oddball round. We have good prices because we buy all of this stuff in bulk. So we only stock the most popular calibers. If we get something like .32 H&R, it won't ever sell. There's a guy somewhere near the middle that carries old guns and ammo. He'll probably have it, but it won't be cheap."

Danny paid for the 7.62x39 ammo. "Thanks."

Alisa helped him put half of it in the pack to split up the weight. "That's not good. I wonder if we should buy another pistol that uses a common type of ammunition."

"Not today," Danny said. "Let's assess what we have, what we need and what it's all going to cost."

"Okay." Alisa looked moderately disappointed.

The three of them decided to split up and meet at the front door. Alisa went to purchase the AK-47, Danny went to find the .32 ammo and the magazine pouches, while Steven went to pick up his shotgun.

"Try to get him to throw in four magazines total for the AK. If not, go ahead and buy two more in addition to the two he is including." Danny kissed Alisa on the head.

"I'll see what I can do." She turned to find the table and walked away.

Roughly thirty minutes later, they rendezvoused at the front door with the new additions to their growing supply of survival items and headed home.

CHAPTER 10

Behold, the LORD maketh the earth empty, and maketh it waste, and turneth it upside down, and scattereth abroad the inhabitants thereof. And it shall be, as with the people, so with the priest; as with the servant, so with his master; as with the maid, so with her mistress; as with the buyer, so with the seller; as with the lender, so with the borrower; as with the taker of usury, so with the giver of usury to him. The land shall be utterly emptied, and utterly spoiled: for the LORD hath spoken this word.

Isaiah 24:1-3

Tuesday morning, Danny glanced over at his

ringing phone in the console of his car as he drove to school. "Steven. I'll call him right back." One of Danny's pet peeves was people texting or talking on the phone while driving. On a rare occasion, he would put the phone on speaker and drive while he talked, but he'd never hold the phone while he drove. And he'd never text while driving, not even at a stop light.

Danny pulled into the parking lot and found a space. He grabbed his backpack and slung it over his shoulder. As he walked briskly toward class, he took his phone out of his coat pocket and returned Steven's call. "Hey. I was in the car. I couldn't pick up. What's going on?"

"Did you catch the financial news before you left this morning?"

"No. Why?"

"It's going to be an absolute bloodbath on Wall Street. Everything is tanking in early morning trading."

Danny's first class was at 9:00, so he knew the markets weren't open yet. "Couldn't the market bounce back after the opening bell rings?"

"Not a chance. Asian markets are down big. Europe is in free fall. Dow futures are down 1000 points right now. This thing will probably be popping circuit breakers all day."

Danny crossed the courtyard and paused outside of the building where his first class was held. "Thanks for the heads up, I'll keep track of what's going on during class. Can you call Alisa and tell her what's happening?"

"Sure. Talk to you later."

Danny put his phone on vibrate and walked into class. He took out his book and listened as his professor began the lecture for the day, but his mind was far from the material being covered.

He opened his spiral notebook and began jotting down a loose inventory of the items that Steven, Alisa and he had accumulated since the dream. On the other side of the page, he tallied up his checking account and the cash he had at home, hidden in his dresser.

Since he regularly came home from work with significant amounts of cash, he kept several hundred dollars tucked inside an envelope, in a hollow space between the two bottom drawers of his dresser. He would typically make a deposit at the bank about every other week so he could write checks for utilities and rent. Since the dream, however, he only kept enough in the bank to cover immediate expenses. He'd heard horror stories of bank closures and capital controls over the past two decades in other countries like Iceland, Cypress, Russia, Argentina, and Greece, during times of economic instability.

Danny checked the financial website from his phone shortly after the markets opened at 9:30. The S&P opened down seven and a half percent which triggered the first circuit breaker within seconds of the opening bell. All markets closed for fifteen minutes.

He texted Alisa. "R U watching this?"

She texted back. "Yes, Steven told me. Not cool. Call me when u can."

"OK. XO"

The markets resumed trading at 9:20. Danny watched the ticker as he tried to pay attention to the rest of the lecture. The major indices rallied a couple of percentage points but turned south again by ten o'clock. The professor dismissed the class, and Danny gathered his things. Once outside the building, he sat on a bench in the courtyard. As he took out his phone and called Alisa, he wondered how many of the other students walking by had even an inkling of what was happening in the financial world.

"Hey," Alisa answered.

"This looks pretty bad. The Dow is down ten percent right now."

"Yeah, I'm watching the news."

"What time is your first class?"

"I have photography at a quarter after ten. I don't think I'm going to class. I'd be late now anyway. I might just play hooky all day. When is your next class?"

"11:30. I couldn't pay attention to the last lecture. I might just go home now."

"You could come over here. We could watch the world end together."

Danny couldn't resist the invitation. "Okay. Maybe we should do some planning as well. Should I invite Steven?"

"You can, or we could just be alone."

Danny smiled. "That might not be very safe. I'm sure it's easier for you, but I have to put a lot of effort into staying pure."

"You're right, I'll call Steven. And it's not easy for me either."

"Should I pick up anything on the way?"

"Yeah, syrup; I'll make French toast."

"Since when do you make French toast?"

"I've been practicing, in secret. I want to master at least three dishes before we get married."

"You're so sweet. What are the other two?"

"I'll tell you as soon as I know. For now, be happy with French toast."

Danny laughed. "I love you, Alisa. See you in a while."

He called Steven who accepted the invitation to the market-crash party. Danny then stopped by the store to pick up a bottle of syrup. As he made his way down the aisle, he wondered if he should be buying more staples to stock up. He resisted the urge, but grabbed the largest bottle of syrup on the shelf and headed to Alisa's.

Once there, he removed his coat and sat the syrup on the kitchen counter. "Smells a little smoky in here."

Alisa waved him away with the spatula. "That was the practice batch. It was slightly more well-done than I wanted, but I've got the temperature figured out now. Go, sit in the living room and watch the markets. I'll bring brunch in when it's ready."

Danny shook his head and smiled as he walked into the living room and took a seat on the couch. He turned the volume up slightly so Alisa could hear the coverage of the financial news network from the other room.

Steven arrived minutes later. "Hey. What did I

miss?"

"If the S&P drop ten more points, it will trigger the second circuit breaker."

Steven laid his coat on the chair near the door. "And that will halt trading for another fifteen minutes, right?"

"Yeah, that's what the commentator is saying. Then, if the S&P drops a total of twenty percent for the day, they shut down the markets 'til tomorrow morning. And there it goes, the S&P is down thirteen percent. We just took out the second circuit breaker."

"Hi, Steven." Alisa walked in the room and studied the television. "That doesn't look good."

"Hey. I brought you some coffee. It was on BOGO." He handed her a bag with two family-sized plastic containers of coffee.

"Thanks. You didn't have to do that."

"I know, but Danny said you were cooking, and I didn't want to come empty handed. I was planning to get you a small package of coffee, but I saw the blinky coupons in the aisle and stacked two of them on top of the buy one, get one deal for the Folgers. Both of the big containers came out to less than one small container. Since we're trying to be frugal, I couldn't resist."

"Smart thinking," Danny said. "I had trouble walking out of the store without buying more supplies when I stopped off for the syrup. But, if we took what we have now to Nana's, it would take at least two trips, and that's with both cars. I suppose if we get anything else, we should take it straight to Nana's, or better yet, just buy it in Anderson."

Alisa turned to go back to the kitchen. "Does Nana have the same selection of grocery stores in Anderson? If not, we might be better off buying stuff here, then carting it out to her house."

"Good point." Danny leaned back and listened to the reporters speculate about the remainder of the trading day. The current question among them was whether the market would make it to the closing bell without triggering the final circuit breaker which would close it down for the rest of the day.

Alisa's face glowed with pride as she brought two plates in and sat them on the coffee table in front of Danny and Steven. "Brunch is served."

"This looks fantastic. Where's yours?" Danny asked.

"Don't worry about me. Mine is cooking; you eat while it's hot." She disappeared into the kitchen again.

Steven said a quick prayer over the food and began eating. "Wow. This is really good. I was worried when I first walked in. It smelled like something was burnt."

"Yeah, she said that was the practice round. I think it's in the trash. But you're right, this batch came out perfect." Danny cut into the next slice of toast.

Minutes later, Alisa came and sat down next to Danny with her plate, just as the market was resuming trading. "Wow, look at the news ticker at the bottom of the screen. It says the Fed, SEC and Treasury are convening for an emergency meeting today at two o'clock. Is that supposed to instill confidence or more panic?"

Steven flipped an invisible coin into the air and pretended to catch it. "Tails, more panic."

The three of them watched the carnage as the losses on Wall Street mounted higher and higher. By three o'clock, the S&P was down by twenty percent and the markets closed for the day. The Dow had lost more than 3,000 points for the day to close at 14,323.

Later that evening, the three friends met back up at work. Danny walked up to the hostess desk where Alisa was hanging up the phone and writing in the reservations book. "New reservation for tonight?"

"No. Party of six just canceled. Looks like we've had a total of twenty cancelations so far."

Danny glanced at the sheet. "We only had about forty to begin with."

Steven walked up to the podium and took a look at the remaining reservations. "Looks like it's going to be a slow night."

Indeed, it was a slow night. The three of them sat at a table near the back and slowly folded napkins for silverware roll-ups, just to look busy. Steven kept his phone on the table so they could monitor the financial news. "The chairman of the Fed is holding a press conference at nine o'clock tonight. I guess he will let everyone know what the plan of action is going to be."

Alisa stood up. "Okay, let's try to get our tables out of here by then, so we can listen."

Danny got up as well. "Do what you want, but I'm going to try to sell my table dessert, cappuccino and whatever else I can to get their check up. I only had three tables all night. I need to make as much as I can off of this last one."

"Yeah, that's smart," Steven said. "The rest of the week might be just as bad as tonight. Besides, it's not like we can't slip back here and listen to the opening remarks right at nine o'clock."

Danny managed to sell his table specialty coffee drinks and two desserts. He still made it to the back table with Steven and Alisa to listen to the speech at 9:00. "Wow. Congress already approved a two trillion dollar bail-out package. That has to be the world record for the fastest thing that ever happened in Washington. And the 500 dollar economic-stimulus package paid out to every American might help business in the restaurant. At least, it didn't all go to the banks this time."

Steven shook his head. "The 500 dollar stimulus check is just a payoff, so people don't riot in the street about the banks getting another bail-out."

Danny took out his phone and quickly did the math. "Yeah. That's only 150 billion dollars in direct stimulus. Out of two trillion dollars, that leaves one point eighty-five trillion dollars to the banks and corporations."

Alisa tapped her finger on her chin. "So if the whole two trillion dollars had gone to individuals, how much would we have gotten?"

Danny recalculated the numbers. "Almost 7,000 dollars."

She crossed her arms. "That would have been nice."

Danny considered the unprecedented bail-out move. "The big question is, what's the dollar going to be worth once the stimulus money gets into circulation."

Steven nodded. "I guess that will explain the part of your dream where the currency was worthless."

Danny pursed his lips. "We should probably spend that money as soon as we get it; to buy things we will need before it triggers massive inflation."

They finished the night at the restaurant, speculating about what the coming days would bring, then headed home.

The huge bail-out package did manage to put a floor in the markets for the next couple of trading sessions, but stocks didn't make a significant rebound.

CHAPTER 11

And they shall look unto the earth; and behold trouble and darkness, dimness of anguish; and they shall be driven to darkness.

Isaiah 8:22

Danny hit the gas when he saw the light turn yellow. He wasn't exactly running late, but he would have to hurry to be on time. He pulled up to the Bryant Street parking garage where he always parked. "Lot full? You have got to be kidding me! Not today."

He quickly drove three blocks south to the garage on Congress. He checked the time on his phone as he pulled in. "It's 5:55. There's no way I'll make it to Lilly's by 6:00." He found a space on the second level, parked his car, grabbed his apron from the passenger's seat, and his pens and corkscrew from the console, then locked the door. Danny dashed for the stairwell rather than wait for the elevator, since he only had one flight of stairs to descend.

Once he hit the street, he broke into a quick jog. The air was very cold, but he could feel himself starting to sweat after he had jogged the first three blocks up Abercorn. He removed his jacket and folded it so he could carry it in the same hand as his apron. Once he reached Bay Street, he opted to take the foot bridge over the River-Street access, rather than jog nearly an extra block up to the cobblestone street, which then snaked back down one block as a ramp that allowed trucks and cars to get to the lower level on River Street.

Halfway across the wooden foot bridge, one of the planks gave way beneath his foot and his entire leg pushed through the hole. "Ahhh!" Danny grabbed the railing to break his fall and in so doing, dropped his phone which bounced off of the plank in front of him and over the side of the foot bridge. The sound of the crashing phone on the cobblestones below added to the sense of doom that he felt in the pit of his stomach from the close call. He slowly lifted his leg out of the hole and pulled himself up by the rails. Very cautiously and very slowly, he walked the remainder of the way across the bridge. He focused his attention on the winged-lion fountain in front of the old Savannah Cotton Exchange. He locked his eyes on the sculpture to keep his mind from panicking about the fall that could have ended his life. Once across the bridge, he took a deep breath and sat down on the circular wall surrounding the fountain. Danny glanced at the old Cotton Exchange to his left and thought about how long it had been standing. The cobblestone streets, the majestic winged lion, even the wooden foot bridge had endured hundreds of years. Everything seemed to be built so solid, and maintained so well. How could the bridge have been neglected and allowed to rot out like that?

Still shaking from the experience, Danny made his way to the stairwell to walk down to the river. "My phone is shot, but maybe if I can find it, I can still get the SD card out and save all of my numbers. I'm late now anyway. At least I have an excuse."

Once at the bottom of the stairs, Danny walked around the building to the cobblestone path which ran beneath the foot bridge. Suddenly the surrounding street lights went dark. "Oh great. I can't see anything now." He looked around at all of the buildings. None of the lights were on. "This is an odd time for a power outage. There's no wind or lightening." Danny carefully walked out toward the river. It was pitch black. He had never felt such total darkness. "Surely some of the people in the restaurants or stores will light candles." None did. Danny regretted not having his phone. At least he would have had his flashlight app.

He felt through his work apron. "Awesome!" He found a book of matches which he used for lighting the candles on the tables at Lilly's. Next, he retrieved a piece of paper from the notebook he used to write down his customers' orders. He twisted it tightly so it would burn at a slower rate. Then, he struck a match and lit a corner of the paper. He held it up so he could see.

There were no people along River Street at all. This was exceedingly curious, on par with the blackout itself. He turned and held the burning paper for light in the other direction. "Nothing. I'll just walk back to my car, and drive by the restaurant. I've got a flashlight in the glove box, at least."

Danny briskly walked up the ramp toward Bay Street. It was the long way, but he wasn't about to risk crossing the foot bridge again. He paused to get another paper torch ready for when the one he was carrying burned out.

Danny passed the flame from the expiring torch to the fresh one as he made his way up Abercorn. He had just enough light to see his next step. Once he reached Reynolds Square, he sat on a bench to twist yet another torch from his pad of paper. Suddenly, he noticed the faintest hint of light coming from above. He looked up. "The moon is trying to peek through the clouds. That would be helpful because I'm about out of paper."

Soon, he could see the towering statue of John Wesley. Danny took a moment to look up at the brazen figure holding a Bible in its left hand and the right hand opened as if he were appealing to passers-by to harken unto the wisdom of the book in his other hand. He smiled. This was the first time he'd passed the statue since becoming a Christian. Now that he had something in common with the man who had been Savannah's first chaplain, he found a sudden interest in the monument. The clouds parted to let in a bright stream of moonlight allowing Danny to read the inscription on the bronze base of the monument. "*Mene, Mene, Tekel, Upharsin.*" Danny knuckled his brow as he re-read the words that appeared as gibberish. "Hmm. Nonsensical. I can't even guess what language that is. Must be an inside joke."

Danny turned his attention away from the monument centered in Reynolds Square to the sound of hooves on the brick streets. "Must be a carriage." The Old Pink House restaurant was right on Reynolds Square and patrons were frequently brought there by one of the city's horse-drawn carriages as it was the destination of many seeking a romantic evening. Danny followed the sound of the clip clop against the bricks toward the street. "Sounds like more than one horse; and they have a very peculiar gait." Something about the timing of the hooves striking the road was off. Danny found himself obsessively curious about what was causing this inconsistency. He scurried through the square unimpeded by the darkness, now that the moon offered a reliable glimmer. His face went pale when he finally came upon the source of the clopping.

Danny immediately turned and ran in the other direction until he stumbled and fell on the rough brick surface of the street. He turned around from his position on the ground to get a second look at the hideous creatures behind him. The radiance of the moon illuminated the faces of three miserable cows. The skin stretched thin across the bones of their head. Their eyes were more lifeless and empty than that of the first such horrific creature he'd seen. "It's another nightmare. It's not real. It's not real. I just have to wake up."

Danny tried to will himself to wake up. "Wake up! Wake up! Wake up!" He shouted repeatedly. Next he just screamed, hoping that someone would hear him and shake him to rouse him from his slumber. Exhausted, Danny sat quietly on the street where he had fallen. The torch he'd been carrying lay on the street beside him, still burning, and the three cows walked slowly toward him.

Convinced he was stuck in the tormented dream, he picked up the remnant of the torch and shook it at the advancing creatures. As they came closer, he could see their eyes with greater detail. They had a milky film over the hollow portal into the emptiness of their souls. He soon realized that they seemed not to respond to the flames of the torch, whatsoever. "They're blind. They're starving and blind."

Almost instantly after Danny had understood the condition of the wretched beasts, he felt a pang of hunger in his own stomach. He backed away from the dismal brutes as if their misfortune was somehow infectious. Soon, the clouds returned and utter blackness once again fell across the street. Danny fumbled for the matches, patted his pockets for the paper, as the torch he'd been carrying was now but a smoldering ember.

He sat up in his bed with a great gasp for air, as if he'd been holding his breath, or as if someone or something had been covering his mouth to suffocate him. His heart was pounding. His first action was to turn on the light next to his bed. Next, he removed the drenched tee-shirt and retrieved a dry one from his dresser. He turned on the hall light, then the kitchen light as he poured himself a glass of cold water from the filter-pitcher in the refrigerator. Danny sat alone, motionless, quiet at the table with nearly every light in the apartment turned on.

CHAPTER 12

I will take away the hedge thereof, and it shall be eaten up; and break down the wall thereof, and it shall be trodden down: And I will lay it waste.

Isaiah 5:5b-6a

Danny tried to go back to sleep after the horrific vision but with no success. He tossed and turned in his bed, readjusting the pillow. "It's no use. I might as well just get up." He looked at the clock. "A quarter after five."

Danny started a pot of extra strong coffee and ate a bowl of cereal. Once finished with his cereal, he sat on the couch with his coffee and opened his Bible. Typically, he would read a few chapters from the New Testament each morning, as prescribed by

Pastor Earl, but this morning he was searching for clues.

He turned to the Book of Isaiah, which he and Alisa had been reading. Pastor Earl said that was good place to start if one wanted to see how God reacted to a nation that had utterly forsaken him. And in every Sunday-morning and Wednesday-night service it seemed that Pastor Earl had no shortage of parallels, teaching how America had followed in the footsteps of ancient Israel.

He turned to chapter 5 and began to read. He pondered the allegory of the vineyard which, according to verse 7, represented Israel. "So God built a fence around the vineyard and caused it to prosper." Danny considered the story of the pilgrims which had come to America in search of a place they could worship freely. "Hmm. Sounds a lot like the Jews who left Egypt for a land of their own."

Danny thought about the Preamble to the Declaration of Independence, "All men are created . . . by their Creator." And the First Amendment to the Constitution, "Freedom of religion . . ." The Pledge of Allegiance, "One nation, under God."

Danny looked up to speak to God. "How did I miss the rich heritage of Christian faith in the founding of this country? Sure, I didn't hear too much about it in school, but when I add it all up, it's undeniable. Heck, it's even on our money, In God We Trust. I bet the founding fathers wouldn't even recognize this place. It looks more like a den of debauchery than a nation founded on Biblical principles. And not only do most Americans want nothing to do with you, as Pastor Earl says, evidenced by taking prayer out of school, removing the Bible from school and replacing it with an atheistic worldview propagandized through evolutionary theory, but the few remaining Christians who dare to say they actually believe what this book says are actively persecuted."

He looked back down at the pages he'd been reading. "I suppose that's what you meant by saying you looked for good grapes but found only wild grapes."

Danny continued to read and silently ponder the Scriptures. *Therefore hell hath enlarged herself, and opened her mouth without measure: and their glory, and their multitude, and their pomp, and he that rejoiceth, shall descend into it. And the mean man shall be brought down, and the mighty man shall be humbled, and the eyes of the lofty shall be humbled. . .* "Is this about your judgment on America, Lord?"

Woe unto them that call evil good, and good evil; that put darkness for light, and light for darkness; that put bitter for sweet, and sweet for bitter! Woe unto them that are wise in their own eyes, and prudent in their own sight! Woe unto them that are mighty to drink wine, and men of strength to mingle strong drink: Which justify the wicked for reward, and take away the righteousness of the righteous from him . . . that certainly sounds like the United States.

Therefore as the fire devoureth the stubble, and the flame consumeth the chaff, so their root shall be as rottenness, and their blossom shall go up as dust: because they have cast away the law of the LORD of hosts, and despised the word of the Holy One of Israel. Therefore is the anger of the LORD kindled against his people, and he hath stretched forth his hand against them, and hath smitten them: and the hills did tremble, and their carcasses were torn in the midst of the streets. For all this his anger is not turned away, but his hand is stretched out still.

Danny took a deep breath. "This is actually more frightening than my dream."

When he came to the final verse of chapter 5, the words stood out on the page as if embossed. They rang through his mind as if they were being shouted from the center of his soul . . . *and if one look unto the land, behold darkness and sorrow, and the light is darkened in the heavens thereof.*

Chills ran up Danny's arms and back. He closed the Bible, stood up, and covered his mouth. He felt that he'd just stumbled into deep water, so intense, so overwhelming, he could not peer into it for a moment longer.

He muttered the final phrase once more through his covered mouth. "Behold darkness and sorrow." If the vision he'd seen just hours before had a title, that was it.

Danny looked out the window. The sun had finally come up. "Alisa should be up by now." He picked up his phone and called her.

"Hello?" Her voice was groggy.

"Are you awake?"

"I am now. What's up?"

"I had another dream. It was pretty spooky."

"Just now?"

"No. A while ago."

"Why didn't you call me? Are you okay?"

"It was like 4:00 in the morning when I woke up. I wasn't going to bother you then. And yes, I'm fine."

"I wish I'd been there. I don't like knowing you're having nightmares, and I'm not there to wake you up."

"We'll be married in less than a month. Then you can wake me up whenever you want."

She giggled. "Don't get mad when I take you up on that offer. So, are you going to school?"

"No, I'm going to go see Pastor Earl if he's available today. This dream was creepier than the last one."

"Do you feel like you can tell me about it now?"

"Sure." Danny proceeded to tell her the dream in vivid details.

"It's an EMP," she proclaimed with a voice of certainty.

"What do you know about EMPs?"

"Not much, but I know that's what your dream was about. I saw a report of some news show a while back, the former CIA director, Woolsey, or something like that was talking about how serious of a risk it is to America. He said, Russia, China, North Korea, or Iran could launch a nuke into space over the U.S. and it would take out our power grid, computers, even cars, everything with chips and microprocessors. He was saying even ISIS or Al Qaeda could launch one from a rudimentary missile hidden in a shipping container or a weather balloon."

"But we can't be sure that's what my dream was about. Ted Koppel wrote a book a few years ago called *Lights Out*. It was about the vulnerability of our electrical grid being shut down by hackers. The dream could be about that. Or, it could be allegorical, the darkness might symbolize a spiritual darkness that's coming."

"News flash, spiritual darkness is already here. Danny, I can't really explain how I know this, but as soon as you said you dropped your phone in the dream, I knew that was the key to understanding it. I knew it was about a loss of technology, communications, electricity and internet access. Even before you said the lights went out, I knew. Then, when you told me about the darkness, I had like a little panic attack. It freaked me out, but trust me, Danny, I just know."

Danny believed her. He completely understood what she meant by freaked out. Next, he told her about his experience while reading Isaiah, chapter 5.

Her voice was shaky. "That's the synopsis of your entire dream, behold darkness and sorrow? Don't tell me anything else. Come pick me up. I want to go see Pastor Earl with you."

"Okay." Danny put the phone down. He hadn't said anything to her about those specific words jumping off the page at him, yet Alisa had sensed the same thing. All of this dream business was getting very interesting and Danny wasn't sure if he was more excited or afraid. He called Pastor Earl to make an appointment to see him, then got dressed and went to pick Alisa up.

The two of them arrived at the church shortly after 10:00 Friday morning. Pastor Earl met them at the door. "Come in, come in. I've got coffee and donuts in the office, follow me to the back."

As they walked into the church office, located in a small room at the back of the little store-front church, Pastor Earl motioned to the small couch next to the desk. "Have a seat and help yourself to the coffee and donuts. So, you had another dream?"

Danny poured himself a cup of coffee from the pot and gave the pastor all the details of the dream. He then explained how he was unable to go back to sleep and went over what he read in Isaiah chapter 5. He shared his personal thoughts about what he'd read and explained Alisa's reaction.

Alisa finished chewing her donut and said, "I can't tell you how I know, but I know his dream is about an EMP attack."

Pastor Earl listened intently to both of them. He sat quietly for a moment after Alisa and Danny finished speaking. Finally, he said, "Well, Alisa, Joseph had a dream when he was younger, but after, he was sold into captivity. His gift was interpreting dreams. Daniel also had the gift of interpreting dreams. It would make sense that God might decide to grant that particular gift to the mate of someone who has dreams and visions. I think your feeling of being absolutely certain about it being an EMP is consistent with someone who has been given an interpretation from God."

Danny scratched his head. "Pastor, if this is

about God's judgment on America, why would he bother causing an economic collapse if he plans to let us be wiped out by way of an EMP? Doesn't that sound like kicking a dead horse?"

The pastor smiled as he nodded. "His ways are higher than our ways. But let me ask you this. How certain are you that your new dream is of a prophetic nature?"

"Pretty sure." Danny's face reflected his confidence in the matter.

"And why is that?"

"Because of the first dream; it was like three weeks before Tuesday's market crash. It was the largest one-day point decline in history."

"What if you hadn't had that dream and seen it fulfilled? How sure about the second dream would you have been?"

Danny rocked forward on the small couch. "I see what you're getting at."

Pastor Earl sipped his coffee. "And all of those people who heard you on Ricky's radio show last Saturday, they saw the markets tank on Black Tuesday as well. I think they'd be inclined to pay very close attention if you choose to go back on his show to talk about this revelation."

Danny nodded. "You're right. You think Ricky would want me to come back on the show?"

"Oh, I'm certain." The pastor rested his head on his hand. "You mentioned that the words *Mene, Mene, Tekel, Upharsin* were inscribed in the bronze base of John Wesley's monument. The statue is bronze, but the actual base of the monument is granite."

Danny shrugged his shoulders. "The base was made out of bronze in my dream. Do you have any idea what those words mean?"

The pastor opened his Bible. "In the Book of Daniel, King Belshazzar is holding a feast, using the sacred instruments from the temple to serve his guests at what amounts to a drunken party. He looks over and sees a giant finger write those words on the wall. Since Daniel had a reputation for having interpreted dreams for Belshazzar's father, Nebuchadnezzar, he was brought in to interpret the message. *Mene*, Daniel said, meant the kingdom had been numbered and finished. *Tekel*, he said, meant weighed and found wanting. *Upharsin*, Daniel interpreted as Peres, which meant the kingdom would be divided. That story is where we get the saying, to see the writing on the wall."

Alisa crossed her legs and leaned forward. "So, how much warning did the king get from that sign?"

The pastor snorted with a grin. "Not much. Cyrus invaded Babylon that very night and killed Belshazzar. It was certainly a message of judgment. And another thing, about the base of the Wesley monument being bronze. In Deuteronomy 28, one of the curses for disobedience is the sky above shall be bronze. It's a sign of judgment. When God judged the Israelites in the desert with poisonous snakes, Moses fashioned a bronze snake on a pole as he was instructed by God. Those who were afflicted could look upon the snake and be healed. To this day, doctors' offices display a bronze snake on a pole, as a sign of healing. At least in those two instants, bronze is associated with judgment.

"And remind me where you were in the dream the moment the lights went out?"

Danny put his arm around Alisa. "Just below the wooden foot bridge, looking for my phone."

"So right beneath the Cotton Exchange and the winged lion."

"Yes, that's right."

"Have you ever noticed the words over the door of the Cotton Exchange?"

Danny furrowed his brow. "Uh, I think it just says Savannah Cotton Exchange."

"Beneath that but over the door, in a horseshoe shape, are the words *Freemason Hall*. The Freemasons, depending on the degree, are the keepers of esoteric wisdom, magic if you will, which traces its roots all the way back to ancient Babylon. All occult belief systems, particularly those associated with sun worship, come from Babylon. And one of the most prominent emblems of Babylon, was the winged lion. Sometimes with the head of a lion, like the one that sits today in front of the Cotton Exchange and sometimes with the head of a human."

Danny was trying to follow everything Pastor Earl was telling him. "So, you think there's a connection between the words on the base of the monument in Reynolds Square, the winged lion and the Cotton Exchange?"

"I do. It all ties back to Babylon. In Revelation, Babylon is called the mother of harlots and abominations. God condemns her for making the nations drink her fornications in Revelation 14. In fact, the word for fornication in the original Greek is *porneia*. It's where we get the word porn. America is the largest exporter of pornography in the world. It covers all sexual acts outside of the marriage covenant. Unfortunately, it's a huge problem even in the church. You may remember, several year ago, a website called Ashley Madison was hacked. The sole purpose of that website was for married people to have discreet, adulterous affairs. The hackers released the names of all the people who used the site and over 400 pastors, deacons and church leaders from around the country were on the list. An article by Crosswalk.com from several years back, cited a survey where fifty-four percent of pastors admitted to looking at porn in the past year."

The pastor took a long deep breath. "So when I sit here and say that America sounds a lot like Babylon and is due for judgment, I'm not excluding the church at large. Whether or not America is the Babylon incarnate of Revelation, our country has certainly taken on many of her attributes. You might say we are possessed by a spirit of Babylon."

Alisa looked down at the floor, then up at Pastor Earl. "So that's the big thing for God? Sexual immorality?"

"That's part of it, but it all feeds back to turning our back on God and forsaking him. The sexual sin is just a symptom of that. It's a tough pill to swallow, knowing that it's so prevalent in the church. I imagine that is largely due to the feel-good messages preachers give in order to keep the pews filled and the coffers full. God isn't some horrific task master that lays down a list of expectations that no one could ever fulfill, but he does call us to a life of holiness. You just don't hear that much in churches today. When folks get caught up in sexual sin, it becomes a sort of addiction. And addiction is just what happens when the flesh is stronger than the spirit."

"As I said before, the one you feed more will be the stronger of the two. A steady diet of R-rated movies, worldly music, a couple more drinks, and going to the lake instead of church; the next thing you know, your flesh is running the show.

"On the other hand, if you make a discipline of praying each morning, reading God's word, listening to worship music, and attending a church where you are challenged to grow, your spirit will grow stronger than the flesh.

"And, the best way of all to break an addiction is prayer and fasting. Fasting is one of those things you don't hear much about in church anymore. It's not pleasant, it's uncomfortable and it just doesn't fit into modern American Christianity. So, now fifty-four percent of our pastors are looking at porn, and they can't break the addiction because they forgot how to fast.

"But it's not just the pastors, it's the congregants, too. The statistics of Christian men who admit to looking at porn are similar to those numbers in the clergy."

"And we're about to be wiped out by an EMP," Alisa reminded him.

"And then there's that." The pastor snickered. "Another sin that God confronts Israel with in the Book of Isaiah is the sin of murdering their children. They would offer babies to Molech. The idols of Molech with hands outstretched would be heated up in a fire and the little babies would be placed in the scorching hands of Molech and burned alive. Much like the millions of babies murdered in abortion clinics today."

Pastor Earl reached over and took Alisa's hand. "And I'm not condemning you for your mistakes. You've repented of your sins and God has forgiven you. That was all he was asking Israel to do throughout Isaiah and all of the Books of Prophecy."

She nodded. "Thanks."

Danny hugged her close. He could see that she needed it.

Pastor Earl continued. "But, once again, abortion could have never stayed on the books if the church hadn't allowed it through complacency and political silence."

Danny asked, "So what do we do now? About the EMP, that is?"

Pastor Earl put his hands behind his head and leaned back in his chair. "Ahhh. That's the million-dollar question, isn't it?"

Alisa crossed one leg on the couch and turned toward Danny, putting her hands on his. "I wonder how long we have to get ready. The market crashed three weeks after your first dream."

Danny held her hands. "I don't know."

Pastor Earl looked at the calendar hanging on the wall. "I'm sure we have some time. God wouldn't issue a warning and then not give us time to react. With that said, I think the inscription on the John

Wesley monument speaks to the imminence of the event, so we should be very good stewards of the time the Lord has granted us."

"Do you think there is any way to stop it?" Danny asked.

Pastor Earl flipped the pages of his Bible. "I think the statue of John Wesley answers that question as well. The actual statue in Reynolds Square stands with a Bible in one hand and the other out stretched, almost as if he is calling the nation to repent and turn to God. Is that consistent with your dream?"

"Yes. I actually thought about that; he looked like he was pleading for people to read the Bible."

"The prophetic significance of the John Wesley statue may go even deeper than that. Wesley was brought to Savannah to be the chaplain of the colony. He was sent back to England after only two years. It could be symbolic of the Gospel being rejected by the majority of our country, as if the Gospel were being told to go back to wherever it came from."

The pastor sighed. "So, the answer to your original question is, yes, it could be stopped. When Jonah finally obeyed God and prophesied over Nineveh, the king proclaimed a fast and all the people repented. God withheld his judgment because the nation had a change of heart. I would love to see that happen to America, but if I were a bookie and had to set the odds on it, they'd probably be somewhere around a billion to one."

"Nevertheless, God's Word doesn't return void, some folks will turn back to him. Ricky sent me an email on Wednesday. He said lots of folks who heard you on his radio show recommitted their life after Black Tuesday. He's been getting calls and emails all week."

"About the timing," Danny said. "If each cow represents a year, is it possible that we have a year of economic famine first, then the EMP?"

The pastor shook his head. "I couldn't tell you, Danny. Because of the way the dreams came, the cows, or years, could just as easily overlap. Either way, I'd rather be a year too early than a minute too late.

"I'm going to start putting together a plan for the church. One of our congregants, Chuck, has a place out on Sapelo Island. It's very remote and he has plenty of room out there. A lot of it is wooded, but it's around twenty acres. We could put some trailers out there to accommodate more people. Plenty of good fishing and wildlife. With a little planning, we could get by. You two would be welcome to come, and Steven of course."

Danny smiled. "Thanks, but we've already discussed going out to my grandmother's farm up in Anderson, South Carolina."

"Good, I'm sure she'll be happy to have you around."

Alisa toyed with the ring on her finger. "But what if it happens before the wedding?"

Danny brushed her hair with his fingers. "Do you want to get married sooner?"

She nodded and smiled.

Danny turned to Pastor Earl. "Would it be possible to move the wedding up to next Saturday?"

"Hmm. Normally, I really don't like to see young folks rush into marriage. How far along are you on those DVDs?"

Alisa sat up. "We've only got two more. We'll watch them both tonight. I promise!"

"And what issues have come up so far?"

Alisa puckered her lower lip. "Nothing really."

The pastor tipped his head low and peered up as if he wasn't convinced. "Nothing?"

"Well, that whole submissive wife thing. That's not exactly the type of girl I am. Besides, I doubt Danny would like that anyway."

The pastor flipped over to Ephesians chapter 5 in his Bible. "Oh, was that part conditional on your personality type and whether Danny would want a submissive wife? I must have missed that last time I read it."

Alisa rolled her eyes and huffed. "No. it wasn't conditional."

"I see." Pastor Earl looked back up. "Some things God says are going to be counter-cultural and other things are going to be downright counter-intuitive, but you're going to have to decide if you're going to trust that He knows best or if you're going to do things your own way. With the challenges that are coming upon us, you're going to need every bit of help you can get. Hard times are either going to push you closer together as a couple or further apart. It all depends on how closely you follow the instruction manual. And Danny, in that same chapter, the husband is instructed to love his wife as Christ loves the church."

"Oh, yes, I've got that!"

The pastor snickered. "You do now. You're dating. But don't let that love grow cold. Some men get complacent with their marriages after a year or two or three. As a sex, we tend to take our wives for granted. We quit saying 'I love you,' because we assume they already know. Women need to hear that. And they need us to communicate. After a long day of work, sometimes we just want to tune out and be quiet. That's okay, but after an hour or so of relaxation, you have to make a conscious effort to engage with your wife. Ask her how her day was. Even if you can't think of much to say, sometimes listening is enough for her. Just try to keep in mind that we're both wired different."

Danny nodded and kissed Alisa on the cheek. "I will."

Pastor Earl added, "And Alisa, in three years when he clams up and quits talking or listening, it doesn't mean he doesn't love you anymore. It just means he needs a gentle reminder."

"So, next Saturday?" Alisa bit her lip in anticipation.

Pastor Earl took a deep breath and paused for a moment. Finally, he said, "Okay, next Saturday."

Alisa squeezed and hugged Danny tight.

Danny, in turn, grinned from ear to ear and said, "I love you."

He then stood up. "Pastor, thank you so much for seeing us on such short notice."

"No trouble at all. Shall I tell Ricky that you'd be available for an interview tomorrow? I'm sure the folks that would hear it and take heed, could use as much advanced warning as possible."

"Uh, sure. If he wants me to come back on, that is."

Pastor Earl got up from his desk. He walked Alisa and Danny to the door. "Have you given any thought how you'd get to Anderson in the event of an EMP?"

Danny shrugged. "Drive, I guess."

"Your car might not function, depending on the source, location of detonation, and size of the EMP."

"Oh, really?" Danny was not very familiar with the effects of an EMP. "How do you know all of this?"

"Several news programs have reported on it over the past several years. Ricky had a former nuclear strategist from the CIA on his show a few times to talk specifically about EMP. The man also served on the Congressional EMP Commission. The government is actually very well versed in how EMPs work and they've made the information readily available. There's just very little interest in it, so not many media outlets cover it."

"Wow. You'd think people would want to know everything they could about such a disastrous effect, so they could prepare for it." Danny rubbed his head.

Pastor Earl stood near the door ready to hold it open for them. "You'd think. I suppose there are other more pressing issues, like who's going to win the Super Bowl."

Danny snickered. "Yeah."

Alisa turned before walking out the door. "So, an EMP, if it were strong enough and in the right location, would disable all cars?"

"They began putting computer chips in cars in 1980. From that date forward, cars become increasingly susceptible to an EMP as the electronics and computer controls become more complex and delicate. Of course, with the power grid down, you wouldn't be able to get gas anyway, since the pumps are electric. But, if you just needed to get to a safe place, like Danny's grandmother's, theoretically, a vehicle built before 1980 would offer your best chance of getting there." Pastor Earl opened the door for them as they walked out.

Danny put his hand in the air to wave good-bye. "Thanks again for everything. We'll see you Sunday."

"Okay, take care. I'll text you to let you know what Ricky says about having you on the show tomorrow, but I'm sure he'll want to get you back on."

Alisa waved. "Bye, Pastor."

The two of them walked to the car and Danny opened the door for Alisa. "I guess we have a lot of stuff to figure out."

CHAPTER 13

A grievous vision is declared unto me; the treacherous dealer dealeth treacherously, and the spoiler spoileth.

Isaiah 21:2a

On the way home from the meeting with Pastor Earl, Danny's mind was busy trying to process all the thoughts swirling around in his head. He needed to get them organized.

Alisa said, "I'm freaking out. We have to get ready for a wedding and the end of civilization, all in one week."

The thought frightened Danny. Either would be quite a task to deal with, but planning for both seemed impossible. Nevertheless, he wanted Alisa to be able to relax. "We'll get it figured out. Let's swing by my place and start brainstorming with a notepad."

"Good idea. I guess we need to call Steven."

"Why don't you call him now? Just tell him the wedding was moved up to next Saturday, and that I had another dream. Let him know we need to talk as soon as possible."

Alisa took out her phone. "In that order? Shouldn't I tell him about the dream first? That will explain why we moved up the wedding."

"Sure, whatever." Danny focused on the road since he was driving a little faster than normal.

Alisa dialed Steven's number. "Hey."

"I'm in the car with Danny. We just left Pastor Earl. Danny had another dream and we moved the wedding to next Saturday."

Alisa held the phone away from her head. Danny could hear that Steven was speaking very loudly but couldn't quite make out what he was saying.

Once Steven's voice died down, Alisa said, "I know, I know, I'm sorry. I shouldn't have told you both of those things in the same sentence. Just come over to Danny's as soon as possible, and we'll explain everything."

"Okay, see you in a while." She was quiet for a few seconds more then said, "No, no more coffee. We've been drinking coffee all morning with Pastor Earl. On top of everything else, my heart is about to jump out of my chest. Bye."

"It sounded like Steven was freaking out too." Danny kept his eyes on the road.

"Yeah. Why don't I call Trish right now and ask if there's any way we can get off work next

Saturday. I don't want to spend my honeymoon night at Lilly's."

Danny smirked. "Me neither."

Alisa called the restaurant and waited for Trish to come to the phone. She explained that she and Danny wanted the following Saturday off, for personal reasons.

"Thank you so much, Trish. We owe you big time." Alisa winked at Danny. "We'll see you tonight."

Danny looked over. "That was easy."

"Yeah, she said she was going to have to make some schedule cuts anyway because it's been so slow. They're considering closing the restaurant altogether on Monday nights. We'll probably all get cut down to three shifts a week."

Danny sighed. "That works out better for everybody. The restaurant will have to pay less staff, and we won't have six servers fighting over a handful of tables. I doubt Lilly's will ever be busy again. We should start making drastic cuts to our lifestyle now."

"Let's make drastic cuts after we get married. At least, I want a new dress, a cake, some flowers, a nice dinner and a honeymoon night at that little Bed and Breakfast over on Gaston. It's my favorite house in Savannah."

It was a once-in-a-lifetime event. Considering the average amount of planning and expenses that went toward a wedding, it was a rather modest list of demands. He couldn't deny her the basics of what would be the beginning of their life together. "Okay, but we'll really have to tighten our belts afterwards."

Alisa shined with joy. "Thank you! For starters, you can move in with me. My parents take care of my rent, cable, internet, and electric. The expenses we'll have to pay will be next to nothing."

"Your place is technically student housing. You'll get in big trouble if SCAD finds out that I'm living there."

"How will they find out? And besides, the worst they can do is kick us out. Then we would have to rent another place and be no worse off than if we moved into your place right now."

"I don't know. It feels dishonest."

"Listen, if it wasn't the end of the world as we know it, I'd agree. But, we have to get in survival mode right now if we want to make it through what's coming." Alisa suddenly quit talking and crossed her arms. Moments later, she said, "But Pastor Earl said I should let you lead, so whatever you decide, I'll go along with it." After a short pause, with her arms still crossed tightly and looking out the passenger's side window, she mumbled, "Even if it kills me, I guess."

Danny fought back a laugh. He was torn between the amusement of the melodramatic performance and the admiration of her commitment to let him be the leader. "Wow. That means a lot to me."

"I'm serious, Danny. It's not a joke."

"I know you are. I don't mean to laugh, it's just "

"Just what, Danny?"

"It's sweet. I've never had anyone place their life in my hands before, even if they don't really trust my decisions. But I promise, I'll do everything I can to keep you safe. I'll take good care of you, Alisa. You can count on me."

"I didn't mean it like that. I do trust your decisions. I know you'll take care of us. That's why I love you." She turned back toward him and put her hand on his arm.

Danny took a deep breath. "Thank you. I love you too. Actually, you're right about being in survival mode. Maybe we should consider living at your place. It probably won't be for that long anyway. Remind me to call my landlord as soon as we get home. This is already going to be short notice."

They arrived at Danny's minutes later. He took off his coat and tossed it on the couch. Next, he dialed his sister's phone. "Cami, hey."

Her voice came back over the phone. "So good to hear from you. How are you?"

"I'm good. The market really got hammered on Tuesday, huh."

"Yeah. Sounds like your dream was a message."

"About that, I actually had another one last night. And I think it's safe to say that it's much worse than the first one."

"Worse than the first one?"

Danny proceeded to tell her about his vision from the night before. Then, he began to tell her the interpretation.

She interrupted. "Danny, stop talking."

He was worried that although the first dream had been fulfilled, she still might not believe him. After all, it sounded crazy, even to him. "Okay. I'm not saying it's true . . ."

She cut him off again. "No, Danny. I believe you, but remember where I work. We need to talk in person. There's no way I can drive down tomorrow, but why don't I come next weekend?"

Danny looked over at Alisa. "Um, okay, but bring something nice to wear."

Cami was quiet for a second. "You're getting married?"

"Eloping would better describe what we had in mind."

"Well, I doubt Nick will be able to come, but I have to bring Nana. She'll be mad as a wet hornet if you don't invite her. And she'll never forgive Alisa. Don't do that to Alisa."

"Hold on one second." Danny quickly explained to Alisa how Cami wanted to talk in person and now knew about the wedding. "And she wants to bring Nana."

Alisa didn't seemed bothered by it at all. "Sure, that's great. Maybe we can have a few people from work and a very small reception at the church."

"Thanks." Danny kissed her on the head and removed his hand from the mic on his phone. "Cami, hey, the wedding plans are evolving in real time, sorry about the confusion. Yes, bring Nana. Where will you stay?"

"I'll take Nana to one of those little Bed and Breakfasts. Don't worry about us, just make sure you carve out an hour or two so we can talk. Do you need help with anything?"

"Not that I know of, but I tell you if I think of something."

"What time is the wedding?"

Danny laughed. "We haven't gotten that far yet."

"Can you make it afternoon? I'll have to drive to Nana's after work Friday, then drive to Savannah Saturday morning."

"Sure. I'll email you the time and address when we get everything worked out."

"Great, talk to you later. And congratulations!"

"Okay, love ya."

"You, too." Cami hung up.

Danny looked over at Alisa. "I didn't mean to mess up your elopement, or whatever you call it."

"Danny Walker, I would marry you in the middle of a hurricane. I don't care. Besides, there are a couple of girls from SCAD that I would like to invite. It'll be fun. We have to have some finger foods."

Danny grimaced at the thought of the extra expense, but what could he say. It was his fault that the wedding would now have guests as opposed to being the clandestine ceremony originally intended. "What if we make the food ourselves? It will be better than anything we could afford from a caterer."

She looked at the light in the ceiling and tapped her finger against her lip. After a moment of contemplation, she said, "As long as it's nice. We can get the plastic plates that look like glass and the plastic forks and knives that look like real silver. If we're going cheap, we're going to go high-end cheap."

Danny knew he'd just dodged a bullet so he had to be happy with that. "Agreed."

"So what will we have? For foods I mean?"

Danny thought. "You like my homemade hummus, right?"

"Yes, and your spinach dip. Can you make that?"

"Sure."

A knock at the door briefly preceded Steven's entry. "So what's going on?"

"We're planning our reception for next Saturday." Alisa grinned.

Steven threw his hands in the air. "I give up. Last night, the wedding was next month, then when I talked to you guys twenty minutes ago, it was Saturday, but still top secret. Now there's a reception?"

Danny pursed his lips. "It's a very fluid situation."

"I can see that." Steven plopped down on the couch. "You can't find a caterer by next Saturday. What are you going to serve, pizza?"

"Not quite." Danny explained the rapidly evolving plan.

Alisa sat in the other corner of the couch and grabbed the cushion. "It's not easy getting married when you're up against the doomsday clock."

Steven said, "Since I'm not in school, I can help with the food. I can make my world famous sausage balls. I also know how to carve a swan out of a watermelon. I watched a chef do it at a hotel I worked at in Iowa. I was so amazed, I went home and tried it myself. It was actually fairly easy."

"Okay, but it better not turn out looking like a chicken." Alisa threw the pillow at him.

"Keep messing with me and it'll look like a frog." He threw the pillow back. "Now, tell me about the new dream."

Danny sat down close to Alisa on the couch and explained everything. He included his confirmation while reading the Bible shortly after waking up, everything Pastor Earl said as well as Alisa's understanding of the interpretation of the dream.

Alisa said, "I hope you're not jealous."

"Jealous?" Steven looked confused.

"You know, because you've been a Christian for a long time, and we come along and start having dreams and interpretations right away."

Steven shook his head. "Read the rest of the book. Do you know how they treated the prophets? Very few people actually listened to them, Jeremiah was thrown in prison, Elijah was hunted down, and Isaiah was sawed in two. I'm happy with being a spectator on this one."

Alisa's face showed her concern as she crossed her arms. "Boy, you know how to take the fun out of it."

"I've got to call my landlord." Danny stood and took out his phone. There was no answer so he left a message. "Mr. Cooper, this is Danny Walker in Unit 206. Due to a personal emergency, I have to move out right away. I apologize for the short notice, but I'll leave the apartment in perfect condition and be out by February first. Just give me a one-hour notice if you need to show it to another renter."

"So, how would we get to Nana's house if both of our cars quit working?" Steven took out his phone and began searching Craigslist for old cars.

Danny looked over Steven's shoulder at the

phone. "I don't know. I definitely don't have money to buy another car."

"What if we sold both of our cars and bought something built before 1980?" Steven kept looking.

Danny sighed. "I doubt I'd get more than 1,500 dollars for my car. How much are old cars?"

Steven shook his head. "I haven't found any yet. The oldest are from the nineties."

Alisa said, "Try searching year by year. Go to cars and put '79 in the search box. Then keep going backwards from there."

Steven followed her advice. "Here's a '79 Trans Am for 2,500 dollars."

"Does it run?" Danny asked.

Steven clicked the ad for the details. "No."

Next, he searched '78. "Here's a '78 Bronco for 5800 dollars. It says it runs and drives great."

Danny looked at the picture. "Kind of rough looking. How much do you think you could get for your car?"

Steven shook his head. "Maybe 3,000 dollars."

Danny stuck his hands in his pocket. "So best case scenario, we sell both of our cars to get an old junker that will probably break down."

"I could tell my dad that I need a car." Alisa said.

Steven smiled. "Really? He'd let you buy an old car?"

"He already knows that I don't feel safe. I'll tell him that I want a classic car as an investment."

Danny pursed his lips. "He bought you an AK. If that didn't make you feel safe, a car isn't going to do it."

Alisa playfully slapped Danny's arm. "He

doesn't know my gun was an AK-47."

Danny shook his head. "Classic cars bought for investment purposes are kept in a garage, not parked on the side of the street."

"Would you let my dad make the excuses?"

"I'm just trying to prepare you for when you get shut down."

Alisa squinted and gave a sneaky smile. "You might be underestimating my leverage with this whole wedding in Connecticut thing. They really want me to have it up there. If I start hinting that I really don't want to, they'll be looking for ways to change my mind. A reasonably-priced classic car for day-to-day driving might not be out of the question."

Steven kept searching for cars. "How would you define reasonably priced?"

"Keep looking. Let's see what's available." She leaned over to look at the screen of his phone.

"Here's a '65 Mustang, rebuilt engine with 10,000 miles on it, needs paint, 6,500 dollars."

Danny looked closer to inspect Steven's latest find. "Does it have a back seat?"

Alisa put her head up against Danny's. "Let's check it out on the computer so we can get a better look."

"Good idea." Danny retrieved his laptop, sat it on the coffee table, and quickly found the ad. "I guess you could call that a back seat, as long as I'm not the one sitting in it."

Alisa put her hands on her hips. "Well, it will be my car, so I'll be driving."

Steven leaned back on the couch. "As long as

Mark Goodwin

I'm back there by myself, I can ride in the back. I'll put my feet up and stretch out."

Alisa protested, "Steven, you are not putting your feet up in the seat of my classic car!"

He pointed to the picture with an open hand. "Look at that piece of junk. I'd be more worried about getting my shoes dirty than the seat!"

"Whatever! Find another car that Steven won't disrespect." Danny shook his head and kept looking. "Wow, this car is nice. '67 Mercury Cougar."

"Ooh, I like it. Nice yellow paint, with a black spoiler, cool wheels. 8,500 dollars. Save it. What else do you see?"

Danny sighed. "Now this is beautiful, '67 Camaro SS, all redone, rebuilt everything. Midnight blue, immaculately restored."

Alisa's mouth hung open as she looked at the classic car. "28,000 dollars. I don't know. That might be more than my dad would be willing to spend. Twenty, twenty-five is probably tops."

Steven took out his phone. "Call the guy and ask if he'd take twenty-five."

"It's all the way in Yulee," Alisa said.

"That's less than two hours away. We could go tomorrow." Steven dialed the number. "Hey I'm calling about your Camaro, would you take 25,000 dollars?"

"Thanks, we'll call you back." Steven stuck his phone back in his pocket.

"So?" Alisa looked anxious.

"He said money talks and bull poop walks, but he used slightly harsher language."

She furrowed her brow. "What's that supposed to mean."

Steven pursed his lips. "It means if you show up with 25,000 dollars, he'll take it. But he won't say he's going to take it until he sees the cash."

Danny said, "I'm sure he'd take a bank check. If you get pulled over with 25,000 dollars, they'll assume it's for drugs and take your money. That whole innocent-until-proven-guilty thing went out of style in the '80s, along with day-glow neon clothing."

"Call your dad," Steven goaded.

"I have to go in the bedroom to do this. I'm going to have to put on an act, so I can't have you two looking at me and making me laugh." Alisa stood up to take the computer to the other room.

Steven raised his fist in the air. "Godspeed!"

"Thanks." She closed the door behind her.

Steven whispered. "Let's sit outside the door and listen in."

Danny growled in protest, but went along with the plan grudgingly. "Don't make any noise at all."

The two of them sat snug, up against the wall so they could each have an ear near the door.

Danny controlled his breath so he could hear Alisa's side of the conversation.

"There are places I have to go that's just not safe to walk. The SCAD campus is spread out all over the historic district and some of my classes don't get out until after dark. I'm going to send you a copy of last year's SCAD security report. You don't want me to be one of the numbers on next year's report do you?"

Steven shook his head as he grinned at Danny.

Danny felt guilty for listening in, but couldn't find the will to move away from the door.

Alisa's voice was faint in the other room. "It's a '67 Camaro, completely restored, so it's essentially a new car, but obviously built much better than a new car."

After a moment of silence, she said, "I'll pay for repairs out of my pocket."

Silence again. Then, "But I don't want a new car, I want this one."

Seconds later, "It could be my wedding present."

After another brief intermission her voice showed her disappointment. "Then maybe I'll just have my wedding down here. All my friends are in Savannah anyway."

Steven mouthed the word, *wow*, in silence as he looked at Danny.

Danny rolled his eyes as he waited for the next response from Alisa.

"I'll take Danny, he knows a lot about cars. I'll call you tomorrow night and tell you who to make the check out to. Thanks, daddy!"

"I love you, too."

Steven gave Danny a high five as the two of them made a hasty retreat back to the couch.

When Alisa emerged from the bedroom, Steven said, "Ma-Nip-U-La-Tive!"

Alisa's face quickly transformed from joy to anger. "You were listening?"

She held her phone in the air as if she might actually throw it at him. "I can't believe you!"

Danny made an immediate move to defuse the

situation and change the subject. "So what did he say? Can we go look at the car?"

"Yes, we can go check it out tomorrow. If we like it, he'll overnight the check on Monday and we can pick up the car Tuesday morning."

"No way! You have to let me drive it part of the way back." Steven's voice was filled with excitement.

She pointed and glared her eyes at him. "You're still in trouble for eavesdropping. You should be thankful that I'm even going to let you ride in it."

Danny read the text on his phone. "I have another radio show interview tomorrow. We can drive down to see the car after church Sunday. But we all have to be at work in an hour. We better get a move on."

"Rats. I still have to get a shower and shave. I'll see you guys there." Steven grabbed his coat and rushed out the door.

"See you later." Danny made his way to his bedroom. "I'll be ready in fifteen minutes, then I'll take you by your house to get ready. How long do you need to get ready?"

"An hour."

"We're not going to have an hour. Can you get ready in thirty minutes? We still haven't eaten. I'd like to get to work early enough to order something to eat."

"Drop me off at my house, then go get something to eat. I'll be ready by the time you come back."

"Okay." Danny absolutely did not want to be late.

The plan succeeded, and they managed to get

something from the drive-thru and make it to work on time, but just barely.

Thanks to Tuesday's market crash, it was another terribly slow night at the restaurant.

CHAPTER 14

Surely the Lord GOD does nothing, Unless He reveals His secret to His servants the prophets.

Amos 3:7 NKJV

Saturday morning, Danny looked at the coffee filter as he anticipated pouring in the grounds for his morning brew. "I was nervous as a long tailed cat in a room full of rocking chairs for the last interview. Maybe I should drink decaf." Of course, being a college student, no such substance had ever crossed the threshold of his dwelling. He threw on his jeans, coat, and shoes and jogged to the convenience store across the street from his apartment.

Since his complex had several other students

living there, the convenience store stayed busy with young people buying a little bit of this and a little bit of that. Danny grabbed a small container of decaf and got in line. He made a mental note of the things the other kids were buying. The girl checking out in the front of the line had a small package of powdered sugar donuts and a pint of chocolate milk. The girl behind her had a small sized laundry detergent, a two-liter of soda and three bags of chips. After her, and just in front of Danny, was a boy who was buying a small box of breakfast cereal and a half-gallon of milk.

Danny thought about what the store would look like the day after an EMP. All of these kids who lived around him bought what they wanted, when they wanted it. None of them had the forethought to have even a week's worth of food on hand. The box of cereal, in the hand of the boy in front of him, probably had four large bowls in it. Danny figured it would make about two breakfasts for the boy which was better than what the girl at the front of the line had. Her breakfast would be gone before she made it back to her apartment.

He looked at the glass doors at the entrance of the store and imagined them busted out, the shelves bare and overturned, the refrigerated section empty and nothing behind the counter except lottery tickets.

By the time he reached the cash register, he'd completely freaked himself out. His mind raced thinking of all the possible survival uses for the items near the counter. A cigarette lighter might start a fire to cook wild game or purify water. Duct tape could be used to repair a backpack, a pair of shoes or a busted hose on a car.

"Five dollars twenty-five cents."

"What?"

"Your coffee, it's five twenty-five!" The man behind the counter looked at Danny as if he were stupid.

"Oh, sorry. I was daydreaming." Danny quickly handed the man a ten-dollar bill, took his change and headed home.

Once back inside, Danny opened the decaf and picked up where he'd left off. "If I don't have any caffeine, I'll get a headache. Maybe I'll do half-caf" He loaded the scoop of regular coffee heavier than the decaf. "Slightly biased toward the caf."

Sure enough, by the time the interview started, Danny was feeling a bit jittery.

The phone rang. "Danny, hi, Ricky Willis. Thanks for coming back on the show. It was unprecedented how fast your last dream was fulfilled after the interview aired. I hope we can get this one out fast enough for people to prepare. Pastor Earl said he thinks it is about an EMP?"

"Yeah. I'm a little spooked by all of this, so if I sound nervous, that's why."

"Well, you didn't sound nervous last time. You did great. But I understand, you didn't ask to be God's messenger of judgment; yet that's probably why he chose you. Either way, it's an intimidating task. Are you ready to go or do you need a few minutes to get composed?"

"I'm as ready as I'll ever be."

"Great. I'll do a quick intro and we'll roll the

tape."

The interview went well. Danny stuttered a few times in the beginning but became more relaxed as the show progressed.

When his account of the dream reached the end, he was suddenly reminded of the intense pangs of hunger and thirst. "I've never felt hungry in a dream. In fact, I don't think I've ever felt that hungry in reality. It was really bizarre, Ricky."

Ricky replied. "I think God is using your dream to warn his faithful remnant to prepare now. Right now, the store shelves are stocked. Right now, you can buy everything you need to keep you alive for several months. People are going to listen to this broadcast, which is syndicated to radio stations all over America and downloaded to phones and mp3 players via our website. Some of them are going to be like Joseph, who after learning of the dreams with the ugly and gaunt cows just like yours, decided to store up the provisions needed to sustain life for himself and others.

"There will be another group of people who will hear this warning and choose to do nothing. They'll finds excuses, like I don't have any place to store it, or I'll die anyway. Well, they will die anyway, and many of them will unfortunately die knowing what those hunger pangs you just described feel like. Famine and starvation are horrific ways to go. I wouldn't wish that on anybody. We read the story in Second Kings, about the women who ate their own children during the siege of Samaria. It is truly a horrific thing that is coming upon America. I pray that all who hear this message will heed the warning."

Danny sighed. "I pray they will also Ricky. When I look around at the other college students in my apartment complex, I wonder how many of them would even survive a week."

Ricky replied, "We had Dr. Peter Pry, of the Congressional EMP Commission on the show several months ago to talk about the commissions finding on the effects of an EMP. He told us that the commission originally thought the mortality rate in America after an EMP attack would be around two-out-of-three, as 100 million was the effective carrying capacity of the U.S. without electricity.

"They reconsidered those numbers after thinking about the state of the country in the wake of such an attack and the skills possessed by the survivors. Very few people have the knowledge to produce their own food or survive a bad winter without electric infrastructure. Most people living in cities wouldn't even be able to get water without electricity. And then there's the contamination of the environment after the nuclear power plants meltdown.

"When they readjusted their calculations with the additional inputs, they estimated the mortality rate to be closer to ninety percent. If you're listening and you want to survive, you should start thinking about where you're going to get water, what you will eat, and how you will defend yourself. This is going to be the biggest disaster this country has ever experienced. It will be the end of America.

"For those of you who missed Danny's first interview, he had a prophetic dream about last week's market crash, days before it happened. Please don't ignore this warning of the judgment coming upon America.

"I know I'm going to get email from listeners claiming that I'm using scare tactics. Folks, when I talk about a ninety percent die off, those are not my arbitrarily created numbers. I got those figures from a former member of the CIA, nuclear strategist, and head of the EMP Commission. Yes, it's frightening but no one buys an alarm clock that makes the tranquil sound of crickets chirping. An alarm clock is meant to startle you so you'll wake up.

"If you don't want to be roused from your slumber, don't set your alarm clock, and if you're not interested in truth, why on earth are you listening to this radio program? This is not shock-value entertainment folks. This is not Orson Wells' OSS social-programing experiment, War of the Worlds. This is real life and if you want to survive, you need to start making provisions right now.

"Danny, I'm sorry you had to endure that lengthy sermon, but I felt the Spirit of God urging me to make one final plea. Unfortunately, even some of our listeners are so deeply entrenched in their complacency that they are almost beyond reaching."

Danny held the phone close to his ear as he continued the interview. "I totally understand. I'm the person who had the dream, yet it seems so surreal. I've never seen anything like what my dream is about, especially not in America. It makes it hard to imagine, such an event happening to us. If it hadn't been for my first dream and the timely fulfilment of it, I would have a hard time believing it myself. But, since I do believe it, my friends and family are making plans to get prepared."

"Danny, without giving away any of the specifics about your location, can you tell us a little bit about what you are planning to do to prepare?"

"After the first dream, we started stocking up food and provisions in anticipation of a currency collapse. We also went to the gun show last weekend, in case we had to defend ourselves due to social unrest. Violence over resources usually erupts in countries when the currency fails."

Ricky commented, "We have no shortage of data on the disorder that follows failing currencies and crashing economies. Russia in the '90s, Zimbabwe, Venezuela, and Greece more recently. Social breakdown has sort of been on a constant ebb and flow in Argentina ever since the peso failed in 2001."

Danny took a deep breath. "But we don't have data on what our modern, computer-dependent culture looks like when the lights go out. While words can't really describe it, I suppose 'unimaginable horror' would point our minds in the right direction."

"The one thing we've been working on since I had the dream is making sure we have a way to get to my grandmother's house in the country. Most cars manufactured after 1980 have computer chips that could be disabled by an EMP, depending on the source, proximity and strength of the blast."

Ricky asked, "Have you considered just going out to your grandmother's now, so you'll be safe when it goes off?"

"My girlfriend, I mean fiancée, I'm going to be in trouble for that remark, but we just got engaged."

"Congratulations, Danny."

"Thanks, Ricky. Anyway, we're both in school, we both work, and our friend that would be going with us works also. The dream could be about an event that happens next week or next year. We can't quit living our lives, you know?"

"I understand your reasoning. I think that's prudent. People have taken drastic measures to prepare for all sorts of imminent events, like Y2K, Shemitah, and everything else. I think it was wise to make preparations, but you're right, you also have to be ready to survive if the event is delayed for several years. Or, the EMP could be a localized event in one section of the country. We don't know, so we have to have the ability to keep functioning in our normal capacity, if we're not directly affected."

"Thanks for articulating that for me Ricky. I don't want to be the reason someone quits their job, moves to the country and then has to file for bankruptcy in six months when the EMP could be decades away."

"You know Danny, the prophet Jeremiah was probably about your age when he started his ministry. His warnings went out for nearly forty years before the walls of Jerusalem finally fell and the city was burned to the ground. Based on the timing of your last dream, I think the EMP is imminent, but we just don't know for sure until it happens. God's ways are higher than our ways. Danny, thanks again for coming on the show to share your vision with us."

"Thanks for having me back on Ricky." Danny clicked off the phone. He had done his part in sounding the trumpet. Now it was up to the people who heard the message to decide if they would take action or ignore the call to prepare.

CHAPTER 15

Some trust in chariots, and some in horses: but we will remember the name of the LORD our God.

Psalm 20:7

Danny, Alisa and Steven had planned to leave straight from church Sunday afternoon to drive to Yulee, Florida to check out the car.

Steven paused in the parking lot, just before they reached Danny's car. "We should stop and pray before we get on the road. I feel like we're depending on this car to get us to Nana's when the EMP pops off. The car is just a tool; we have to keep our faith in God."

"Okay. Do you want to pray?" Danny asked.

"Sure. Let's all hold hands." Steven took hold of

Danny's and Alisa's hands and bowed his head. "Lord, we pray that if this car is your will for us, you'll give us a sense of peace about it and make everything go smoothly today. We also ask that if this is your will, you'll bless this car and help it to stay mechanically sound. If, however, it's not your will, we pray that you'll close the door on this deal and grant us the wisdom to recognize that it was your hand that shut it. Amen."

"Amen. Thank you, Steven." Alisa got in the car and shut the door. She sat up front with Danny and Steven sat in the back.

Danny started the car. "There's ham sandwiches and sodas in the cooler next to you Steven. You can hand those out if you like."

"Great. What type of Coke do you want Alisa?" Steven rummaged through the cooler.

"Diet, please."

He handed her a can. "You know that Diet Coke is like drinking poison right?"

She popped the top and took a sip. "And regular Coke fights heart disease right?"

"Touché." Steven opened a can of regular Coke and passed it to Danny.

Alisa took a sandwich as Steven handed it to her. "So what happens if the EMP goes off while we're driving today?"

"I put our bug-out bags in the trunk." Danny sipped his pop.

"Why didn't you tell me to bring mine?" Steven asked.

"I guess I just thought you would." Danny took some chips from the bag in between him and Alisa.

"Besides, statistically, it's not likely. We'll be there for less than an hour looking at the car."

"But it could happen while we're on the way." Alisa took the bag of chips.

"If it happened right now, it would take us an hour to walk home. If it happens while we're fifty miles away, I think we could get home in two days. Each bag has three days of food in it." Danny took a bite of his sandwich.

"You don't have the guns back there do you?" Alisa asked.

"Yeah."

"All of them? The AK?" Her mouth hung open.

"It's not illegal. There's nothing wrong with having a rifle in the trunk."

She shook her head. "Just, please, don't get pulled over."

Steven leaned forward. "Three days of food for two people."

Danny finished chewing. "Two days of food for three people. But quit worrying about it. It's not going to happen while we're gone."

"Are you saying this as a prophet or as someone trying to keep his girlfriend from freaking out?" Alisa jerked the bag of chips away as Danny reached for them.

"Both, now give me the chips!"

The playful bantering soon died down and a sense of melancholy fell over Danny. He watched the other cars as they passed him one by one, wondering which of their drivers would survive the coming calamity. Statistically speaking, he knew the answer was not many.

Alisa stared out the window. "What 'cha thinking about?"

"Nothing, you?"

"I'm just wondering what these roads will look like afterwards. You know?"

"Yeah." He knew alright. He couldn't help but wonder.

They made good time on the road and reached Yulee in just under two hours. Steven called the seller when they exited I-95, so he was waiting outside when they arrived.

The middle-aged man wore a ball cap, tee-shirt and jeans with just enough grease stains to indicate he was probably the one who had restored the classic car. "You guys drove all the way down from Savannah?"

Danny got out. "Yeah. We really liked the pictures." The midnight blue paint was deep and rich with sparkles. The chrome wheels glistened in the sun, and the tires had just been shined.

"You're the one who wants it?"

"Her, actually." Danny nodded his head in Alisa's direction.

The man started to laugh as if Danny was kidding, but seemed to quickly recognize that Alisa really liked the car. "Oh. Okay. It's good to see a girl with an interest in classic cars."

"I love the color. Can I drive it?"

The man handed her the keys and said, "Sure, let's go."

Alisa drove, Danny sat up front with her, while Steven and the seller sat in the back. The engine roared when she turned the key. The vibration of the idling motor caused the car to tremble with power.

Alisa drove fairly fast, considering it wasn't her car. She glanced at the seller in the rearview mirror when they came to the second stop light. "Sorry, the gas pedal sort of goes down by itself."

The man chuckled. "Yep. Most of these old muscle cars have that problem."

When they returned to the man's house, Danny, Steven and Alisa took a look under the hood. The man explained all of the different things he had done to the car.

Danny recognized most of the things he said; for the others, he just nodded. "Can you take 25,000 dollars?"

The man exhaled. "You have 25,000 dollars today?"

"I'll have it Tuesday," Alisa said. Then she proceeded to explain the arrangement to get the check from her father.

The man stood and stared at the car as if it pained him to sell it. Finally, he said, "My bank is the one right after you turn back on the main road. If you can get here before 4:00 on Tuesday, give me a call and I'll meet you up there. If you show up at 4:01 or if you have a check for 24,999 dollars, it's off and I walk away. I have to have my bank verify that the check is good before I hand over the keys."

Alisa stuck her hand out. "Then we've got a deal?"

The man put his hands in the air. "If someone comes along tomorrow afternoon and offers me full price, I'll have to take it."

Alisa huffed, then stuck her hand out again. "If

no one offers you more than 25,000 dollars before I get here Tuesday with the check, we've got a deal?"

The man cracked a smile and shook her hand. "Yes, ma'am."

"Thanks so much. We'll see you Tuesday." Danny waved as he, Alisa and Steven got back in his car.

The first hour of the drive home was spent talking about how cool the old '67 Camaro was. Once the adrenaline wore off, they all settled down. For the remainder of the trip home, they discussed making a trip out to Nana's with some supplies.

CHAPTER 16

A prudent man foreseeth the evil, and hideth himself: but the simple pass on, and are punished.

Proverbs 22:3

Tuesday came and once again, Danny and Alisa skipped class to go pick up the car. This time, Steven brought his bug-out bag, as well as his shotgun.

"Does everyone have everything they need? If the EMP happens while we're on the way back, we would just take the Camaro straight to Nana's. We wouldn't come back to Savannah."

Alisa tossed an extra bag in Danny's trunk. "I brought some more clothes, like you asked, but I thought you said it was statistically unlikely."

"I was just trying to keep you from tripping out."

"Thanks." She punched Danny's arm. "Steven, did you take your plate off your car so I can use it to drive the Camaro home?"

"It's my plate. I'll have to drive it back." He winked.

"Not fair. Where's the law that says that?"

"In my law book. Do you think I'm going to trust you to drive a car with my plates on it? You might rob a bank and I'd be blamed for it."

"Or, I might kill somebody. And you couldn't be blamed for it. Because you'd be dead!"

He held the license plate high in the air. "My plates, my rules. You decide."

"Fine Steven. You drive my car home, but you'll never drive it again."

Danny shook his head. "Let's go children."

They were on the road shortly thereafter.

Alisa looked over at the speedometer. "Slow down, we've got a trunk full of guns and ammo, not to mention a bank check for 25,000 dollars. I love hearing you explain your EMP dream, but I'm not in the mood to watch you present it to a cop, who may or may not believe one word that comes out of your mouth."

Danny hadn't realized how fast he was going. "Thanks, I'm not in the mood to convince a cop that I'm a prophet with a trunk full of guns either. I'll set the cruise control."

"So you're calling yourself a prophet now?" Steven snickered.

"It was meant as a joke." Danny glanced in the

rearview.

"I didn't mean to bust your chops." Steven reached forward from the back seat and put his hand on Danny's shoulder. "Everyone else is calling you a prophet. But you seemed resistant to the title. I'm glad to see you coming around."

Danny cracked a faint smile. "Thanks, but I don't think of myself as a prophet. I'm just some guy who has weird dreams."

"Weird dreams from God," Alisa added.

"Weird dreams from God that come true," Steven said.

The three of them were silent for the next several miles as they continued south on I-95.

Danny broke the solitude. "I'm thinking of getting a cheap bike from Craigslist."

"You can have mine. I'm getting a car," Alisa teased.

Danny reached over to mess up her hair. "I'm buying one so we will all have bikes to take to Nana's."

"I just talked my dad into buying a 25,000 dollar car that will still work after the stuff hits the fan. Why do we need bikes?"

"There won't be gas to run the car when the grid goes down. We'll have the gas we're able to store and that's it."

Alisa huffed. "Maybe we shouldn't have spent so much money on a stupid car that we're only going to drive one time."

Danny had wrestled with that same line of reasoning in his own mind, but eventually came to the conclusion that they were doing the right thing.

"If you'd spent any less, you would have been looking at cars that either needed paint, were full of rust, or still need some other things done to the engine. We might not have the time to do a lot of work to a car. This thing is totally rebuilt. We know it's going to be a dependable car and that's the most important factor. On top of everything else, let's say nothing happens, you still have a really nice, very cool hot rod."

"That's true." Her arms were still crossed, but she sounded as if she was coming back around.

"Plus, I saw three cows in my last dream, which, according to Pharaoh's dream in Genesis, represent three years. Let's say the worst is over and things are getting back to normal in three years. You'll have one of the few working cars. And, because you didn't get a clunker, it will still look nice and run great. Spare parts are going to be tough to find after the apocalypse, and this car is in pristine condition, it isn't going to need any repairs for a long time."

"You're right. Thanks. I guess I'm just stressed out over all of this. I want to make sure we make the best decisions possible." She reached over and kissed him on the cheek.

Steven said, "Not to be insensitive to the matter, but all of your dad's cash isn't going to be worth the paper it's printed on after all of this is over. It's not like you're wasting his money. In fact, from an investment point of view, the value of this car is probably going to jump a thousand percent in the first ten minutes after all the other cars quit working. You should try to talk him into buying a few more just like it."

She flopped back in her seat and groaned. "Ugh. I tried to tell him about me going to church and Danny's dreams. He cut me off and started talking about how he smoked pot in college. He went on and on about how it was okay to experiment with life when you're young, but to keep a firm grip on the big picture and not let stuff interfere with the future."

Danny quickly looked over at Alisa with concerned eyes. "Wait. Your dad thinks I'm on drugs?"

She huffed. "I don't know what he thinks. Maybe he was comparing our encounter with Jesus to him smoking pot. Who knows? I should have known better than to try and tell him anything anyway."

Danny reached over to take her hand. "Sorry the conversation went so poorly. I didn't know."

She stroked the top of his hand with her index finger. "I didn't bother to tell you because I didn't want you to not like my dad."

"He's buying us a 25,000 dollar bug-out car, I think I can forgive him for thinking I eat mushrooms and my dreams stem from a drug-induced trance."

She laughed. "He never said that."

Steven chuckled loudly. "Yeah, but that's what he thinks. He thinks Danny is a hippy, who wants to go back to the golden days of tripping on acid and following the Grateful Dead. That's why you want a car from the '60s."

Alisa unbuckled her seatbelt and turned around to slap Steven with her coat. "My dad knows Danny is pursuing a master's degree. He knows he's not a hippy Steven!"

"Stay seated, and keep your seat belt on, with your hands inside the ride until it has come to a complete stop!" Danny yelled.

Alisa faked a pout as she turned back around and fastened her belt. "He called you a hippy."

Danny couldn't fight back his smile. "I've been called worse."

"If we're going out to Nana's soon, we should buy some gas cans to take out there. Every gallon we can stock up is going to extend the usefulness of the car. Do you guys know how long gas will store?" Alisa asked.

"No. Look it up," Steven answered.

"How long will gas store?" She queried her phone for the information. "It says about six months. Hmm. This site says you can put an additive, called Stabil, in gas which will keep it fresh for up to two years. Wow, that would almost get us through the entire three years."

"Great. We'll try to get several gallons. I wonder if it would be cheaper to buy one larger container than a bunch of small ones." Danny kept driving.

"Five-gallon gas cans are pretty heavy when they're full. If you buy anything bigger than that, you'll have trouble picking it up, unless you run back and forth, filling it with gas from the smaller cans. Of course, then you'll need some type of pumping apparatus to get the gas out when you need it," Steven said.

"Good point. I guess we should start off with five-gallon cans, then we can buy something bigger, in addition to the smaller cans, if we have time."

Danny contemplated the costs of the cans, the gas and the stabilizer.

"Back to the conversation about bikes." Steven's voice came from the back seat. "What kind of bike are you looking for?"

Danny shrugged. "I don't know. Some type of road warrior. It doesn't have to be pretty, but I want something sturdy, with thick tires."

"I put Tuffy tire liners in my bike. Before I got my car, I went everywhere on my bike; work, school, grocery. Of course, you're always riding on the side of the road, which is where all the garbage winds up. After changing tires several times from picking up screws, nails and whatever, I bought those liners. Never had another flat since. They go between the tire and the inner tube. It doesn't matter if the tire gets a hole from a nail, the tube is what holds the air in."

"I had no idea there was such a thing," Alisa said. "I get flats all the time. It's like thirty bucks a pop, every time I have to take it to the shop. I wonder why they never told me about the liners?"

"Because that'd be the end of your thirty bucks a pop," Steven said.

Danny looked over at Alisa. "It would probably be a good idea to put the liners in your bike also. Does anyone have a bike rack for the back of a car?"

"I do, but it only has spaces for two bikes," Steven answered.

Danny devised a plan to get three bikes to Nana's. "Once I buy a bike, I'll take mine out to Nana's first. Then we can take both of yours when the EMP hits."

"Yeah, good idea. I was thinking of selling my car to buy some more survival supplies. So, I'll probably be using my bike for transportation until it's time to go," Steven said.

Alisa turned around to look at Steven. "So, it's settled. You're going to stay with us until things get back to normal. You're not going back to Iowa?"

Steven's voice revealed his apprehension over the choice. "The only way I could go back to Iowa is to leave now. And it's like Danny said, the EMP could be a year or ten years from now. I love my family, but I don't want to leave my job or you guys."

"Aww. That's so sweet." She tilted her head to one side. "You're like a brother to me, Steven."

"Ditto," Danny smiled and glanced into the rearview mirror.

"Thanks. You two are like family to me also," Steven said.

Shortly before they arrived at the seller's bank to complete the transaction, Steven called him on the phone to let him know they were nearly there. He met them in the parking lot when they arrived, and they took the check inside to verify.

Once the check was deposited, the man signed over the title to Alisa and Steven, and put the tag from his car on the Camaro to drive it back to Savannah. Danny and Alisa followed Steven in the Camry and the trip went smoothly, without incident.

CHAPTER 17

Therefore shall a man leave his father and his mother, and shall cleave unto his wife: and they shall be one flesh. And they were both naked, the man and his wife, and were not ashamed.

Genesis 2:24-25

Danny's face was pale and small beads of sweat formed on his forehead as he sat in the chair, silently.

"Keep breathing, brother. You don't look so hot. Let's take your tie off and unbutton that top button." Steven unfastened the clip to the bowtie under Danny's collar.

He went to retrieve a glass of water for Danny and returned. "You're sure you want to go through with this right?"

He sipped the water. "Yeah, there's just a lot of stuff going through my head right now. This is a big step, everything changes today. Tomorrow, I'll be responsible for her going into the toughest period in the history of America. I wonder if I'm up for it. I don't know if I'll be able to provide for her or keep her safe. It's frightening."

"Hey, you've got a really good girl. She's smart, so are you. Together, you'll greatly increase each other's odds of survival. And more than that, you've got God leading you. Of all people, you should know that. Have faith in God. Have faith in Alisa, and have faith in yourself." Steven handed him the bowtie.

Danny stuck it in his shirt pocket. "Thanks. And thanks for being my best man, and for helping out with the food."

"You got it. I'm glad Chef Eric opted to help out with the hors d'oeuvres. Can you imagine what a wreck you'd be if you were the groom and the caterer?"

Danny chuckled and looked toward the front door of the small store-front church to see who was arriving so early.

"Hey." Cami walked in with her arms outstretched.

Danny stood to greet her. "Thanks for coming. How was the trip?"

"Good. I'm ready for a break from driving, but it was a good trip."

Nana came in next. "What is this place? It don't look like no church I ever saw."

Danny fought back his laughter and gave her a hug. "God's not as picky as you, Nana."

She looked over at Pastor Earl, who came up front from the small store room in the back, where the food was being kept for the reception. "Is he supposed to be the preacher?"

Danny couldn't contain his laughter. "Yes Nana, this is Pastor Earl. Pastor Earl, this is Nana and my sister, Cami."

"Pleased to meet you. I'm so glad you could both make it." Pastor Earl smiled warmly.

Danny explained, "Pastor Earl was kind enough to allow his office to be turned into the bride's room."

"That was very nice." Cami smiled then said, "Danny, we've got about an hour. Is that enough time to swing by your place and pick up the stuff you want me to take back to Nana's? I'm sure you'll have other things on your mind after the wedding and the reception."

"Yeah, thanks. Nana, do you want to come with us?"

"I've been in the car for four hours. I think I'll just stay here with the preacher."

"Okay, and this is Steven. If you need anything, he'll get it for you."

She looked at Danny and pointed to Steven. "He's the one coming out to the farm with you and Lisa?"

Steven looked curious. "Who's Lisa?"

"Alisa." Danny nodded at Nana. "Yep, that's him. We'll be right back."

Danny and Cami hurried to the car. It was a short

trip, but Danny still wanted to get back as soon as possible. Cami let Danny drive since he knew the way.

He started the car and pulled out of the parking lot. "I hope I didn't get you in trouble by saying the wrong thing over the phone the other day."

"No, it's not that at all. The EMP threat has been out to the public for years. In fact, the Congressional EMP Commission published all of their findings and the EMP Taskforce has continued to try to inform Americans about the threat so they'll urge their elected representatives to pass funding to protect our grid."

"It would be expensive?"

"No. It would cost less than the amount we give to Pakistan in foreign aid for a single year."

"So greasing the pockets of a country that has banned the Bible and incarcerates Christians is more important than hardening our electrical grid?"

"The American public is too busy fussing over who should have been chosen on the Bachelorette to bother with such trivial matters as calling their representatives to tell them what to do; so the lobbyists on K Street take care of that for us."

"If everyone knows about it, why couldn't you talk?"

"Because Nick will be expected to go to one of the bunkers for continuity of government, but we have plans of our own. If an EMP occurs, we'll head straight to Nana's, as should you and Alisa. Every conversation we have on the phone is recorded and reviewed because of our jobs."

"Wow, I thought government employees were

immune from warrantless surveillance."

"Ha! The top echelon of government are more worried about us than anyone else. Anyway, continuity of government after an EMP is a pipe dream, and everyone who sits around trying to hang on to a system that no longer exists will just die a slow death. Off the record, most of the military and law enforcement who understand what an EMP would do, are planning to bug out and abandon ship within minutes of an attack.

"Danny, this is the nightmare scenario that keeps everyone at the Pentagon up at night."

"But who could do this to us?"

She let out a dry laugh. "Who couldn't? An EMP can be generated with relatively low-tech devices. Of course, sovereign actors like China, Russia, Iran and North Korea could detonate a nuclear device at a high altitude and take out the grid of the entire country."

"Why would they do that? China needs us to buy their cheap garbage. No more Walmart means no more Chinese economy."

"That might be true for China, but not for Russia, especially since the sanctions placed on them by the US. The cold war is back on, and in full swing. Ever since relations started deteriorating over the Ukraine and Syria, we've continued to poke the bear. Continued sanctions, crashing their economy by manipulating the oil price downward, power outages in Crimea, disagreements and mishaps in Syria, backing Turkey, the list goes on. Sooner or later the bear is going to do more than growl."

"But what about mutually assured destruction?

Don't the Russians still respect that concept?"

"They do, but America and Russia engage in proxy wars now rather than escalating to direct conflict. It worked so well in Afghanistan that we're doing it again in Syria. Russia's military intelligence, GRU, could easily hire a group of terrorist lackeys to set off an EMP attack against us, without it ever being traced back to them."

"I thought they were backing Assad? How could they hire Al Qaeda or ISIS to come after us?"

She shrugged, "They wouldn't have to. Hezbollah is Shia, just like Assad and they hate America every bit as fervently as ISIS. But, all Muslims hold the doctrine of my enemy's enemy is my friend, so working with ISIS or Al Qaeda for a one-night show, especially one of this magnitude, wouldn't be off the table for either side."

Danny knuckled his forehead. "China and Russia are the only two on the list with ICBMs. What type of delivery system would a terrorist organization use?"

"A scud could be deployed out of a shipping container right off the coast. It just has to get up to altitude before it detonates. We don't have any defense against that."

"Does the U.S. have any way to check shipping containers at sea?"

Cami shook her head. "In 2013, Panama stumbled upon a North Korean freighter in the Panama Canal with missile components capable of delivering a nuclear warhead which could have reached altitude to produce an EMP. The Panamanian government suspected the ship of having drugs. It was pure luck that those were found.

"And Kim Jong is a psychopath. He thinks North Korea is still at war with America. The Pentagon watches him like a hawk. In addition to Russia and China, we suspect North Korea also has what's called a super EMP. North Korea's two KMS satellites are supposed to be for agricultural studies, but some people in the DIA think it could house a warhead capable of producing a super EMP."

"Why don't we just shoot it down?"

Cami sighed. "We don't have any proof that it's for nefarious purposes and it would create an international incident, possibly on the level of Archduke Ferdinand's assassination. The next thing you know, everyone starts picking sides and voilà, World War III."

"I guess talking about how it's going to happen or who is going to set it off is an exercise in futility. The end result is the same."

Cami cocked her head to one side. "Yes and no. If we knew who was going to set it off or what type of device they were using, we'd know if it were going to be a localized event or if it were going to take down the entire country's grid. I don't suppose you left out any clues from your dream, huh?"

Danny pursed his lips. "No. I told you everything I can remember. Does Nick believe me?"

"I told him about your first dream, then we saw what happened. He knows it wasn't a coincidence. In fact, we're dipping into our retirement fund to buy some other supplies to take to Nana's. We'd just closed it out, but since it's a government retirement account, it would set off too many red flags.

"Nick is putting together a list of things we'd need after an EMP. We'll see how much cash we can take out without triggering any alarms, then we'll see how far we can make it stretch."

Cami turned toward him. "But, you're positive it's an EMP, right? You're sure it couldn't be a coronal mass ejection from the sun? A CME would generate a similar effect, at least on the grid. The difference is the wave length of the pulse. A CME is much longer, so it wouldn't couple into smaller electronics unless they were plugged into the grid. Cars would still operate, laptops that are not plugged into a wall socket, phones, battery operated radios; most of that stuff should still work. The grid would go down, because the power lines would act as long antennas that would carry the pulse to the transformers and SCADA systems that control the grid power stations."

"Cami, I had a dream about a blackout in Savannah, I lost my phone and saw cows that were blind and starving. There's no way to tell you what caused it, who caused it or when it is supposed to happen. The person who was most sure that it was about an EMP was Alisa. You can ask her if she thinks it could be triggered by the sun. I guess if cars were able to survive a CME, that's the best way to get hit, right?"

Cami sighed. "CME, EMP, six of one and half a dozen of the other. A CME would leave cars and computers which would allow us to recover faster once the power came back, but there's a good chance that it could be global. If everyone's power goes out, there will be no one to rebuild and help us out.

"Which, in and of itself, becomes a sort of blessing and a curse. If the global playing field is leveled by a CME, we wouldn't have any help in getting back on our feet, but we also wouldn't have to worry nearly so much about a subsequent invasion.

"On the other hand, if we were hit by an EMP, we know hostile action has been taken against us and we have to expect a physical attack. Most military hardware is protected against EMP, but there'd be no national infrastructure to keep it running, no nation for it to protect and no tax payers to keep it funded. It might take a few months for us to completely fall apart, but we eventually would. Then, our resources would be easy pickins for an aggressor to take."

Cami shook her head. "For a few measly dollars, all this could have been avoided, but the politicians and K Street lawyers got in the way of the ounce of prevention we so desperately needed."

"It's almost like God confused their thinking to prevent them from taking action to keep us safe. Like he was setting us up for judgment." Danny pulled into the parking lot of his apartment building and cut the ignition.

Cami opened the door and chuckled. "Trust me, it didn't take an act of God to cause Washington to take the worst-possible course of action. They do that every single day."

When they arrived at Danny's apartment, he

unlocked the door. "Don't get freaked out by all the boxes. They're not all for you to take back today. We're planning to take two more car loads out to Nana's next week."

Cami looked at everything Danny had stacked against the wall. "Wow, it looks like you guys managed to stock up a lot of food."

"Yeah, we have more at Alisa's and Steven's. I think we bought everything Nick told us to get for bug-out bags also. All three bags don't have every single item he said to get, but we have at least one of each between the three of us." Danny grabbed a box of clothing and took it down to the car.

Cami grabbed another box and followed him. "That's fine, you don't necessarily need three water filters or three compasses as long as you don't get separated and no one loses their gear. But, you should have redundancy for the critical items like shelter, water, fire and food.

"Did you get some more ammo for Pop's old gun?"

"Yeah, and I think I mentioned to you that Alisa bought an AK. We bought ammo for that too."

"That's fantastic. You should probably give me some of your ammo to take to Nana's. Guns don't weigh much compared to the ammo. If you have to bug out on foot and carry the guns, at least your ammo would be there when you arrived."

"Thanks, but Alisa just bought the Camaro. We'll be coming in that. The ammo doesn't take up much room."

Cami stuck the box in the trunk. "The best-laid plans of mice and men, you should have a contingency plan. If you have fifty rounds of ammo for the pistol and a hundred for the AK, that should be plenty. You should let me take the rest back to Nana's."

Danny stuck the box he'd been carrying in the trunk, closed the lid and led the way back to his apartment. "Okay, I can see the wisdom in that recommendation. I'll take you up on the offer."

Cami followed. "Do we need to go by Alisa's to get the ammo for the AK?"

"She's been keeping it over here. She's not supposed to keep guns at her place. She lives in student housing."

Cami tittered. "I can just imagine what her housemates would say if they saw her carrying an AK-47 into her apartment. I would imagine most of the kids at SCAD are pretty far left politically."

Danny nodded his head and grabbed another box from the stack near his door. "Oh yeah, she'll be lucky if the green police don't kick her out of school for buying a car with an eight-cylinder engine. Forget about carrying a rifle case in the house.

"I'm going to be staying over there so we can save money for more supplies to survive the blackout. Fortunately, she bought an under-folding AK so it will slip right into a large backpack and none of those commies where she lives will ever know it's coming in the apartment."

Cami grabbed a box and walked right behind him. "Yeah, well, desperate times call for desperate measures. I'm just glad to see you guys taking Nick's advice and getting prepared."

"I'd have to be a moron not to." Danny stuck the box in the back seat. They had room for four more boxes, which they loaded up, then headed back to the church.

Danny pulled in and handed the keys back to Cami. "Thanks for taking all of this stuff out to Nana's for us, it will save us a trip. And thanks for the chat. I needed to distract myself, I was getting nervous about the wedding."

Cami took the keys and got out of the car. "Nothing like discussing the end of the world as we know it to settle those anxious nerves."

Danny smirked. "You know what I mean. The wedding is here, it's happening in the next few minutes. Hopefully, we've still got some time on the apocalypse."

Cami winked. "I love you little brother. You and Alisa are going to make each other very happy. You've got nothing to be nervous about."

"Thanks." Danny walked back into the church and headed for the restroom. He had to check the mirror and put his bow tie back on.

Fifteen minutes later, Steven approached Danny inside the entrance doors of the small church. "Last chance to run out the back door. Are you good?"

"Yeah, I'm good. And I'm going to tell Alisa you offered to let me run out the back door."

"Awesome, I'll tell her why. Because you were sweating profusely and turning pale at the thought of getting married."

"Hmm, let's call a truce."

"It's your call." Steven walked next to Danny up to the podium as the processional music played softly in the background.

Pastor Earl stood at the front and greeted Danny when he arrived. "You look more relaxed. That's good."

Steven stood next to Danny. "Yes, I'm sure Alisa will find it comforting to not find him passed out on the floor when she comes in."

Soft music continued to play over the church PA system. Dana, Alisa's maid of honor and good friend from Lilly's Restaurant came up to the podium. "She needs a few more minutes."

Pastor Earl asked, "She's okay, isn't she?"

"Big-day jitters. You know. We'll have her out here in a bit." Dana turned and walked back toward the office.

Pastor Earl kept Danny engaged in small talk which kept him from getting nervous again. Minutes later, the man who worked the church sound board changed the track to play the Bridal Chorus.

Dana proceeded down the aisle to take her place near the podium.

All of Danny's anxiety melted away when he saw Alisa coming down the aisle. Chef Eric from Lilly's, had always taken an interest in their relationship and he walked Alisa down the aisle. She hadn't bought a formal wedding dress nor ordered expensive flowers from a florist, but she still looked stunning. She wore a new, pretty white dress and held a bouquet of beautiful red roses from Publix. Dana fixed her hair and makeup, and had her looking like a model from a bridal magazine. Moreover, she glowed with an ear-to-ear smile as she made her way down the aisle.

Danny smiled and silently mimed his greeting to her. "Hi."

She did the same. "Hi."

Pastor Earl read a few passages about marriage from the Bible and briefly expounded upon the reading. Next he said, "Alisa and Danny have both written their own vows. Danny, I'll let you lead."

Danny fought to keep his hand steady as he took the note card out of his pocket.

"In all its grandeur and its bitterness too,

"The life I live, I will live with you,

"As we honor our God, and keep his ways,

"I will lead and serve you, all of our days,

"Through all of our poverty, through all of our wealth,

"Through all of our sickness and all of our health,

"When summer is hot, when winter is cold,

"I'll be yours to have and you'll be mine to hold,

"I take thee Alisa, by my side,

"I take thee Alisa to be my bride,

"To love, honor and respect, I promise to you,

"'Til death do us part, I say 'I do'."

Danny put the card back in his pocket.

Steven handed the ring to Danny.

Danny slid the ring on Alisa's finger.

Dana handed two small three-by-five cards to Alisa.

She read from them aloud. "Danny, I knew you were the one because of the way you showed your love for me, so gentle, honoring and dedicated. You're my best friend, you are the one I want to be married to for the rest of my days. Only God could have created a man like you who wants to love me and whose heart was designed to unite with mine for eternity.

"I want to serve the Lord by your side and live for his glory. I believe he made you just for me and I promise to love you, submit and honor you for the rest of my days."

Dana handed Alisa the other ring which she placed on Danny's finger.

Pastor Earl prayed a prayer asking God to protect them as a couple and to bless them throughout their marriage. Then, he looked up and said, "I now pronounce you Husband and Wife. Danny you may kiss your bride."

Danny kissed her for a good long while, then whispered in her ear. "Thank you for marrying me."

She hugged him and whispered back. "No, thank you. Sorry my vows weren't quite as poetic as yours."

Danny held her close. "Had they been penned by Shakespeare, they couldn't have possibly made me any happier."

Danny escorted Alisa down the aisle while the music played, followed closely by Steven and Dana.

Steven and some of the other men who were in attendance quickly rearranged the chairs to convert the sanctuary into the reception hall. They brought out folding tables and moved the chairs around. Dana and some of the other girls from work scurried to get them decorated with white candles, red roses and white tulle.

Danny tried to help Chef Eric set up the plates

and food, but he would have none of it. Cami grabbed the newlyweds and took them outside for some pictures. "I got some really great shots of the ceremony. We'll just get a few quick shots outside. I know it's cold, but the sun is shining and the light is beautiful."

Danny and Alisa followed her outside to a patch of evergreen shrubbery near the corner of the strip mall where the small store-front church was located.

Cami took several shots instructing them where to stand. "I'm going to get these printed up at the CVS over on Victory. I'll prepay and you can pick them up as soon as they're ready. Don't dilly dally. If the lights go out, digital prints might not ever be viewable again, and you'll want to remember this day. Bring the pictures out to Nana's on your next trip. I have a nice album for your prints waiting for you there."

"Thank you Cami. I'm so happy to have you as a sister, now." Alisa was beginning to shiver from the cool brisk air.

Danny took off his jacket and put it around Alisa's shoulders. "Thanks so much. Can we head back in now?"

Cami grinned. "As soon as I get a few shots of her with your jacket on. This is adorable. Would you mind taking it off and putting it back on her for the camera?"

After everything Cami was doing for them, he couldn't exactly refuse. Besides, it would make a nice picture. "Sure."

A few more shots and they headed back inside where the church had been totally transformed into the reception hall. A very small space at the front was even reserved for a dance floor. Pastor Earl prayed to bless the food and the attendants began making their way through the buffet-style line for punch and a selection of finger foods.

Danny and Alisa made themselves plates and sat down. Pastor Earl followed behind them through the buffet line and sat down with them. "I'm so happy for the two of you. How are your daily Bible-reading plans coming along?"

"I'm staying on track, keeping up with what I'm supposed to cover each day. Danny, on the other hand, is powering right through it. He finished the New Testament, the Books of Prophecy and has started from the beginning in Genesis, plus he's reading the Books of Prophecy again."

Danny finished chewing his finger sandwich. "Yeah, some of the stuff in the Books of Prophecy sounded very familiar. It reminded me of the things you said about America's judgment, when you were helping me understand my first dream. But some of it goes over my head. I'm trying to figure out the context of what was going on and when it was written."

"As you read through the Old Testament, that will become clearer. Particularly when you get to the books which deal with the history of ancient Israel, like Samuel, Chronicles, and Kings. I have something for you that might help. I'll be right back." Pastor Earl got up, went to his office, and returned with a book.

Alisa said, "We'll get your office cleaned up in a few minutes. There's probably makeup, curling irons and clothes all over the place."

Pastor Earl put his hand in the air. "No trouble at all." He handed the book to Danny. "This is Halley's Bible Handbook. It will give you a little background information on the authors of the different books, a timeline of when they were written and what was going on politically. This will be a big help in understanding the Books of Prophecy. You'll read about the kingdom split, the idolatry and influence of the pagan cultures in the southern kingdom as well as the northern kingdom, and the empires God used to punish them both."

"Thanks." Danny opened the book and began studying the pages.

"I'm happy to see someone with as much interest as you, Danny. I'm glad to help. But there will be plenty of time to study it after the honeymoon."

Danny closed the book and looked at Alisa. "It would take more than a book to distract me from the honeymoon. The EMP could go off tonight and I'd never even notice."

"Don't say that, Danny. I hope it doesn't go off tonight. I've been dreaming of staying in that little Bed and Breakfast on Gaston Street. Where are Cami and Nana staying tonight?"

"At the same Bed and Breakfast we're staying at. They're in the room next to ours."

"Danny! It's our honeymoon! Nana scares me already. We have to try to get another room."

"I'm kidding. They're actually staying at a Bed and Breakfast near your apartment."

"Danny Walker! If it wasn't your honeymoon, you'd be sleeping on the couch, so don't push it!"

Pastor Earl chuckled. "I can tell you two are going to make a good couple. If you'll excuse me, I'm going to go say hello to some of the other guests."

"Thanks again Pastor, for everything." Danny shook his hand before he walked away.

Cami took a seat at the table after Pastor Earl got up. "Nana looks like she's having fun."

Danny looked over. "She does. I'm glad everything worked out the way it did. Who knows if we'll ever have the big fancy wedding in Connecticut, and I'm not sure Nana will want to go to that one, even if we do."

"So, Alisa, Danny and I were discussing his dream earlier. I was wondering if you thought it could possibly be a coronal mass ejection from the sun or do you think the EMP has to come from a man-made source."

"Why are you asking me?"

"Danny seems convinced you are his official dream interpreter."

"I don't know about that. When he was telling me the second dream, I immediately knew it was about an EMP, but I don't know how I knew. And, I don't have any secret insider information on what causes it. Sorry."

"About being his interpreter, I'm still not sure I understand everything from the first dream and I hope there aren't any more dreams to interpret."

"But the cows, Pharaoh's dream had seven. Danny has only seen four so far. It makes sense that he would dream of three more, right?" Cami ate one of the prosciutto and melon balls on her plate.

"I hope not. I worry about him every time he has another dream." Alisa put her hand on Danny's.

"Okay, just thought I'd ask. I didn't bring your wedding gift inside, so remind me to give it to you before you leave. I wasn't sure how agreeable the other guest would be to what we got you."

Alisa put her hand up. "No, no, no. I can't handle surprises. You can't lead up with that kind of cryptic statement and then not tell us what it is."

Cami didn't rush her response. She finished chewing the pimento cheese finger sandwich she was eating, then took a drink of her sparkling water. She blotted her mouth with a napkin. "Well." She took another drink. "I suppose I should tell you anyway."

Alisa sat motionless through the theatre that Cami was using to build the suspense. "What is it? Tell us!"

Cami toyed with the sandwich as if she might take another bite before revealing the gift. "Nick was the one who insisted we get it for you, so it's not a typical wedding gift."

"Okay, now you're torturing me too," Danny said.

Cami fought back a mischievous grin. "We're really proud of the effort you guys are making to get all of your preps put together and out to Nana's. We knew you had to make choices because of finances, especially when it came to your selection of firearms, and you did good, considering what you had to work with."

Alisa's face appeared pained by the mystery of the gift, but she managed to thank Cami for the compliment. "That's so sweet. You and Nick really helped with that. We're very grateful for the advice. So, bottom line, what did you get us?"

"Well." Cami stalled again and took another drink. "Your buddy has a shotgun, great for self-defense and hunting. You guys have an AK; very intimidating if you ever have to use it to defend your lives. It will also drop a deer or any other animal in this part of the country for that matter. You've got Pop's old pistol, which is reliable and concealable but it has a limited shot capacity. We thought the one thing your little arsenal was lacking was a good semi-automatic pistol with a double-stack magazine; something that holds several rounds and is easy to reload."

Alisa was bursting at the seams with anticipation. "You bought us a gun!"

Cami smiled. "A Glock 19; very dependable, easy to clean. It's small enough to stick in the back of your jeans if you have to, but large enough to hold fifteen rounds, seventeen if you use the magazine from the Glock 17, and nineteen if you replace the magazine floor plate with a two-round extender."

"Twenty if it has one in the chamber?" Danny was trying to keep up with the math.

Cami nodded. "Twenty, with one in the pipe. But we don't typically max out our mags. It's better to leave an empty space, so I'd take nineteen and be happy with it."

"The Glock 19 will take the same magazines as the Glock 17?" Alisa seemed confused.

"Glock magazines are standard sized, so that the

compact or sub-compact sized models will hold the magazines from the full size models, provided they're the same caliber. So the magazine from the seventeen, the full size 9mm Glock, will fit in the nineteen or the twenty-six. The reverse isn't true though. The mags from a smaller model would be too short to fit in a larger model."

"So it sticks out the bottom?" Danny tried to visualize what Cami was talking about.

"Right, and I brought you two of the nineteen-round mags in addition to the 2 fifteen-round mags that came with it. We also got you a hundred rounds of ammo. We've got plenty of 9mm ammo at Nana's which is part of the reason we decided to get it for you. Nick said not to expect another present if you have another wedding in Connecticut."

Alisa chuckled. "No problem. Can we go see it now?"

"Sure." Cami stood up and led the way out to the car.

Danny got into Cami's passenger seat and Alisa sat in his lap, since the back was full of boxes that Cami was carting back to Nana's.

Cami took a neatly wrapped gift from beneath her seat and passed it over to Alisa. "Here you go."

Alisa tore into it, since Danny couldn't do much with her sitting on his lap.

Danny helped her lift the flaps to open the case.

Alisa took it out, remembering the basic firearms safety tips Nick had taught them at the farm. "Wow! Thanks."

Danny held it for a moment. "Can you show us how to change the magazine and rack it?"

Cami gave a brief tutorial, with the gun unloaded, and had them both practice dry firing the weapon to get used to the amount of pressure that it took to drop the hammer.

"Where is the safety?" Alisa looked the pistol over.

"The safety on a Glock is, don't put your finger on the trigger until you're ready to shoot." Cami winked.

"This is awesome. Thanks so much, sis." Danny couldn't wait to get the pistol out to Nana's so he could shoot it.

"Put it in your trunk. You don't want something like that sitting in your car seat, tempting anyone." Cami opened her door and got out.

"Yeah, thanks." Danny got out of the car after Alisa, then took the gift straight to his car which had been uniquely decorated with streamers and window paint to advertise the fact that he and Alisa were just married.

"Steven! I'll kill him." He put the pistol in the trunk and slammed it shut.

They went back inside. Alisa and Danny mingled with the guests for a while then danced to a couple of songs.

At Last by Etta James played over the speakers and they swayed close together.

Alisa nudged Danny. "Look who Steven is dancing with."

Danny slowly turned as they danced. "Maid of honor, best man, they're sort of obligated to, aren't they?"

Alisa shrugged, then whispered in his ear. "I'm

glad we stayed celibate. Well, since we committed our lives to Christ, I mean."

"Yeah. Me, too." Danny held her near while she lay her head on his shoulder.

"But, it's been long enough. I'm ready to get out of here."

Danny's heartbeat quickened. "Yeah, me, too."

They said their goodbyes and escaped to their romantic room at the Bed and Breakfast, to love each other as God intended.

The next morning, Alisa ran her finger through Danny's hair to wake him. "Did the bomb go off last night?"

The warm light of morning poured into the room through floor-to-ceiling windows with magnificently-ornate molding and original, wooden, plantation shutters. "Yeah." He reached over to the night stand and grabbed his phone. "But my phone still works, so no EMP."

"You're bad." She lobbed her pillow across his head. "I'm starving, what time is breakfast?"

"At 8:00, we've got a half hour to get to the dining room."

"Then we can come back to bed?"

"Check-out is at 11:00. We could come back to the room for a bit. We've got all day."

She stretched out under the sheets. "Great."

Danny got up and put his clothes on. "Trish said she'd buy us dinner if we wanted to go by Lilly's later. We eat there all the time, but it would be nice to sit at a table as customers."

"Plus, we wouldn't have to cook, or clean up."

"Who is this 'we' that cooks?"

"Shut up, Danny. I'm trying to learn. Don't I always help you clean up when you cook?"

He lay back down on the huge, four-poster bed, put his hands in hers and kissed her. "Yes, you do. I'm just giving you grief. Actually, I prefer cooking to cleaning up afterwards, so I'm quite happy with our current arrangement."

"But you like my French toast, right?"

"I love your French toast." He kissed her neck. "I love everything about you."

"Stop it, Danny. You're tickling me." Alisa pushed him away, got out of the bed and got dressed.

She pulled him up from the bed. "Come on, let's go get some coffee."

The newlyweds spent the rest of the day enjoying their first day of being husband and wife. The worries of the world would all still be there tomorrow, so they purposed not to let it dampen this one day that was dedicated to being their honeymoon.

CHAPTER 18

Come, my people, enter thou into thy
chambers, and shut thy doors about thee:
hide thyself as it were for a little moment,
until the indignation be overpast. For,
behold, the LORD cometh out of his place
to punish the inhabitants of the earth for
their iniquity: the earth also shall disclose
her blood, and shall no more cover her slain.

Isaiah 26:20-21

The following weeks were spent hurrying to and
fro, trying to get everything accomplished on their
respective EMP-preparation-to-do lists. Danny
made several trips out to Nana's, both for the
purpose of pre-positioning survival supplies and to

minimize the amount of belongings that he took to Alisa's apartment after he moved out from his place on January 31st.

The reduced work schedule allowed the three friends to have more time for prepping, but with school, church and everything else, they stayed very busy. Danny continued to save his money as if he still had to pay rent. That money was pooled with whatever Alisa earned from the restaurant to buy more ammo, batteries, storable food, and other supplies to take out to the farm.

Steven sold his car to raise funds for purchasing more shelf-stable foods, which also went to Nana's.

Danny found a rugged bike on Craigslist and had it serviced at the bike shop. He changed the tires and tubes with heavy-duty replacements and also added Tuffy tire liners. He took the initiative to have the liners put into Alisa's bike as well.

The three of them perfected the art of maximizing calories while minimizing costs in their long-term-food-storage program. The bulk of the food purchased was rice and beans, both because those two foods were inexpensive and because they stored for years. The white rice, bought in twenty-pound bags, was less than ten dollars a bag and would keep for twenty years if stored properly. The dried beans, which provided an excellent source of protein and fiber, would store for five to ten years and cost about a dollar per pound.

Additionally, they stored large amounts of jellies, pancake mix, flour, dried fruits, coffee, grits, sugar, pasta and pasta sauce. The one item that was noticeably missing from the growing stockpile in

Nana's house was canned meats. The calorie count was simply too small and the cost too high for them to purchase a lot of canned meats on their meager budget.

Instead, they bought four rabbits, a buck and three does, and put together a small rabbit hutch near the woodshed behind Nana's house. The rabbits alone would soon produce a steady supply of meat that didn't require preserving, since one or two rabbits could easily be consumed by the group in a single meal.

Nana's cattle would provide an additional meat source, but most of the meat would have to be canned or turned into jerky, except during the coldest part of winter when outdoor temperatures would keep the meat frozen without the use of electricity.

The breed of cattle that Nana kept on her farm were Hereford, which were bred specifically for beef, but all cows produce milk. In a pinch, they could certainly be milked.

The chickens could also be eaten for meat, but it was decided that they were generally more valuable as egg producers.

Besides being fantastic sources of meat, eggs and dairy, all of the manure from the individual animals would produce excellent fertilizer.

While there was still much left to do, Danny was breathing a little easier because of everything they had accomplished since his first dream just six weeks earlier.

He took Alisa to lunch for Valentine's Day. It was the first time they had done anything besides work, school, church and prep since the honeymoon. They walked to Mrs. Wilkes' Dining Room at ten o'clock. They'd been there plenty of times to know that you had to be an hour early if you wanted to eat at the first seating.

"It's a little chilly in the shade." Alisa sat on the metal bench out front of Mrs. Wilkes.

"We're going to be out here for a while. Are you sure you want to wait? This isn't the most romantic place for Valentine's Day, sitting at a table full of strangers. Of course Valentine's Day lunch doesn't lend itself to affectionate passion, like a candle lit dinner. Sorry we have to work tonight."

"It's romantic to me. I'll always remember the first time we came here. And don't worry about it being lunch, we'll light some candles when we get home from work tonight." Alisa winked at him.

He kissed her on the forehead. "Happy Valentine's Day."

She kissed his lips. "Happy Valentine's Day to you. I know sitting with strangers isn't very romantic, but I wanted to come here because I know this might be the last time we ever eat at a restaurant. And if I had a chance to eat at only one place in Savannah, this would be it."

Danny nodded. "I agree."

By 10:45, the line was growing to the end of the street. It was a mild fifty-two degrees, but the occasional breeze made it feel cooler. "Not much longer now," Danny glanced at his watch.

"Good. I skipped breakfast so I'd have plenty of room."

"So did I." Danny stood up to move around as he

was feeling the chill himself.

At eleven o'clock, the doors opened and they made their way to the table.

Once the table of ten was filled with guests, the host welcomed everyone at the table, and said a prayer to bless the food. Then, the servers began bringing plates and bowls of home-style food to the table. Danny filled his plate with fried chicken, meatloaf, black-eyed peas, collard greens, fried squash, cornbread, biscuits, mashed potatoes, gravy, macaroni and cheese, and cooked cabbage. With a few exceptions, Alisa did the same.

Forty-five minutes later, Danny polished off a small dish of banana pudding. "I'm stuffed. I'm going to need a nap."

Alisa sat back in her chair. "I'm too full to lie down. Can we take a walk through Forsythe Park first? It's probably not so cold now, and we'll be moving."

"Anything for you, my Valentine." Danny stood up, took out his wallet and walked to the register to pay.

They took a long stroll through the park which was only a few blocks from Mrs. Wilkes, then headed home to get ready for work.

That evening, the two of them arrived at work together. Trish instructed them on how to cut and place the roses in the small vases for each individual table. Additionally, they were to replace the regular candles on each table with red ones and sprinkle rose petals on the white tablecloths.

Minutes later, Steven came in and began helping Danny and Alisa cut the stems and fill the vases with water. "Looks like you guys could have held out and had a Valentine's Day wedding after all."

Danny smirked. "Maybe from an EMP standpoint, but I don't think Alisa could have made it."

"I can't believe you, Danny." She slapped his arm.

"Sounds like he struck a nerve." Steven giggled.

"Shut up, Steven!" Alisa threatened him with a vase full of water.

Steven winced. "Just sayin'."

Danny wisely redirected the conversation. "Trish said we've got quite a few reservations on the books. More than we've had since the market crash."

"It'll be nice to make some cash for a change." Steven stuck the roses in a vase and placed them on a serving tray.

Alisa continued to cut more roses to the proper length with the scissors. "I've never seen Lilly's offer such deep discounts, much less on Valentine's. It'd be tough to cook dinner at home for what they're charging tonight. But, I guess it's working. They have to do something to get people in here."

Dana arrived next. "Hey guys. What are we doing?"

Steven picked up the tray of vases and walked off abruptly without a word.

Danny turned to watch his friend, then relayed Trish's instructions on the table set up for the evening to Dana.

"Great. I'll get started on changing the candles."

Dana took the box of red candles and walked away to switch them out.

Danny waited 'til Dana was gone. "Did you see that? There must be some serious friction between those two."

Alisa stopped and looked at Danny with her mouth hung open. "Seriously?"

"What?"

She put her hands on her hips. "You don't know. He didn't say anything to you?"

"About what?"

Alisa covered her face. "They hooked up at the wedding."

"Hooked up?"

"She offered to give him a ride home after the wedding. He offered to buy her dinner for taking him home. They went out to eat, then ended up making out in her car, when they were parked out front of his apartment. She invited him to come back to her place, he wouldn't. He tried to get her to go to church the next morning, she wouldn't. He explained your dream, everything we're doing to get ready, but she doesn't really buy it. They decided it wasn't a good match and moved on, but the tension between them is getting worse and worse. I can't believe he didn't tell you. She talks to me about it every time we work together."

Danny huffed. "He never said a word to me about it."

The restaurant was set up and ready to go twenty minutes before the first reservation. Danny made himself a glass of water at the service station near the bar. In hopes of a busy night, he wanted to be well hydrated.

Steven came back and poured a Coke. "I hope we're slammed. Even with no car insurance or gas to buy, money has been tight."

"Speaking of not having a car, how did you get home from the wedding?"

"Got a ride."

"From who?"

"Uhh, Dana."

"Hmm. I saw you guys dancing at the wedding. I meant to ask you about that."

"Nothing to tell."

"Nothing?"

Steven exhaled and sat his glass down on the counter. "No, not really. Why? What did you hear?"

"I heard something."

"Look, I made a mistake. I thought, maybe, she'd be interested in coming to church, learning about God. But it was a mistake. Missionary dating."

Danny chuckled. "What's that?"

"Trying to convert someone, basically because you think they're cute. Not a good thing to do. Bad plan, bad motive. Can we talk about something else?"

"Sure. I wasn't trying to rub your nose in it, I was just surprised you didn't tell me."

"Sorry, I wasn't trying to hide it, but I'm embarrassed about the whole thing."

"No worries, I understand. Looks like you're getting a table."

"Let the games begin!" Steven patted Danny on the arm as he walked away to his table.

The night progressed and by 8:30, nearly every

table in the restaurant was full. Alisa stood at the register and waited for Danny to finish ringing in his order. "How are you doing?"

"The same as everyone else, I guess. All two tops, everyone is getting the special, no big spenders. Better than what we've been doing the past couple weeks, but far from the good old days. What about you?" He sent his order and stepped out of the way so she could ring in her order.

She looked at her notepad and began entering the order on the computer. "Ditto."

Suddenly, the music stopped, the computer screen went blank and the lights went out.

CHAPTER 19

And I will bring the blind by a way that they knew not; I will lead them in paths that they have not known: I will make darkness light before them, and crooked things straight. These things will I do unto them, and not forsake them.

Isaiah 42:16

Danny immediately took his phone out of his pocket. "My phone is dead. This is it. Get your coat and purse. I'll grab Steven, we need to leave right now."

"What about our tables?"

"They need to leave, too. Hand Trish all of your closed checks. Better yet, give them to me and I'll give them to her."

Alisa made a rough estimate of how much cash she'd made in tips and took that out before handing the wad of credit card slips and cash to Danny. "Here. I'll meet you up front."

The candles provided adequate light to see his way through the dining room. He walked into the storeroom where his coat was. He took the small flashlight from his apron pocket so he could find it. He took it from the rack and put it on.

Steven walked in right behind him. "Can you put some light on the rack so I can find my coat?"

"You got it." Danny held the flashlight.

Trish walked in. "Hey guys, can y'all help me bring some candles to the kitchen so they can see? Since we've got gas stoves, they can keep the food coming out."

Danny handed Trish his and Alisa's credit card slips. "Trish, this is the EMP I tried to tell you about. We're leaving, and you need to get out of here too."

"Danny, this is a temporary power outage. The lights just went off. They'll be back on in a few minutes, probably."

"No, they won't be back on for years. Look at your phone. It's dead also. Why would a power outage shut your phone off? Anyway, I don't have time to argue with you. We've got to go."

"If you guys walk out, you're both fired." Trish's voice was harsh.

Steven put his coat on and handed her his receipts. "You should have listened to him before, but at least listen to him now. Take care of yourself Trish. Get some supplies from the restaurant and try to find a safe place to go."

She took the slips but said nothing. Her face showed that she was concerned about what they were telling her, but she seemed unwilling to accept it.

Danny put his flashlight back in his pocket and grabbed one of the candles from the table. Steven and Alisa followed him and also took candles. They briskly made their way up the cobblestones on River Street. Many of the restaurants had candles burning, so it wasn't pitch black. People wandered around trying to figure out what happened. Some were looking at their phones and trying to guess why they were dark as well.

Danny led the way up the road to the street level. When they arrived, brilliant white light arched from the pad mounted transformer at the corner of Bay and Drayton. The light reflected from the low-hanging limbs of the live oak above the transformer showed that the surrounding area of Bay Street was littered with stalled cars. The transformer hummed and glowed brighter, then with a loud pop, shower of sparks, and puff of smoke, went dark.

As the people got out of their cars, they stared at the three friends because they held some of the only sources of light anywhere around. A few people had flashlights in their cars, but they were a very small minority.

Steven's bike was locked to a public bike stand at the top of the incline. He handed his candle to a frightened young couple standing nearby, unlocked his bike and walked with it next to Danny and Alisa.

"Hey, where did you get those candles?" another man called out.

"Just keep walking," Danny said.

A faint voice, barely discernable from the clamor of the confused people milling about, called from the distance. "Alisa, wait up!"

"Wait, someone is calling for me." She grabbed the arm of Danny's coat.

He turned. "Who is it?"

Steven blew out a deep breath of disdain. "Dana."

Alisa scolded him. "Be nice, Steven. She's frightened."

"Hey!" Dana was carrying a candle from the restaurant. She panted to catch her breath from sprinting. "Can I come with you guys?"

"Absolutely not! I tried to warn you about this, and you laughed it off. You wanted nothing to do with preparing for it, you wanted nothing to do with God and nothing to do with me." Steven's voice was indignant.

"I'm sorry Steven. I should have listened. It was a tough thing to accept, but you were right and I was wrong. Please let me go with you guys."

"No. We have a plan and we have to stick with it. You have to accept the consequences of your decision," he scorned.

"Okay, but it's not fair to say I didn't want anything to do with you. You're the one who said we couldn't see each other and told me not to call you." Dana looked at the light of her candle and began to cry.

Steven's tone lightened. "You should try to get

somewhere safe and you should try to do it fast. Things are going to get really bad. Pack a bag, get a bike and go to your folks place in North Carolina."

"They're in Marion, it's in the mountains and over 300 miles away. I couldn't get there on a bike in summer, much less in the dead of winter." Her sobs grew louder.

"Shhhh, it's okay." Alisa put her arm around Dana. "Danny, didn't Nick say we would need a lot of people to keep everything running out at Nana's? You know Dana is a hard worker, she'd pull her weight around the farm."

Danny looked at Steven. "What do you think?"

He walked out of earshot from the girls, leaned his bike against a tree and sat down on the pavement. "It's your grandmother's farm and Alisa's car. I'm just a guest myself. I don't really have any say in the matter."

Danny took a seat next to him. "That's not true, this is the big event. We've planned for this together and we make decisions together. What's your recommendation?"

Steven shook his head. "I don't know. On one side, I feel like all of this is happening to America because people like Dana wanted nothing to do with God. They're the ones who have elected the politicians, who chose the judges that have protected a woman's right to have her unborn baby murdered. They're the ones who wanted God out of the classroom, out of the courtroom, and out of public spaces. They're the reason that our military men and women can't pray in Jesus' name or tell their fellow soldier about salvation without fear of being court-martialed.

"I worry that intervening on her behalf may be getting in the way of God's judgment."

"And on the other hand?" Danny glanced over at his friend.

"On the other hand, the Book of James says mercy triumphs over judgment." Steven pursed his lips. "Then, I have so many personal emotions tied up in the decision. I was so disappointed in her when she showed no interest in even hearing about God, and I was disappointed in myself for trying to convert someone for my own selfish desires. I'm really ashamed of what I did and having her around is a constant reminder of my failure."

Danny put his hand on Steven's shoulder. "I think you're being too hard on yourself."

"And, I'm letting my self-loathing influence my decision about whether we should take her with us.

"Then there's the logistics side of the equation. We're already going to be cramming stuff in the car."

"Someone could sit in someone else's lap," Danny said. "That would conserve some space."

"She's not sitting in my lap!"

Danny held up both hands. "I didn't specify. That's fine. We'll work something out. The girls are both small framed. They could sit in the back, close. You'd probably need to be in the front anyway with a weapon, in case anything happens on the way."

"I guess so."

"Do you want to tell her?"

"No way. You tell her."

Danny got up, picked up his candle and walked

back over to Dana and Alisa. "We talked it over. You can come out to the farm with us, but."

Dana cut him off and gave him a big embrace. "Thank you so much."

"Wait, wait, wait! Let me finish. It's contingent on Nana letting you stay and she can be pretty cantankerous, especially when it comes to strangers. You can only bring one bag, so make it count. If Nana lets you stay, you'll be doing a lot of farm work, so keep that in mind when you're deciding what clothes to bring.

"If she says no, there's nothing we can do about it. But her place is in Anderson South Carolina. You'll be a heck of a lot closer to Marion, North Carolina than you are now; probably only about a hundred miles or so. If Nana says no, we'll do what we can to help you get there. We'll give you a bike and some supplies and help you map out the safest, easiest route. But her decision is final and there's nothing we can do about it.

"This isn't a negotiation. Like Steven said, you had your chance to work with us so now this is charity. And, it's going to cost us provisions and space that we had planned for ourselves. So take it or leave it. Do you understand?"

"I totally understand. I'm so sorry. Thank you so much." Dana dried her eyes.

Danny said, "Go to your house, pack a bag, one bag, and get to Alisa's as fast as you can."

"Are we leaving tonight?" she sniffed.

"At first light in the morning, but the streets are going to get less safe with each passing minute tonight. The more people figure out what just happened the worse it's going to get."

"Thanks. I'll be there in an hour, no more than two." She hugged Alisa and walked off toward her apartment.

"Come on, let's move." Danny took Alisa's free hand with his and began walking toward the apartment.

Alisa said, "Maybe we should take Steven by his place in the car tonight so he can pack."

Steven shook his head. "I don't think you should be driving around tonight. I can walk home. I'll be okay on my bike."

"I'd at least like to find out if the Camaro is going to start. Maybe you should come by while we test it," she replied.

Danny nodded. "That's a good idea. Start it up, and shut it right off as soon as we know it works. If it didn't survive the EMP, the sooner we know, the better chance we'll have at coming up with a new plan to get out of here."

Alisa's apartment wasn't far and they soon arrived. Even before they went inside, she got in and stuck the key in the ignition.

"Let's make sure no one is watching." Steven said.

They all looked around and determined the coast was clear.

"Here it goes." She turned the key. The engine fired right up and purred with power.

"Great, turn it off, fast!" Danny's voice was imperative.

She cut the ignition, climbed out of the car and locked the door. "Thank you, daddy!"

Steven smiled. "Thank you, Jesus!"

"We did the best we could. It's all in God's hands from here on out. Do you want to come back here tonight?" Danny asked.

"Why don't you guys pick me up on the way out of town?"

"We need your bike rack to pack our bikes on the car." Alisa toyed with her keys. "I know it will be uncomfortable staying here with Dana, but you'll probably be living in the same house for the next few years. You're going to have to get over it."

Steven paused. "I'll come back by with the rack in a while."

"So you'll stay here?" Danny asked.

"Let me think about it. But I'll definitely bring the bike rack over for the car."

"Once it's on and the bikes are mounted, we won't be able to open the trunk. It would really be best if you brought all your stuff back over. Then, we could leave straight from here. Every street we drive down is going to bring us more undesired attention."

Steven took a deep breath and let it back out. "I'll come back over and stay here. I'll have to make at least two trips. I have to bring my bug-out bag, plus all those shotgun shells are heavy."

"Why don't you take my revolver, so you'll have something if you get in a pinch?" Danny followed Alisa up the stairs to the entrance of her apartment.

Steven nodded slowly. "I think I'll take you up on that."

"Great. Wait there and I'll bring it out."

"Okay."

Danny went in, grabbed the pistol and wrapped it in a bath towel, so it wouldn't draw any attention if another student was coming in or out of the apartment. He took it outside and unfolded the towel to show Steven. "It's ready to go."

Steven looked both ways before taking the pistol, then stuck it in the back of his pants. He untucked his white oxford work shirt and let the tail hang over the pistol to conceal it. "This is totally illegal."

"Cop cars and radios aren't working, so you don't have much to worry about." Danny folded the empty towel and tucked it under his arm.

Steven creased his forehead. "Cop cars and radios aren't working, so we've got a lot to worry about."

"On second thought, you're right. Be safe out there." Danny waved as Steven rode off into the darkness.

Just before he reached the door, he heard a faint scream off in the distance. He walked inside and looked at Alisa. "We probably should have walked with Dana to her house."

"She'll be okay."

"I don't know. It sounds like it's already starting." Danny sat down on the couch for a moment. There was so much to do, but he just didn't have the energy.

Alisa, on the other hand, changed out of her work clothes and was using the candle from work to light her closet as she rummaged through her clothes. "There are so many things that I really like, stuff I don't want to get rid of, but I know it won't be practical for the end of the world."

Danny called back from the couch. "Why don't you pick your three favorite outfits. Save those, and then stick to practical attire for everything else."

"And my shoes. I have so many nice shoes."

"Didn't you already take most of the things you really liked to Nana's?"

"No." Her voice came back from the other room. "I took all the stuff that would be good for the farm. Old jeans, old sneakers, and hiking boots. It was mostly clothes I was going to throw out."

"At least you didn't throw it out."

She walked into the room and saw him sitting on the couch. "Aren't you going to pack?"

Confronted on his lack of ambition, he sat forward and sighed. "Yeah. I'm just thinking about what the next few days are going to be like and it is exhausting to consider."

"One day at a time, Danny. That's what you tell me when I get overwhelmed. Just focus on what you need to do right now. Come on, get up." She took his hand and pulled him from the sofa as if she were prying weeds from a garden bed.

Reluctantly, he stood. He went to the bedroom and changed out of his work clothes. Next, he began packing a few of his everyday clothes into a duffle bag. He had already taken most of his clothes to Nana's, so it took him only a few minutes. "I guess I'll start boxing up the rest of our long-term storage food."

"Let's eat the ice cream from the freezer before it melts. We might not ever have ice cream again."

"Okay." Danny loved ice cream. Eating his last bowl would feel like a funeral for a dear friend.

"In fact, we should eat everything in the fridge that we can tonight."

"I'm sure Steven and Dana will be hungry. When they get here, we'll all sit down for one last meal. I'll put the milk in the freezer. That will help it keep 'til morning. Then we can eat some cereal before we head out tomorrow."

"Good idea." Alisa brought her bug-out bag and sat it near the door.

Danny retrieved his from the hall closet and sat it next to Alisa's. He heard a loud pop in the distance. It could have been a transformer blowing up or it could have been a gun. Considering the EMP had happened nearly an hour ago, he figured that it was most likely a gun. "I'm going to load all of the empty magazines. It will save a little space, and they'll be ready if we need them."

Alisa came back out of the bedroom with a small carry-on suitcase. "Okay, is the AK loaded?"

"I'll load it." Danny went to retrieve the Glock from the dresser drawer. He placed it in the front of his pants. He stuck the extra loaded magazine in his back pocket, then loaded the other two spare magazines. He put those in the small backpack he used for school. He also placed his cash, Bible, flashlight, change of clothes and the extra ammo in it. He planned to keep it right by his side at all times.

Next, he loaded the two extra AK-47 magazines and stuck them in the magazine pouch attached to Alisa's bug-out bag. He took the AK from between the mattress and box spring, stuck in a magazine and racked a round into the chamber. Danny did a very bad Scarface imitation. "Ho kay, I'm reloaded."

Alisa walked in the room. "Cute. Is the safety on?"

Danny smirked, switched on the safety and worked the AK, barrel first, into her bag.

"It fits with the magazine on?"

He put his hand on the handle. "Yep, if you have to get it out fast, it's probably going to pull some of the other contents out as well. Of course, if you have to get it out fast, other stuff falling out is going to be the least of your worries."

Another pop rang out from somewhere in the darkness. This time it was closer. Alisa picked up her bug-out bag. "I'm actually going to keep this by the bed tonight."

Danny and Alisa emptied out every spare container that could be used to box up food, toiletries or other items of value. They filled the boxes and put them by the door.

Danny paused to look at the items pilling up at the door. "I doubt we'll be able to fit all of this stuff. We should arrange it in order of most important to least. Once we start putting things into the car, the clock will be ticking. Anyone who sees us loading up is going to figure out that we have one of the last functioning automobiles in Savannah."

Alisa stood next to him. "You're right. For food, let's start with the densest items since they'll have the most calories for the space they occupy."

Danny began sorting the things into different boxes. "Good call."

They soon finished the task and sat down on the couch.

Alisa's stare looked distant.

"Are you okay?" Danny put his arm around her.

She cracked a faint smile. "Yeah, mostly just thinking about how different everything is going to be. And I'm worried about my folks."

He didn't know what to say to comfort her. Her parents weren't interested in listening when she'd tried to tell them about the dream, and their odds of survival were likely slim. He just pulled her closer and swept her chestnut hair out of her face with his fingers.

Steven's tell-tale knock was at the door. The door knob rattled as he tried to let himself in.

"Hold on, it's locked." Danny stood to unlock the door and let Steven in.

Steven pushed his bike into the living room with his bug-out bag on his back and a trash bag filled with something.

"You don't want to lock your bike up outside?" Danny took the garbage bag and sat it near the end of the row of boxes. He guessed it was a sleeping bag and a pillow.

"No way. People are stealing everything that isn't tied down."

"Locked up would pretty much be tied down, right?"

Steven shook his head. "No. They might not get the bike frame, but they could take the wheels, which would render it useless to me. I'm telling you, it's getting pretty bad out there. I think the criminal element is starting to figure out there are no sirens, no helicopters, no radios, no cops and no repercussions for their actions."

Steven took a seat on the living room chair. "Did you guys take a shower?"

"No, did you?" Danny asked.

"Yeah, the pressure was weak, but it was still hot from the hot water tank. I figured it would be the last one for a while."

Alisa looked toward the bathroom door and sighed. "I took one right before work. I guess I'll just have to savor the memory."

A frantic knock was at the door. "Alisa! It's me!" Dana's shaky voice called out.

Danny stood to let her in. "Hey."

Her face was white and she was visibly upset. She sat her backpack, a small overnight bag and her cat carrier on the floor. "I just saw someone get shot!"

Alisa jumped up. "You're all shook up. Take a seat on the couch. Danny will get you some water."

Danny took his cue to go get a glass of water.

Steven followed him to the kitchen. "Looks like it's getting worse out there."

"And it looks like we picked up a cat for the journey. I don't think Nana is going to let a cat stay in the house and I'm not sure how Rusty, the old farm dog is going to feel about one being outside, but what am I going to say about it now? Look at her, she's a mess." Danny instinctively went to the faucet for a glass of water. He turned it on, but only a trickle came out.

Steven handed him one of the jugs of water they'd stored in the pantry. "The cat situation will work itself out. I'm wondering if we should leave tonight. I wasn't expecting people to start killing each other for a couple of days."

"Yeah, me, too. Nick said most cities would have about seventy-two hours before society went into full meltdown."

Steven leaned against the counter. "He may be right, this might just be the preview for the main event."

Danny capped the water jug off and sat it back in the pantry. "I still think we'd be better off waiting until day break. Right now, it's mostly the criminal element. They tend to scatter like cockroaches when the sunlight hits them. The decent people won't get desperate enough to be violent for a few more days."

Dana took the water when Danny brought it to her and sipped it. "He just shot them."

"Who?" Danny put his hand on her shoulder.

"The guy. Some guy and his girlfriend were coming out of the convenience store with a few bags of groceries. I guess the store was still selling stuff to people who had cash. I saw candles burning inside the window."

"Anyway, four young guys, one of them had a knife, came up to him and told him to give up his groceries and his wallet. The guy handed them the groceries and it looked like he was getting his wallet to give them, but he pulled out a gun and shot the one closest to him in the chest. The other three dropped the groceries and took off running. He shot at them. One dropped dead in his tracks, he hit the other in the leg and the last one got away.

He walked over to the man he shot in the leg and told him to go pick up the groceries and put them back in the bag. The injured guy was begging him not to shoot him, his girlfriend was crying; it was insane. The mugger crawled over and put the groceries in the bag, begging the guy the whole time not to shoot him.

The man with the gun took the groceries, handed them to the girlfriend and shot the injured criminal in the head. He said something to the effect that he was doing him and everyone else a favor."

Steven turned to Danny. "Are you sticking to that theory about decent people not being violent yet?"

Danny sat with his eyes wide open. "That guy sounds like he was blood-thirsty to begin with. He was probably hoping to get a chance to blow somebody away like that. I mean, if someone is mugging you, sure, shoot them. But once they're not threatening your life or property, how do you just waste them?"

Alisa was now sitting by the cat carrier. "Poor little thing, your cat is shaking. Can we take her out?"

Dana dried her eyes with her shirt sleeve. "Yeah, that's Puddin'. She hates loud noises; I can't imagine what she thought about the shooting."

Alisa opened the top of the carrier and a fluffy, blonde flash of fur shot straight under the couch. "Wow. I can't believe such a fat animal fit under that small space!"

Dana sniffed and finally cracked a smile. "It's

mostly fur."

Danny asked "Is she a Ragdoll?"

Dana shrugged. "No. Ragdolls are bigger, and more docile. She's just a feral cat I started feeding, who finally made her way into my apartment. She probably has some long-haired breed mixed in, maybe Himalayan or Ragamuffin.

"I know you said I could only bring one bag, but that cat is my life. If there's no room, I'll leave my belongings and take the cat."

Danny felt horrible for the girl. "We'll make room for your cat in the car, but like I told you, I can't make any guarantees when we get to Nana's."

Dana lay down on the floor so she could stick her hand under the couch. "I understand. Puddin' lived outside for several months, even after I started feeding her. She's pretty resourceful, so even if she has a barn or something, she'd be okay."

Danny nodded. "That might work out. We'll see."

Steven stood to look out the window. "So it's settled. We should wait 'til morning to leave?"

Danny looked at Alisa who didn't seem to object. "I think that's our best bet. We're keeping our guns close by the bed. You should do the same Steven."

"Dana, you can have the couch. I'll roll my sleeping bag out on the floor." Steven retrieved his shotgun from his bug-out bag in two separate pieces. He screwed the barrel into the tubular magazine.

"Wouldn't that fit if it were already put together?" Danny asked.

"No. The barrel would stick out of the top an

inch or two. Since I had your pistol, I thought it would be best to keep it as concealed as possible. I'll stick a sock over it or something in the morning when we leave." Steven then loaded the gun and racked the pump to send a shell into the chamber.

Dana stared at the weapon with fearful eyes.

Alisa seemed to notice and asked, "Have you ever shot a gun?"

"No." Dana answered quietly.

Danny winked at Dana. "You're from North Carolina. How is that possible? Alisa is from the land of the liberals, she has an excuse."

Dana forced a grin. "I must have slipped through the cracks."

Danny chuckled. "Well, I suppose you've been made painfully aware, it might be a good skill to have in the coming days. Do you mind if I show you the basics?"

Dana sat up. "I guess."

Danny turned toward Steven. "Can I see the revolver?"

"Sure." Steven passed it to Danny.

Danny opened the cylinder and emptied out the bullets. He proceeded to give Dana the basics of firearm safety, just as Nick had done for him. Next he passed the unloaded weapon to Dana. "Go ahead and find a target on the wall, then pull the trigger."

Dana tried to do as he asked. "Like this?"

"Cup your right hand with the left and straighten out your right arm a little more. You want a good firm grip on it." He gently helped her adjust her form.

She pulled the trigger. Click. "That wasn't so

bad."

"Good job." Danny took the pistol and reloaded it.

Alisa stood. "Let's eat. We've got a ton of stuff in the fridge that is either getting eaten tonight or not at all. Then Danny wants to have a memorial service for his last bowl of ice cream."

He rolled his eyes. "That's a little exaggerated."

Steven finished flattening out his sleeping bed on the floor near the boxes. "Ha. I doubt it."

Alisa asked, "Do you have food for Puddin'?"

"Yes, I have a half bag of dry food for her."

"Will she eat people food?" Alisa opened the fridge and looked inside with the flashlight.

"Sure." Dana made scratching sound on the floor near the edge of the couch to try to coax her pet to come out.

"We've got cold vegetable beef soup, homemade, by Danny. A slice of cold pizza, hot dogs that have been in here since before Danny moved in; he won't eat those."

"Puddin' loves hot dogs," Dana said.

Steven raised his hand. "And Steven loves cold pizza."

"Technically, hot dogs are fully cooked, so you could eat them cold, if you want one. I have buns."

"Sure, I'll try it." Dana smiled.

"I'll have some of the vegetable soup. But I'm not eating it cold." Danny took his flashlight and dug his folding stove and a can of Sterno from his bug-out bag.

"I'm having cheese and bread. If anyone else wants some, there's plenty to share." Alisa began taking things out of the fridge and passing them around.

Steven lost his playful expression. "Can we pray before we eat? We should be thankful for what we have. A lot of folks aren't going to live through the next few weeks."

"Good idea." Danny stooped what he was doing. "Steven, would you like to ask the blessing?"

"Sure." He bowed his head. "God, we're so grateful that you gave us a heads up before this calamity hit us. We thank you for all of the provision that you've provided for us and the wisdom you've granted us in helping us prepare. We hope that through this hardship, folks will recognize their need for you, and perhaps, they will call on you for assistance and you will hear them and help them. The streets are restless tonight, I ask that you'll protect us 'til morning and give us a safe journey tomorrow. We love you God. Thanks for everything. Amen."

Dana looked at him curiously. "Heads up? Thanks for everything? You talk to God like that?"

"Why? I thought you didn't believe in God. How do you think I should talk to him?" Steven bit into his cold pizza.

She broke off a small piece of hot dog and laid it on the floor, near the edge of the couch. The hot dog vanished under a quick brush of yellow fur. "I never said I didn't believe he existed. I don't know how you should talk to him. I never thought about it. I wasn't being critical of how you did it, it just surprised me, that's all."

Danny stirred his soup over the folding multifuel stove. "I think he is more concerned that we talk to him at all, rather than how we talk to him."

She placed the subsequent pieces of hot dog farther and farther from the edge of the couch, forcing Puddin' to come out in the open to keep eating. "I guess I would have felt silly talking to God. Why would he care about anything I had to say?"

"Even if you don't believe in Jesus, if you just think God exists, he cared enough to make you in the first place, right? I mean, that's something." Alisa ate a piece of the cheese she was using for her sandwich.

"Yeah." Dana was finally able to pick up Puddin' and hold her.

Danny tasted to see how hot his soup was. "Look at your cat. What can she do for you? She can't make you breakfast, she can't build you a house, she can't buy you a car, but you love her."

Dana snuggled her nose in the cat's fur. "I get your point."

"Then you'd admit it is at least conceivable that God could love you for the sole purpose of being loved in return. That's why he cares what you have to say." Steven took the piece of cheese being offered to him by Alisa.

"I guess, but you guys don't all have to gang up on me." Dana took a bite of her hot dog.

Danny didn't say anything, but he felt like that was a good start. He remembered how stubborn he'd been about the matter. He ate his soup and silently thanked God for how patient he'd been in waiting for him to come around.

They finished eating most of the things from the fridge, then they polished off the two different flavors of ice cream. Alisa gave Puddin' a taste of her dulce de leche ice cream, which earned her an instant friendship with the creature.

Alisa put her empty bowl in the sink and went to rinse it, but of course, no water came out of the spigot. "It's going to take a while to get used to not having water."

"Can we flush the toilet?" Dana asked.

Danny said, "We stored about thirty gallons of water. I'd like to take at least ten gallons with us, just in case. The rest, I suppose we can use to brush our teeth, wash our face and flush the toilet."

Steven lay down on his sleeping bag. "We should try to get some sleep. Daybreak is going to come early and we need to be able to think."

Alisa said, "I've got a battery operated alarm clock. What time should we set it for?"

"Six. The sun comes up around 7:00. That's when I want to be pulling away from the curb," Danny replied.

Alisa brought a pillow and comforter out for Dana. "Sleep tight."

Dana spread out the comforter on the couch. "Thanks. Puddin', come here."

The cat was walking across Steven's sleeping bag to inspect it.

Steven gave the animal a scratch behind the ear. "She's not bothering me."

Danny sighed. The cat introduced a new set of challenges, but being the perfect intersection of an alley cat and a high-bred aristocrat, Puddin' was too cute to ignore. And that offered a valuable distraction from the ongoing meltdown of the world that was.

"Good night." Danny followed Alisa into the bedroom and closed the door.

CHAPTER 20

Because thou hast made the LORD, which is my refuge, even the most High, thy habitation; there shall no evil befall thee, neither shall any plague come nigh thy dwelling. For he shall give his angels charge over thee, to keep thee in all thy ways.

Psalms 91: 9-11

Danny turned over as Alisa shook him. "What?"

"Wake up. There were gun shots outside. It sounded like it was on our street!" her voice was frantic.

Danny grabbed his flashlight and his Glock from the night stand. Then he heard a bump in the living room. He hurried to the door. "Are you guys okay? What was that noise?"

Dana sat up on the couch. "It was my cat. The gun shots scared her and she ran under the couch."

"Smart cat. Steven, did you hear where the gun shots came from?"

Steven lit a match and held it high so he could locate his candle. "No. I didn't even hear them. I was out cold."

"I heard them. They came from right out front. I was wide awake." Dana shielded her eyes from Danny's flashlight.

Danny lowered the light. He hadn't noticed that he had it pointed right in her face. "Sorry. I'm going to check and make sure the car is okay."

Alisa came out in her robe. "No Danny. Stay inside."

"I'm just going to the entrance door where I can see the Camaro."

Steven put on one shoe, then the other. "I'll be right behind him."

Danny grabbed a jacket so he could conceal the pistol in the pocket then quietly opened the door.

Steven grabbed the shotgun and followed him. "Keep your flashlight off. There should be enough moonlight to tell if the car is okay or not."

Danny pointed at the shotgun. "Put that thing away. Grab the pistol and keep it hidden. All we need is for one Alisa's neighbors to walk out of their door, see that and start screaming."

"Where did you put it?"

Danny shinned the flashlight to the kitchen counter. "Right there."

Steven went to grab it. He propped the shotgun up against the inside door frame. "This will be close by if we need it. Are you sure you reloaded the revolver?"

"Positive." Danny made his way to the entrance door and peeked out.

"Do you see anything?"

Danny scanned the area thoroughly. "No. Nothing."

Steven looked over Danny's shoulder. "The car is still there."

"Yeah."

The two of them waited to see if there was any more activity, then went back inside.

Danny closed the door and locked the dead bolt. "What time is it?"

Alisa was sitting on the couch, next to Dana's feet. "4:30, no use trying to go back to sleep now."

"It's going to be a long day." Danny made his way to the kitchen area and picked up the coffee pot. "I wish we had an old percolator like Nana's."

Alisa walked in behind him and took out the coffee filters. "I have an idea. Start boiling some water in a sauce pan."

Alisa's creative side allowed her to think outside of the box in finding solutions. Danny suddenly had a new appreciation for that aspect of his young wife. It would be very helpful in getting through the days to come. He lit the Sterno in the folding stove and filled a pan with a jug of the stored water.

Alisa took the flashlight to her room and returned shortly with a stapler. "We'll just fill the coffee filter as usual and then staple it shut, like a tea bag."

"Good thinking." Danny took some bowls out of the cupboard and called out to Steven and Dana. "I put the milk in the freezer last night, so it's still cold if you guys want cereal."

Dana came to make a bowl for herself.

Danny pulled out another small bowl. "Would Puddin' drink some milk?"

"Thanks, but she'd probably rather have a piece of hot dog."

"Sure." Danny took out the remaining hot dogs from the now, room-temperature fridge and handed them to her.

Once breakfast was finished, they still had over an hour before it would be time to start loading the car.

Danny went over the seating arrangements again, specifying that he would have the Glock, Steven would be in the passenger's side with the AK-47, Alisa would be in the driver's side back seat with the shotgun and Dana would have the revolver, and sit behind Steven.

They finished packing everything and getting it by the door. Alisa looked at the bike rack that would go on the trunk. "How will we get all three bikes on here?"

Steven demonstrated using the plastic clasps with the Velcro straps. "These two on the back of the rack are static, so they'll hold the bike on the outside. The other two can be moved back and forth on the rail, so we can split them between the two inside bikes, which are less likely to fall off anyway. This rack fits two bikes comfortably, but we can squeeze three if we position the handlebars and pedals just right."

They all sat quietly in the living room, watching

the flicker of the candle while they waited for the minutes to tick away and for daylight to appear.

Steven said, "We could spend this time asking God to protect us. We're going to need it."

Steven, Danny and Alisa said a short prayer, one at a time.

Danny was ready to raise his head when he heard Dana's voice.

"God." She paused for a moment. "If you're there, if you're listening, please keep us safe." She was quiet again for several seconds. "And thank you for letting me be part of this group."

"Amen!" Alisa put her arm around Dana.

Danny picked up the small battery-operated clock from Alisa's nightstand. "6:45. Let's load up. We'll all take what we can carry. Steven, you stay downstairs and watch the car from inside the entrance door. You'll have the pistol and Alisa's bug-out bag with the AK by your side. We need everything that we're putting in that car, so if someone tries to take something, it's the same as putting a gun to our head and pulling the trigger. Do what you have to do to protect it. If you don't think you can, let me know and I'll take that position."

Steven breathed in as if he was processing what Danny had said. Then he gave a confident nod. "I can do it."

Dana coaxed Puddin' out from under the couch and put her in the carrier.

"Okay. Let's bug out!" Danny took two extra magazines from his pack and stuck them in his back pocket. He grabbed his bug-out bag and led the way down the stairs. He looked out the entrance door before opening it. The faint orange glow on the horizon offered just enough illumination for him to verify that no one was walking around in their immediate area. He opened the door and walked silently down the stairs and to the car. He carefully put the key in the trunk and opened it. Danny took each person's load and positioned it in the trunk. Danny lowered the trunk but didn't lock it. He made eye contact with Steven, pointed at his eye, then at the trunk.

Steven nodded that he understood, walked up the stairs and placed Alisa's bug-out bag next to his feet. He opened the top flap so the AK would be easily accessible if need be.

Danny led the girls back to the apartment for the second load. They gathered the next batch of high-priority items and headed back toward the car. Steven held the door open for them as they went in and out loading up as much as possible. Once the trunk was filled, they mounted the bikes on the back.

As day break progressed, the details became more apparent. Alisa covered her mouth and pointed at the street.

"What?" Danny looked at a dark spot on the pavement.

"Blood!"

Danny grimaced. "Let's keep moving so we can get out of here."

There was room for a few more boxes and some spare water jugs on the back seat between the two girls, but they had very little leg room and not an inch of extra space on the seat. Dana held the cat carrier in her lap. Each of them closed the doors as quietly as possible, but the big heavy doors of the classic hot rod were made of thick metal, and there was a limit to how softly they could be shut.

Danny took the pistol out of the back of his pants and stuck it under his leg. He put the keys in the ignition and started the car. "God, keep us safe, please!"

He pulled out into the street and didn't get far before he was blocked by several stalled cars. "Oglethorpe is going to be like this all the way to the highway. The median keeps me from being able to go around."

Steven said, "If you go down to Broughton, you'd be able to drive on either side. No median."

Alisa leaned forward. "Or you could take the alley, then cut over to Hull. Smaller streets but less used on a Thursday night, which is when the cars died."

"Good plan." Danny backed up and took Alisa's advice.

When they turned onto Hull, Danny had to stop the car again. A horse and buggy was trying to maneuver its way between two stalled cars. Three men, all in dark hoodies, were in the buggy and they avoided eye contact with Danny.

"I'm guessing they aren't the legal owners of that carriage," Dana said.

"You're probably right, but it's not our concern." Danny waited for them to pass then navigated the Camaro through the same small path.

They made it to the Highway 17 on-ramp before they encountered another blockade of disabled vehicles.

Danny pulled to the side. "We have to get through this. Alisa, you drive. Steven and I will move the cars."

"How are you going to do that?" she asked.

"It's an on-ramp. We'll put them in neutral and they'll roll backwards. Just make sure the Camaro isn't in the way when they start rolling."

"How will you get in the car to change the gear?"

"Bust the windows," Danny said.

"With what?" Danna asked.

Steven took out his keys. "A bike lock will do it."

Danny got out. "Dana, sit up front. You're the primary security person until we get these cars moved."

Steven removed the U-shaped Kryptonite lock from the frame of his bike on the back of the car.

Danny checked the door. "Locked."

Steven stepped forward and smashed the heavy end of the lock into the window and it shattered.

Danny stood back. He half expected the alarm to go off. Of course, it didn't. He opened the door, and carefully brushed the shattered glass out of the seat with the sleeve of his jacket. He sat down, put his foot on the break and tried to put the car in neutral. "Locked."

"Got a screwdriver?" Steven asked.

"In the glove compartment." Danny waited for Steven to return with the screwdriver.

"Stick this in the ignition and give it a few good whacks." Steven handed him the screwdriver, then separated the heavier locking mechanism from the

U-shaped bar of the bike lock. He handed the heavy, straight-bar for Danny to use as a hammer.

It took Danny a little more than a few good whacks, but with a little brute strength, he was finally able to put the car in neutral. "Tell Alisa to back it up a little more. I'm not sure how fast this thing is going to roll."

Steven did so and called out once she was well clear of the rolling vehicle. "Okay, you're good!"

Danny let his foot off of the break and stepped out. The car rolled backwards down the on-ramp until it careened into the guard rail. They repeated the process for one more car then they had a clear path onto the highway. Everyone resumed their original positions in the Camaro and they continued the journey.

Once they reached Highway 17, he was able to drive a little faster as it was somewhat more open. The occasional cluster of stalled cars would require him to slow to a crawl, but they became less frequent as they got farther and farther away from Savannah. It took over an hour to make the short twenty-mile drive to Eden, but after he turned onto U.S. 25, he was able to open up the engine and make up for lost time.

It was after 10:00 when they reached Waynesboro, Georgia. The U.S. 25 Bypass allowed them to avoid going through the center of town. As they neared the point where the bypass intersected with the main road, Steven pointed forward. "You might want to slow down, people are walking around in the middle of the road up here."

Alisa leaned forward from the back seat. "What

are they doing?"

"Looks like they're pushing shopping carts." Dana's voice came from the rear of the car.

As Danny got closer, he could make out more details about what was happening. "That's a Wal-Mart around the curve. I guess they're looting in broad daylight."

Approximately fifteen people were pushing shopping carts, south in the northbound lane, back toward town. Since Walmart was on the right, the looters were following the path of least resistance in using the northbound lane. Danny slowed down, and drove across the median, which simply consisted of grass and provided little to no hazard to the vehicle. The people pushing the carts pointed at the Camaro as it drove past. Danny had to maintain a moderate speed, as there were quite a few cars littered about in the southbound lane. On top of it all, he still had to deal with the physiological aspect of driving into oncoming traffic. Although the cars that were facing him hadn't moved for hours, and the odds of other cars coming were slim, something in his brain didn't want him in that lane. More looters waved their hands and shouted something as they passed. One man on a bike gave them pursuit, but stood no chance against the suped-up classic car.

Steven chuckled as they drove past the crowd. "Did you see that lady's cart? She had a flat screen television."

Alisa giggled. "She can tear out the back and do a puppet show through the screen."

"The cart I saw was filled with what looked like

electronics; video games, DVDs, CDs," Dana said.

Danny shook his head. "I guess the fact that their cars, phones, and battery operated devices don't work still hasn't sunk in. Or maybe they can't figure out that if those items don't work, the ones at the store probably won't either."

"Live and learn." Steven gazed out the window.

"More like die and don't learn," Alisa retorted.

Once Danny passed the mayhem, he quickly crossed back over the grass median into the northbound lane. "Unfortunately, you're probably right Alisa. Anyone in that group with half a chance of surviving would have stocked up on any remaining food. Next, they'd make a run for camping, hunting and fishing items. Then, gone back for any remaining consumables, like soap, shampoo, cold medicine, pain relievers, and first aid supplies. Finally, they'd go back and get clothes."

"What about toilet paper?" Steven turned toward Danny. "I'd be stocking up on that."

"And trash bags. I'd get trash bags, and duct tape, and canning supplies," Alisa added.

Danny stayed focused on the road ahead. "Yeah, all of that stuff will have more utility than a flat screen."

"But, aren't all of you supposed to be Christians? Doesn't the Bible say thou shall not steal?" Dana quizzed.

Steven quipped, "You're a believer now? Listen to this, Danny, she's quoting Scriptures!"

Dana's voice was surly. "It wasn't a criticism, Steven. I'm only looking for an explanation."

Steven turned around toward the back seat. "I

was just busting your chops. But you have to understand, from our perspective, people who couldn't care less about what the Bible says and have no desire to understand the context, are always so quick to whip out Scriptures to bash Christians with."

"But, to answer your question, yes, it's wrong to steal. That's the short answer."

"We're stuck in the car for the next few hours, I guess I've got time for the long answer if you feel like telling me." Dana sounded as if she had a genuine interest in hearing what Steven had to say.

"Okay, well, the Bible is very clear in Proverbs chapter 6 that we should take lessons from the ant and store up provisions in the summer, so we'll have food for the winter. So, I suppose that would be the higher road. Since the majority of Americans learn more from Wimpy than the ant . . ."

Alisa cut him off. "Wimpy? Who's Wimpy? Is he in the Bible?"

Steven busted out laughing. "Seriously? Wimpy! From Popeye."

"Popeye?"

"The guy who eats the spinach and get super strong. You know, the cartoon."

She replied, "I've got nothin'; I guess we didn't get that channel."

"Forget about Popeye, but he had this friend, Wimpy, his shtick was that he was a moocher and he would always tell people I'll gladly pay you Tuesday for a hamburger today."

"I don't get it. Did Popeye have a hamburger stand?"

"You're missing the point. Wimpy is the quintessential American who wants goods and services today and wants to pay for it later."

"Oh, that was a long way of explaining it."

Steven rubbed his head. "Back to the question; is stealing wrong? Had folks followed the fundamental example of the ant rather than Wimpy, they'd be in much better shape."

"Couldn't you say grasshopper instead of Wimpy? I think more people are familiar with Aesop's fable of the ant and the grasshopper than Popeye." Alisa continued to pester Steven with this line of contention.

Steven ignored her statement. "Since they didn't, now they aren't in a position to provide for their families, which is also a directive given by Paul in First Timothy chapter 5.

"Being forced to choose between stealing and watching your family starve, most people, even Christians, will decide that stealing is the lesser of the two evils. In fact, when faced with starvation, most people will choose a lot of things which they come to think of as lesser evils."

"Like what?" Alisa asked.

Steven paused. When he spoke again, his voice was much more reverent. "In Second Kings, during the siege of Samaria, women were eating their own children. There are also records of women feeding one of their children to their other kids to keep them alive during the Holodomor."

"What was that?" Dana's voice sounded horrified.

"It was when the Soviets tried to starve off the

ethnic Ukrainians during the 1930s. Millions of people died.

"Then, after World War II ended, Germany was wrecked. Women would prostitute themselves for the occupying soldiers' food. For like one meal, and I'm not talking about trashy women, I mean high society women. They were doing anything they could to not starve or watch their children starve.

"Even now, before the EMP, the going rate for a prostitute in Greece had sunk all the way down to four euros an hour. And once again, not trashy druggy chicks, girls that would have otherwise been in college. Since the Greek economic crisis, they have no options. There's no work and no way to get by.

"So, yes, stealing is wrong, but when it comes down to dying of hunger or watching their kids die, people, even Christians, are going to be doing a lot worse things than stealing before we get through this crisis."

No one said a word.

Then, Steven sighed. "Unfortunately, most Christians who weren't prepared for this, will try to cling to a higher moral standard longer, so by the time they decide stealing is the lesser evil, there won't be anything left to take. They'll have to skip directly to the subsequent phase of depravity."

"Which is?" Alisa pried.

"Worse than stealing, but people will do whatever they have to when they're desperate," Steven said.

The inside of the car was silent, except for the hum of the tires against the pavement, for the next several miles.

The first break in the soundlessness came from Alisa. "I have to pee."

"Okay, we'll find a place to pull over." Danny scanned the road.

Steven said, "We should avoid the standard pit stops. I'd look for a spot off the beaten trail."

"Yeah, I'll try to avoid people."

"Well, I'm not going on the side of the road. I'm not a boy," Alisa protested.

Danny grinned. "I'm quite aware of that."

He continued on for a couple more miles, then took a right onto Northlake Road. It was a well-to-do neighborhood that was heavily wooded.

"This is a subdivision, Danny." Alisa's voice showed her disapproval.

"The houses are pretty spread out. Look, there's a lake with woods all around. I can drive right up into the tree line." He pulled off into the grass and parked at the opening of the woods.

"Yeah, no one will notice a purple Camaro with a loud eight-cylinder engine roaring." She opened the door.

"It's midnight blue, not purple. Just hurry! Everyone should go if they can. Obviously, every time we stop, it creates a security issue." Danny tucked the Glock in the back of his pants, got out and headed in the opposite direction from Alisa.

He returned to the car soon after and waited for the others to return. Steven, like himself, hadn't gone far for his break, so he was next to return. Alisa and Dana returned together about a minute later, walking leisurely.

Danny waved for them to hurry, and shortly thereafter, they were back in the car and the group was on their way.

As they approached Augusta, Georgia, Danny had to slow down as the amount of stranded vehicles strewn about the road increased.

Steven held an open Atlas in his hand. "520 is up here on the right. You can take it around Augusta. If people in that little town were looting already, I suspect Augusta might be getting pretty rough by now."

"Good call. Which way?"

Steven looked at the map. "Southeast is the more direct route. Northwest takes you farther from the center of town, but looks like it is just as populated around the highway. In fact, I'd say it might even expose us to more people than the direct route."

The last few miles before they turned onto the 520 Expressway were increasingly congested. People were outside and took notice of a working automobile. An old, rusted out pickup truck from the '70s was coming off the Bobby Jones Expressway as they were coming on.

Steven commented. "I bet his friends don't make fun of his truck anymore."

"Still, not as cool as our car." Alisa said.

The expressway had a moderate amount of stalled cars, so Danny could only drive about twenty-five miles per hour. In multiple instances, he had to come to a crawl to work his way in between the cars or pass in the emergency lane. It took over an hour to reach the interchange where they would link back up with US 25 north.

As they came down the exit ramp, once again, they were completely blocked off by stalled cars.

"Okay, everyone knows the drill." Danny put the car in park and opened the door.

Alisa came up front to the driver's seat, Dana came to the front passenger's side and Steven got out, carrying the U-shaped bike lock.

Danny instructed Alisa. "We're trying to push the stalled cars in the other direction this time, so stay close. We might need you to nudge them forward a bit."

"Okay." She blew him a kiss.

"Ya'll need any help?" A man's voice called from the top of the ramp. He and another man were walking toward them.

Danny froze in his tracks. His heart began pounding.

Steven looked over at him. "Why would these guys be walking on the expressway?"

"This isn't right." Danny turned to face the men and put his hand on the handle of the Glock. He called to the men. "No thanks. We're fine."

"Why don't you let us give you a hand." The men kept advancing.

Adrenaline pulsed through Danny's veins. His hands were shaking like a leaf. He pulled the pistol out and pointed at the man closest to him. "I said, no thank you! Walk away!"

"Hey, that's no way to treat people. We were just trying to help." The man put his hands in the air.

Steven motioned for Dana to give him the AK. She opened the door, handed the rifle to him, took the bike lock and shut the door.

Steven leveled the rifle at the second man. "Danny, what do you want to do?"

"Let's get back in the car, get back on the expressway and find another exit that's not blocked." Danny kept the pistol aimed at the men.

Alisa had the window down so she could hear Danny's instructions "Do you want to drive? Should I get in the back?"

"I'm going to need you to drive, sweetie. Steven and I are going to need to watch these guys while you back up the ramp."

"I'm scared."

"I know, baby. It's going to be okay. Once we get back on the expressway, I'll switch with you." Despite his fear, Danny tried to make his voice as soothing as possible.

Danny and Steven got in the back and rolled down the windows so they could keep their weapons trained on the men.

The two men stepped behind a stalled vehicle and yelled. "We're going to teach you some manners."

Two other men stepped out with long guns and blocked the path of the car. Then the first two men retrieved rifles from behind the car and came back out.

"They've got guns! What do we do?" Alisa's voice was cracking.

The first man yelled. "We just want the car. No one has to get hurt. Get out of the car."

"Put it in reverse and go, as fast as you can drive, go!" Danny shouted.

"But they're in the way!" Alisa protested.

"Then run them over. They'll move." Danny said.

Dana was crying. "Let's just give them the car."

"No. We need this car and everything in it to survive. Besides, there is no guarantee they'd let us live anyway." Danny's mind was made up. The topic was closed for discussion.

"Alisa, go! Now!" he yelled.

She hit the gas and began speeding backwards toward the men. One took a shot but missed. Danny stuck the pistol out the window, facing the back and took a shot. He missed, but fired several other times. One of the men went down in the road. Steven was leaning out the passenger's side and firing the AK-47 as fast as he could. The remaining men ducked behind the stalled vehicle. Alisa drove right over the downed man. The car popped up in the air and back down as both of the driver's side tires thumped over the fallen attacker. It was just enough to cause Alisa to lose control of the car and the Camaro bashed into the concrete barrier at an angle and came to a complete halt.

The car was now pressed up against the barrier, just passed the stalled vehicle the men had been using for cover. The remaining assailants leaped up and began firing.

Steven called out, "I'm up against the wall. I can't get out to shoot. Alisa, you have to go forward a little to get off the wall so you can keep backing up."

"Okay." She was crying, but managed to follow Steven's instructions.

Danny kept firing until his magazine was empty.

"Steven, trade me."

Steven took the Glock and handed Danny the AK.

"Thanks," Danny made the exchange and tossed a new Glock magazine from his back pocket to Steven. He stuck the rifle out the window, took aim and fired. He watched two of bullets find the chest of one of the men; another one of the aggressors went down. He continued shooting until the rifle was empty.

Alisa kept a steady even speed as she fled, in reverse, up the exit ramp and back onto the expressway.

Steven reloaded the Glock and took several more shots as they moved out of range of their assailants.

Alisa continued to drive backwards on the expressway. "What should I do?"

"If you see a good spot to flip around so you can go the other direction, do it." Danny watched to see if any of the men were still pursuing them on foot.

"Okay." She slowly backed up to the shoulder and turned the car around. "I think the car is smoking, Danny."

Danny whipped his head around toward the front to see steam pouring from under the hood. "Rats. They hit the radiator. Keep driving but keep your eye on the temperature gauge."

Steven pointed over the back seat. "There's an exit. Take it. Dana, pass me the Atlas next to your seat."

Alisa had to make a sharp turn since the car was now traveling south in the northbound lane.

Dana passed the Atlas back to Steven.

"Thanks." He took it and began scanning the page it had been opened to. "This road should run right into US 25. We'll have to go through town, but if we keep moving, I think we'll be okay."

"The temperature is climbing. Should I keep going?" Alisa asked.

"Keep going. We need to get out of here." Danny peered over the seat to see the gauge. It was still registered below the red zone.

Ascauga Lake Road, the street they'd exited onto ended only yards from the ramp. "Is this US 25?" Alisa looked for signage. "It says Edgefield."

"This is 25, I saw a sign back there. Hang a right." Steven said.

They continued through the outskirts of North Augusta. Soon they came to an intersection. "This is where we would have come through if it hadn't been for the ambush." Danny looked toward the interchange on the right.

"It's getting really hot now. What should I do?" Alisa's voice was still frantic.

Danny looked around. They were still in a populated area. "It's thinning out around here, but let's try to go another mile." He held his breath as he watched the temperature gauge creeping deeper and deeper into the red zone.

"It's been a mile Danny," Alisa said.

"I'm watching for a good place to pull off." Danny's eyes bounced back and forth from the gauge to the road ahead.

Finally, he spotted a location that might offer a safe harbor temporarily. "Pull into that church parking lot ahead. Drive around to the back of the building."

The tiny church had a thick coat of chalky white paint directly over the cement blocks. The empty parking lot, which could accommodate perhaps ten cars before congregants would have to park on the grass, was surrounded by woods.

Alisa turned into the lot of Mt Zion Baptist. "It looks like less smoke is coming out of the engine."

"That was steam. If it's not coming out, that means there's no more water in the engine." Steven's voice was not overly optimistic. "But we're alive. Thank God for that."

Danny got out, as did everyone else. He popped the hood. Only a trickle of steam poured out of the large hole in the radiator.

Alisa walked over by him. She put her arms around him and burrowed her head in his neck. "I'm so scared."

He turned away from the car. "It's okay. We're alive. God protected us."

Danny looked over at Steven and Dana who were both sitting in the grass. Dana was bawling her eyes out and Steven had his arm around her and was pulling her long, strawberry blonde hair out of her eyes. He whispered to Alisa as he pulled her close. "Everything is going to be just fine."

CHAPTER 21

These things I have spoken unto you, that in me ye might have peace. In the world ye shall have tribulation: but be of good cheer; I have overcome the world.

John 16:33

Danny put his hand near the radiator cap to see if it was still hot. The car had been sitting for nearly an hour. He touched the cap lightly to check if he would be able to open it. "Feels pretty cool. Do you think it's okay to open it now?"

"Yeah, the pressure is what's dangerous. I'd say that bullet hole pretty much took care of that." Steven leaned over to look around the engine.

"Any chance we can patch it up?"

Steven shook his head. "I don't know. The good

news is, the bullet hole is just under the midpoint of the radiator. Theoretically, it should allow us to fill it to about forty percent. If we had screws roughly the size of the holes, we could patch the holes, but it would probably fail as soon as the radiator starts building pressure."

"How far could we go before that happens?"

Steven shrugged. "Maybe a mile, maybe five."

Alisa walked up to where the boys were standing. "I need to get that paracord out of your bag."

"Don't you have some in your bag? It's up front," Danny said.

"Nope. I checked already. I'm going to make a little harness for Puddin'. She needs to get out of the carrier to go to the bathroom. Dana is afraid that the gunfire stressed the cat out. She thinks if she lets her out, she might run off into the woods."

Danny smirked. "I know the feeling. We have to pull everything out try to find a way to patch the radiator any way. I'll get it for you."

"Thanks." She kissed him on the cheek.

The three of them walked to the back of the car and began unloading the bikes from the bike rack so they could open the trunk. Danny pulled the paracord out for Alisa.

"What about the bolts holding the trunk on? Could we use any of those to patch the radiator?" Danny scanned all of the connected parts inside the trunk to see if there were any salvageable screws.

Steven looked at the bolts. "It would have to be exactly the right size, and we'd need two of them."

"If it was little too small, couldn't we wrap them

with duct tape?"

Steven's face showed his despair. "I don't think so, Danny. It would have to be a short, fat screw that gradually gets larger. A bolt won't work."

"What if the bolt were long enough to go all the way through the radiator so we could put a nut on the other side? We could cut a piece of rubber from the spare tire to make washers." Danny was desperately trying to think of a way to fix the car.

Steven sighed. "If the entrance and exit holes were lined up perfectly, which they probably aren't and if you could find a bolt and nut that are approximately the same diameter as the holes, which I seriously doubt, that might work for a couple of miles, but I still don't think it would hold up under pressure."

Discouraged, Danny took a seat on the ground next to the bikes. "Could we keep pulling over and filling the radiator all the way back to Nana's?"

"Not the way we just did it. We would have to pull over every two or three miles and give the engine an hour or two to cool off. And we have to do that, regardless of whether it's a safe place to pull over or not."

Danny thought for a while. "I'm going to grab the map and see how much farther we have to go."

Danny retrieved the map from the car and brought it back over to where Steven was sitting. "Looks like we've got about a hundred miles left. I guess we could make it on the bikes if we had to."

"Three bikes, four people. That'll be a heck of a ride."

"And a cat."

Steven looked at Danny. "We have to be sensible. We'll be lucky if we can get all four people home safely."

Danny shook his head. "She'll never forgive us if we make her abandon the cat. Besides, I'm not convinced she will even go without it."

Steven took the map from Danny and studied it. "We'd have to abandon that much more gear if we took the cat. How could we get everyone back on three bikes anyway?"

Danny stood up and inspected the bikes. "The girls could take turns riding on the handlebars. The cat carrier can dangle off the handlebars of one of the bikes, and not one with a person already riding on it, obviously. All we need to take are the guns, and enough supplies to get us home. We have food and clothing at Nana's."

"I vote that we drive the Camaro as far as we can. Trenton looks like the next town, if you could call it that. It doesn't look like it's very populated. After that, Edgefield is the next town, a little bigger than Trenton from the looks of the map. It's about fifteen miles from here. It will probably take us the rest of the day to get there, moving in three-to-five-mile jumps at a time, letting the car cool off and refilling the radiator."

"Okay, let's give it a shot." Danny walked over to the girls. "Ladies, we're loading up and heading out."

Steven and Danny filled the radiator to the top of the lowest hole, then filled the overflow tank. They put the bikes back on the rack and everyone got in the car.

Danny turned the key and the only noise it made was the sound of the starter clicking. "That can't be good."

"Give it some gas," Steven said.

"I hit the pedal when I turned the key." Danny turned the key, but got roughly the same result.

"Sounds like it's done." Steven leaned back and looked out the window.

"What? My car won't start back up? I thought you guys said this was a good car and that it would last for many years." Alisa sounded upset.

"We didn't take into account that it would get shot and we'd have to flee for our lives while the engine overheated," Steven said.

"I know, I'm just upset," she said. "Can we fix it?"

"No. We'll have to get to Nana's on bikes," Danny answered.

"I don't have a bike." Dana's voice was worried.

"I think we figured all that out." Danny laid out the plan for how they would work the bikes.

"How long will it take us to get to Nana's?" Alisa asked.

"We could probably walk there in about five days, or less than that, I hope." Danny opened the door and got out.

Everyone else did as well. They walked to the back of the car and took the bikes off the rack, again.

Danny opened the trunk. "We need to figure out how much stuff we can carry, then decide what to take and what to leave behind."

They began the process of going through everything. Unpacking and repacking the bug-out bags to make them as light as possible yet keeping the most critical items.

Alisa tied 2 one-gallon jugs together with paracord so they could dangle off each side of a bike, with each jug acting as a counter weight for the other.

"We should eat a huge meal and drink a lot of water before we head out. We'd have that much less to leave behind or carry," Steven suggested.

"Yeah, I'm getting hungry anyway." Danny glanced at his watch. "Wow, nearly two o'clock. Time flies when you're surviving the end of the world."

Dana looked at his watch. "How is your watch working?"

"My brother-in-law Nick, you'll meet him at Nana's, recommended that I get a G-Shock. I guess it was good advice. Anyway, from what I understand about EMPs, the wave can't couple directly into something as small as a watch."

She crossed her arms. "My phone wasn't much bigger, and it's fried."

"It has an internal antenna, which is specifically designed to catch a radio wave; that's essentially what an EMP is," he explained. "The EMP destroys the circuitry, the microchips; but the EMP wave is too long to directly affect them. Something has to act as an antenna and pull the pulse into the chip."

"Hmm. I wish I'd known all of this a month ago." She put her finger to her lips.

Steven put his hands in the air and started to

speak.

Dana cut him off. "Don't even say it. You tried to tell me. I know."

Alisa put her arm around Dana. "Let's eat."

Danny picked through the boxes of food that weren't packed. "Ravioli, granola bars, tuna, beef stew, cheese crackers. Grab whatever you want. Steven, will you ask God to bless the meal?"

Steven said a quick prayer and took a can of Spaghetti Os. He pulled the tab to remove the top and ate straight from the can. "Cold Spaghetti Os leaves something to be desired."

Alisa opened a can of beef stew. "Anything straight out of the can leaves something to be desired, even if it's hot."

Dana found a can of ravioli. "I'm glad we have something to eat. Thank you guys so much for sharing with me, and letting me come with you; and for letting me bring Puddin'." She picked up the cat and stroked her head. "You saved our lives."

Steven looked over at Danny and bit his lip. His eyes got glassy as if he was about to cry. He lowered his eyes to the can of food.

Danny just smiled at his friend with a wink and a nod. Danny was certain that they'd done the right thing by helping Dana and her cat, and he knew Steven felt the same. What was more, Dana's gratitude reminded Danny to be thankful for what they had. In the same way that they'd helped her, God helped Danny and his friends by granting him the dreams and giving them the means to prepare.

Danny opened a can of tuna and sat it in front of Puddin' who seemed very grateful for the gift.

"Thanks, Danny." Dana kept her end of the cat's make-shift harness wrapped firmly around her wrist as they both ate.

Danny finished his ravioli and then ate a can of peaches. Afterwards, he checked his watch again. "Best case scenario, we get another three hours of travel time before we have to find a place to make camp. I'm mentally tired from all the action today. What would you guys say about just sleeping here and getting a fresh start in the morning?"

Alisa stuck her hand in the air. "I vote we stay."

"Me, too." Dana's hand went in the air.

Danny looked at Steven. "What about you?"

"It's already a majority."

"If you don't agree, at least let us know why. If it's a good reason, you know we'll listen," Danny said.

"We're not that far away from Augusta. I don't think it's very safe. There could be roving bands of marauders running around after sunset and we'd be completely exposed. I would feel better if we took advantage of the daylight to get farther away from here."

"Good point." Danny raised his eyebrows and stuck his hands in his pocket. He looked around. "Would you feel more comfortable if we slept inside the church?"

"You're going to break into a church?" Dana covered her mouth in disbelief.

Steven looked at the back door. "It's definitely safer. And, the sun has been shining on the roof all day. It would keep us warm for the night; at least warmer than a tent." He looked at Dana. "You do

313

realize, God doesn't live in the building, right? He cares more about you than the building."

Alisa added, "Plus, we can leave all of the extra food and supplies that we can't carry for the people of the church. They'll find it the next time they come."

"Then it's settled. We'll sleep here and head out first thing in the morning." Danny shook the door knob.

"I think we should arrange a watch schedule, so someone is on lookout all night. It's too dangerous for all of us to be asleep in case someone slips up on us during the night." Steven examined the lock.

"Sounds like a plan." Danny looked through the glass in the door. "Looks like we're going to have to break it."

Steven retrieved his trusty bike lock. "Hopefully they'll understand. I'm sure the supplies we leave behind will put them in a more forgiving mood."

He smashed the pane of glass nearest to the latch of the dead bolt, then knocked out the remaining shards with the straight portion of the lock, so he could reach through and unlock the door.

The guys went in and the girls began hauling in the supplies.

Danny looked around. "I want to find a broom and sweep up the broken glass, so we don't track it all over the place. I also don't want to push the bikes over it, even with the heavy duty tires and liners."

Soon the glass was swept, Steven had duct-taped a piece of cardboard over the broken pane of glass, and all the supplies were inside the small church.

The little sanctuary was carpeted which made it a comfortable place for them to sleep. They still had several hours before dark, but Danny insisted that everything be done well before hand, so they wouldn't attract any extra attention by using flashlights or candles after sundown.

They positioned their sleeping gear in the front of the sanctuary, near the podium. Then, the boys took advantage of the remaining light to reload the spent magazines for the Glock and the AK-47.

Dana let Puddin' roam freely through the church and inspect the various items. The cat had to smell the piano, the podium, the mic stand and the bases of several pews.

"First time in a church, huh?" Dana followed closely to make sure Puddin' wouldn't get spooked and hide where she wouldn't be able to retrieve her. "Me, too."

Steven pulled a deck of cards from his backpack. "You guys know how to play spades?"

"I might need a refresher, but I've played before," Danny replied.

"Is it easy to learn?" Dana watched as Puddin' jumped up in a pew to get comfortable on the cushion.

"Super easy." Steven shuffled the cards. "Two teams."

"Great," Alisa said, "Me and Danny, and you and Dana."

"Guys against girls." Steven wasted no time in making the correction.

Danny noticed Dana's expression. She acted as if she couldn't be happier with the teams, but he knew better.

After a few hands of cards, the light dissipated.

Alisa said, "Dana and I are going to sit up and talk, so we can take first watch."

"Okay, wake me up in four hours." Steven said.

"I'll take the last shift." Danny took off his watch and handed it to Alisa.

"Good night." She kissed him.

Danny rolled over in the sleeping bag and closed his eyes. As he drifted off to sleep, he saw the horrible scene of the day replaying in his mind, the gun shots, the men falling, the tires running over the assailant. Each time he would see it, the vision stirred him from his sleep. But with each passing episode, he fell back to sleep faster and faster, until the dark visions no longer roused him from his slumber.

CHAPTER 22

Thus saith the LORD; Cursed be the man that trusteth in man, and maketh flesh his arm, and whose heart departeth from the LORD. For he shall be like the heath in the desert, and shall not see when good cometh; but shall inhabit the parched places in the wilderness, in a salt land and not inhabited. Blessed is the man that trusteth in the LORD, and whose hope the LORD is. For he shall be as a tree planted by the waters, and that spreadeth out her roots by the river, and shall not see when heat cometh, but her leaf shall be green; and shall not be careful in the year of drought, neither shall cease from yielding fruit.

Jeremiah 17:5-8

"Your shift, big guy," Steven nudged Danny gently.

It took Danny more than a minute to fully grasp where he was and what was going on. The memories of what had happened the day before slowly fell into place, like the pieces of a puzzle coming together to form a complete picture. "Wow, it's cold."

"Yeah, I think the temperature really dropped last night." Steven laid his shotgun on the floor next to him and nestled into his sleeping bag.

"Did you hear anything last night? Any movement on the road?"

"No, the girls didn't hear anything either."

"Good. I think I'll build a fire right before the sun pops up. Everyone can stand around it and get warm before we head out. Alisa made several of those coffee bags by stapling the grounds inside the filters. I'm sure that will help warm us up and get us motivated."

Steven handed the watch back to Danny and covered his head. "That should be okay. I'm sure the smell of smoke from fires is going to be all over the place with these temperatures, so I don't think it will make us stick out. Wake me up at first light."

Danny put his watch on and got out of the sleeping bag. He quickly began layering clothes from his bug-out bag. He did a few pushups to get his blood flowing and to generate some body heat. Next, he rolled up his sleeping bag and began packing up his things to move out at dawn.

Danny found a comfortable chair near the window where he could see out. He leaned the AK-47 up against the wall and sat silently as he watched and listened. Sorting his thoughts would be more than enough of a task to fill the next couple of hours. Who were the men they had killed? How long is it going to take to get back to Nana's? Was Cami alright? Would they survive the winter? And if so, would they survive the coming year?

Soon, Danny felt overwhelmed by the thoughts and worries. He remembered a sermon on the power of prayer by Pastor Earl. Despite the supernatural revelations Danny had received through his dreams, he wasn't so sure about prayer. Sure, he did it because he was supposed to, but could it actually make a difference. Danny sighed and whispered, "What have I got to lose?"

He kept his eyes open as he began to pray silently, taking his concerns and insecurities to the one who had given him the revelations. It wasn't long before he felt less worried. He remembered the peace of God that Pastor Earl spoke of. Peace that wasn't contingent on the circumstances, but came from inside, from a place that the storms of life couldn't reach.

As the first hint of daybreak appeared in the distant horizon, behind the bare tree limbs, Danny got up from the chair. He laid the rifle near the place where Alisa was still sound asleep and took his pistol to tuck in his pants. He found his lighter and went outside to locate some tinder for a fire.

The occasional breeze was frigid. He had no

thermometer, but he was sure the temperature was well below freezing. He gathered up several bunches of dried leaves and small twigs. Next, he found a few larger limbs. He skipped looking for large logs, both because he had no means of cutting them to size, nor would they be around long enough for them to catch fire.

Danny lit the leaves and carefully fed the small twigs into the burning debris. He added another handful of leaves and laid the larger branches atop the flames in an A-frame fashion. The warmth immediately dispelled the chill and made him feel much better. He successively placed larger sticks into the blaze, until it burned bright and hot. Then, Danny retrieved a pan, filled it with water, dropped in one of Alisa's coffee bags, and positioned it on the most stable logs to heat.

He walked back inside and gave Steven a push. "The sun is coming up. Rise and shine."

A muffled response came from the recesses of the sleeping bag. "I don't want to go to school today, mom."

Danny chuckled and woke up the girls. "Where's your cat?"

"At the bottom of my blanket, by my feet." Dana didn't have a sleeping bag. She used the comforter Alisa gave her the first night.

"It's cold." Alisa squinted as she rolled over to look at Danny.

"Yeah. Bundle up with several layers. I've got some coffee brewing." Danny began taking the bikes outside. He slung two connected water jugs over the frame of the one he would be riding and tied a length of paracord around them so they wouldn't knock up against each other. Each bike would carry two gallons, giving them a total of six before they had to locate a water source to refill them.

Ten minutes later, Danny went back inside to see how well the rest of the group was progressing with getting up and preparing their gear for the journey. He grabbed a box of granola bars, took two and passed the box to Alisa. "Everyone eat as much as you can. After this morning, we'll have to make the food last."

Dana opened another can of tuna for Puddin'. "You heard Danny, eat up." Dana looked up. "How much food are we taking with us?"

Danny folded the stock of the AK-47 and helped Alisa situate the rifle into her backpack. "We've got four days of ready-to-eat stuff; MREs and canned goods. Then we've got another three or four days' worth of dehydrated food for backup. Dehydrated food has to sit in water to rehydrate and it has to be cooked; so it has a longer cook time, but also takes up a lot less room, and weighs only a fraction of what the ready-to-eat stuff does."

They decided to keep the long guns stowed, as they would be cumbersome to ride with otherwise, and they didn't want to draw unnecessary attention. Steven put his shotgun in his backpack and kept Danny's revolver tucked in his pants.

Danny kept the Glock in the back of his jeans, and all of the extra magazines loaded and readily accessible in his inside coat pockets. If they got into more trouble, he would be able to lay down cover fire while Steven and Alisa retrieved the long guns from the packs.

Everyone ate as much as they could, had a cup of coffee and brushed their teeth. Danny stomped out the coals. "Dana, let's practice getting you up on my handlebars."

"Okay, Alisa, you've got Puddin'?"

"Yeah, she's safe with me."

Dana turned around with her back to the bike. "Now what?"

"Jump up and lean back against my arms." Danny got his foot in place to get the bike rolling as soon as she was up. The bike had a lot of weight with his backpack, the water and now a passenger.

She jumped up and Danny started pedaling. It was a slow start, but they were soon rolling along. Steven and Alisa fell in behind them and they were on the road.

The first few miles were relatively flat. That was good, because the slightest incline required Danny to shift to the lowest gear on his bike. Alisa had been using her bike for transportation for over two years in Savannah. Steven had just recently sold his car and began using his bike, but he also seemed to be in decent cycling shape for the first leg of the journey. Danny guessed they'd covered about five or six miles, then he asked Steven to carry Dana on his handlebars for a while. The group made a quick pit stop for the exchange and quickly got back on the road.

As they moved steadily along, another old truck, perhaps a late sixties model, passed but didn't slow down to bother them nor pay them any mind at all.

Alisa said, "I wonder if I had bought a truck instead of the Camaro, maybe it would have survived the attack and we'd already be at Nana's."

Danny sighed. "I wonder if we had left the night before, maybe we could have avoided the incident on the exit ramp altogether. Or maybe I should have planned a different route that would have completely avoided Augusta."

Steven shook his head. "Nothing good will come of second guessing yourselves. We all did the best we knew how, and God took care of us. If Alisa had bought a truck instead, it might have broken down before the EMP ever went off. If you would've had us leave the night before, we could have all been shot before we ever got out of Savannah. Who knows the terrors that could have awaited us if we'd taken another route? The plan we made got us out of Savannah and half way home. God used that car to keep us alive. We have to be thankful."

"You're right. Thanks," Alisa said.

Two hours later, they reached the town of Trenton. It was small, but they kept moving through it. They saw only one functioning vehicle as they passed through town, a 1979 Cutlass. It looked like a car that someone was in the process of restoring.

Once they were well outside Trenton, they stopped for a break.

Danny pulled out the map and calculated how far they'd gone. "Looks like we've covered about fourteen miles. How is everyone feeling?"

"I could easily go for three or four more hours; after a break, of course." Steven said.

"Me, too, I'm good." Alisa took a big drink of

water. "Dana can ride my handlebars for a while."

"Okay, I'll carry the cat." Danny stretched.

Steven looked at the map. "Edgefield is about five miles out. We should take it easy until we get there, so we'll have enough energy to pick up speed through town."

Danny found the town on the map. "Looks like about two miles to get through it. We'll keep moving until we're another mile beyond, then stop for another quick break."

They all shared a box of vanilla wafers, hydrated and took bathroom breaks, then prepared to get back on the road.

US 25 skirted the perimeter of Edgefield, so they didn't see much action, which was exactly what Danny had hoped for.

They cleared Edgefield as planned roughly an hour later, then found a quiet spot for lunch. It was a clearing off a gravel path which ran along a wooded lot. It was concealed by the surrounding trees, but the sun beamed down on them and kept them warm. The heavy exercise prevented them from getting cold while they were moving, but once the group stopped, the cool air quickly sucked away the body heat they had built up.

After they had eaten, Danny placed the map on the ground so everyone could see it. "This is Kirksey, it looks like it's about twenty miles from here, give or take. This green area right before Kirksey is Sumter National forest. That should mean that we'll be able to find water and hopefully a good camping spot. It will be about three o' clock which gives us about three hours before sunset to get water, eat dinner and set up camp. I think that's going to be about as far as I can make it today anyway. What do you guys think?"

Steven looked closer at the map. "I think that's a good place to stop for the night."

"How far to Nana's from there?" Alisa asked.

"About fifty miles, maybe a little more," Danny answered.

"Can we make it in one day?" Dana asked.

"Not at the rate we're going. With the amount of cargo and people we're moving, we have to move slow and steady. But we can definitely do it in two days." Danny stretched his legs which were getting tired.

"Lord willing, we can make it in two days," Steven added.

Danny smiled with a nod. "Lord willing."

The group mounted up and prepared to finish the next leg of their journey.

Dana would pedal Alisa's bike and Alisa would sit on the handlebars for the next few miles.

A handful of vehicles passed by. Some were going north and the others south. None of them stopped or even slowed down as they traveled by. The group progressed along their way, and clouds began to move in.

"Did you feel that?" Alisa called out to Danny.

He felt a few drops of precipitation but hoped that it would stay dry. "Rain?"

"Snow," Alisa replied.

Danny grimaced as he looked at the dark clouds gathering in the north. While snow wouldn't drench their clothes, any accumulation would certainly put a damper on their travels.

Twenty minutes later, they stopped briefly so Alisa and Dana could switch positions. Danny took advantage of every break to stretch out his back which was feeling the burn of the long journey.

"My butt is asleep. Riding the handlebars is a lot tougher than pedaling." Alisa stretched her legs against a tree, one at a time. "Looks like the flurries are getting heavier."

"Feels like the temperature has dropped another ten degrees, too." Dana put her hand over her nose to warm it.

Danny pressed his foot into the fallen snow which was beginning to accumulate in the grass along the side of the road. "It's not sticking on the road yet. But it will soon if it keeps snowing. We should go as fast as we can. Once it starts sticking to the roadways, we'll have no choice but to go slow."

Steven took a drink from his jug. "The water is starting to get slushy. Everyone should hydrate before it freezes hard."

Everyone followed his advice, then mounted up to get back on the road.

Danny pushed as hard as he could to lead the pack in hopes of inspiring the others to go a little faster. But since he wasn't accustomed to riding, his muscles had their limit. He made a conscious effort to breathe through his nose. Otherwise, the frigid air sent a chill deep into his lungs.

The flurries turned into a steady snow fall and Danny watched the individual flakes as they fought to survive the impact with the road. As more and more snowflakes fell, they held on longer and longer before melting on the pavement.

The group moved as fast as they could and finally reached the intersection of US 378, which marked the beginning of Sumter National Forest. The team would continue up US-25 which cut through the forest.

Danny got off his bike for a short break. "The snow is starting to stick on the road, but we've got another seven miles before we reach the distance we'd hoped to complete. If anyone starts to slide, just give us a holler and we'll all slow down. This isn't the best condition for riding, but if the weather keeps up, tomorrow is really going to be a tough row to hoe."

Danny took another drink from his jug, which now had the consistency of a half-melted slushy. The ice-cold water sent chills through his body and he wished for a hot cup of tea, or coffee, or cocoa. Anything hot, or even lukewarm would have been better than icy water, but he knew he had to stay hydrated. He watched as the girls forced themselves to drink also. "We'll make some hot soup after we set up camp."

Dana asked, "How will you build a fire if everything is wet?"

"I've got my little fold-up camping stove and a few cans of Sterno. We can cook and boil water on that," Danny replied.

"But that's not enough to keep us warm all night." Alisa sounded very concerned.

"We'll just have to pile up together under the covers to conserve body heat. The tent will block the wind." Danny saw Steven purse his lips at the suggestion.

He made his way over to his friend while the girls were busy checking on the cat. "Do you have a better idea about how to keep from freezing tonight?"

Steven crossed his arms. "I just don't want to be snuggled up next to Dana."

"Steven, you and I will have to be on the outside, in case there's a noise and we have to get up. By necessity, the girls have to be in the middle. The only other option is for Dana to be next to me and Alisa to be snuggled up to you, which is wrong on a multitude of levels."

Steven huffed. "I understand."

"What's up with you? You were comforting her at the church after the shootout. One minute you seem like you like her, and the next minute you treat her like a pariah. If I'm confused, I can just imagine how she feels."

"It doesn't matter how she feels or how I feel. It just won't work, okay?" Steven checked his gear, put his backpack back on and saddled his bike.

"Sure." As he walked away, it occurred to Danny that Steven might actually be as confused about the matter as he was acting. He decided he wouldn't confront him about it anymore. If Steven wanted to talk about it, he would be there, but for now he'd give Steven his space.

They were soon back on the road and the snow continued to come down harder and harder. Fifteen minutes later, a thin, even sheet of snow was forming on the road. The buildup caused them to move progressively slower, until they came to a crawl, but they eventually reached their desired destination point, near the northern edge of the forest.

Danny looked toward the line of pines which were about fifty feet off the road. "Let's walk back through there and look for a good spot to camp. I want to be far enough from the road that we won't be visible to passersby."

Alisa pointed at the tracks Danny was leaving with his feet and his bike in the snow. "If anyone wants to find us, they won't have to look too hard."

Danny looked up at the falling snow, which was now greatly reducing visibility. "Those tracks will be covered in fifteen minutes. We better get a move on if we want to be set up by dark."

The group followed Danny back into the woods.

Dana looked at the snow piling up on the branches overhead. "Can those limbs break off from the weight of the snow and hit our tent?"

"Pines don't reach very far out so that's probably not much of a threat. However, they can bend and dump a pile of snow on us all at once. We'll take that into consideration when we pick our spot." Danny trudged forward.

"Look! A downed tree. The dirt sticking to the roots formed a sort of natural wall. Maybe that would be a good spot." Alisa paused as she looked at the uprooted pine.

Danny headed in that direction. "Good call. If we could build three more walls, we could greatly reduce the wind that will be pounding the tent all night and conserve a good deal of heat."

Alisa looked at the clearing beyond the fallen tree. "Did you ever build a snow fort?"

"I did," Dana replied.

"What if we built a wall of snow around the tent?" Alisa leaned her bike against a tree and dropped her pack.

Danny thought for a moment. "What would we use to make the bricks? We don't have much to work with."

"It doesn't have to be aesthetic, just functional," Steven said. "Remember when we used to build snowmen? You just roll up a ball. We can roll up balls of snow, like building a snowman, and pack snow in the open spaces. We can stack smaller balls on top and build it up to the height of the tent."

"We could lay branches across the top and make a roof. That would help to hold the heat in." Dana checked the strength of the branches on the downed tree.

"Good idea. We need to be sure the branches across the top are strong enough to not collapse under the weight of the snow as is collects on the roof." Danny looked around the forest. "A couple good limbs for cross beams would help mitigate that risk."

Steven began pulling out the tent. "I'll get this set up, if the rest of you want to start on the snow wall."

The girls went to the open field to start rolling large snow balls.

Danny looked at the spot where Steven was working on the tent. "A bed of pine needles would help to insulate us from the ground."

Steven paused. "Yeah, but they're covered by the snow."

"We have plenty of low hanging branches all around us. I'll cut the ends off with my knife."

"I'll give you a hand with that." Steven took out his knife and began cutting.

Once Danny and Steven had an adequate pile of pine needles gathered at the tent site, Danny retrieved his wire saw out of his pack and began cutting limbs to make a roof. Meanwhile Steven finished setting up the tent.

The girls began rolling three-foot-tall snow balls to the camp site fairly quickly, as the snow was accumulating rapidly.

Alisa stood next to her giant snow ball. "Where do you want them?"

Danny marked off a perimeter in the snow with his foot. "If we go wide, like this, we'll have enough room to keep our gear in the igloo, plus a little extra space to cook with the folding stove."

Dana rolled her first snow ball to the line Danny had drawn on the ground. "Won't the camping stove melt the walls?"

Danny looked at the camp site. "We'll cook against the wall of dirt formed by the up-rooted tree. The roof is going to be made of branches, so we don't have to worry about the ceiling melting either."

Steven drove the tent pegs in the ground to keep the dome tent from blowing away. "The wind is coming heavy out of the northeast. We should put the entrance of the igloo on the southwest."

The bottom row of snow balls were put in place.

Alisa said, "We used most of the snow in that clearing. Where should we get the snow for the second tier?"

Danny looked at Steven. "Back by the road, I guess."

Steven nodded. "Visibility is pretty low right now. If it keeps snowing like this, the tracks will be covered in twenty minutes."

"We'll give you a hand." Danny led the way back toward the open field near the road.

In just over an hour, the four of them had a crude igloo set up with a thick layer of pine branches for a roof. Steven cut open a trash bag and used it as a door flap for the entrance, securing it into the snow with several small twigs, carved with sharp points to easily pierce the snow wall of the igloo.

"Let's put the bikes behind the fallen tree. If anyone happens to come along, they won't be out in the open." Alisa took her bike and began moving it.

"I doubt anyone will be walking around in this, but better safe than sorry." Steven grabbed his bike and followed her.

"After that, we should start melting snow to refill our water jugs. We don't have much daylight left." Danny followed with his bike, then went into the igloo and set up his stove.

The only other thing that went in the tent, besides the four friends, was Puddin' and the water jugs. Everything else was stored in the empty space between the tent and the igloo wall. They were all very happy that they'd provided the extra space once they saw how tight the quarters were with four people and a cat in a dome tent.

After the jugs were filled with the melted snow, Danny began making dinner. Since they weren't going anywhere for the night, he cooked several of the dehydrated meals of southwest beans and rice. "Do you think Puddin' will eat beans and rice?"

Dana held her cat, wrapped up in a corner of the sleeping bag. "If you pour the juice from a can of tuna on it, she'll eat anything."

Danny smiled. "We can do that. Then the rest of us can share the tuna."

It took a long time for the food to cook and rehydrate, but waiting for dinner made for a good time killer. It would be a long, dark night in the cramped little tent.

Despite the tight quarters, Danny slept well that night. His layered clothing, the combined body heat under a stack of sleeping bags, and the igloo to block the cold kept him warm. He turned on his flashlight and glanced at his watch when he awoke. "Seven."

Danny crawled out from beneath the warm sanctuary of the covers. He exited the tent and pulled the pegs securing the trash-bag flap in the entrance of the igloo. The diffused light of morning poured in. Nearly twelve inches had built up at the entrance of the shelter and heavy snow was still falling.

Danny put his shoes on and went outside. He looked around but was barely able to see ten yards in front of him. He went to find a tree to relieve himself, then headed back to the igloo.

"What's it like out there?" Alisa poked her head out from beneath the covers.

"It's bad. Looks like we got about a foot last night and it's still coming down. Visibility is terrible. I can't imagine trying to get anywhere on bikes in this."

Steven rolled out from his side of the tent and put his shoes on. "Maybe it will let up later."

Danny handed him the large cooking pan. "Can you fill this with snow while you're outside? I'll make coffee in it first, then I've got some packages of brown sugar oatmeal."

"Sounds great!" Dana smiled.

"Where's Puddin'?" Alisa got out from under the covers and put her shoes on.

Dana stuck her head under the sleeping bag. "By my feet. She's awake, but doesn't want to come out. I'll take her out to go to the bathroom when I get up."

"I'll be right back." Alisa zipped her coat and left the shelter.

Steven returned minutes later with the pan, packed with snow. "The bikes are completely covered. So is the roof."

Danny took the pot and sat it on the stove. "Should we clear some of the snow so the roof doesn't collapse?"

Steven pushed against the roof. "It's not bowing at all. I think it's pretty sturdy. Besides, the snow is acting as an extra layer of insulation."

Dana put her hood over her head and tied it tight. "But how much more snow can it handle? I can sweep half of the snow off, then the rest can remain to keep out the cold."

"Good idea. Go ahead and do that." Steven

looked through his bag which was against the igloo wall.

"Okay, I'll hand Puddin' to you guys when I get back and then sweep the roof with a branch or something." Dana took her cat and left the igloo.

By nine o'clock, everyone had drunk the coffee and eaten their oatmeal. Danny cleaned the pot, and melted snow to refill the water jugs, so there was nothing more to do.

"Still coming down pretty hard out there." Dana peeked out the entrance, which was left partially open to allow some light into the structure.

"Spades?" Steven held up a deck of cards.

"Nothing worth watching on television; why not?" Alisa retrieved a pen and pad from her bag, then found a comfortable position inside the tent.

Hours later, they had lunch. The flurries kept falling, so they continued playing cards. Danny made several pouches of the dehydrated chicken alfredo pasta for dinner. It didn't really have chicken in it, just chicken flavoring, but no one complained; including Puddin'.

Darkness fell Sunday night, and they were still stuck in the same location, over fifty miles away from Nana's.

CHAPTER 23

And not only so, but we glory in tribulations also: knowing that tribulation worketh patience; and patience, experience; and experience, hope.

Romans 5:3-4

Once again, Danny was the first one up at 6:30 on Monday morning. He repeated his routine from the morning before. Over two feet of snow covered the ground. What was worse, it now had a layer of ice on top of it. "This isn't good." He punched the ice gently, but it didn't break. He exited the shelter and put his foot on the ice. It cracked under his weight and gave way to the powdery snow beneath. The sky was clear, but the ice would not make for a good day to travel. Danny lifted a section of broken ice and filled the pan with packed snow to melt for coffee and returned to the shelter.

"Still snowing?" Steven was up second.

"No, but it looks like a skating rink out there. I'd say we have about a half inch of ice on top of the snow."

Dana rolled over. "How can we ride bikes in that?"

"I don't think we can." Danny lit the Sterno in the small stove.

"We can't stay here another night. We have to make some progress." Steven put his shoes on.

"Steven's right. We have to get moving, even if we have to push the bikes." Danny moved the brick of melting snow around in the pan with a spoon as it heated up.

Alisa stuck her head out from under the covers. "Yeah, we'll be out of coffee soon. We need to get to Nana's to resupply."

Danny chuckled as he shook his head. "We'll get there, eventually."

"How far can we go in one day, if we have to push the bikes and walk?" Dana slowly came out of the covers.

"At least ten miles, maybe twenty. And who knows, maybe the sun will melt it off after noon." Steven put on his hat and left the shelter.

"The sun might melt the ice and it could refreeze with a thicker layer of ice tonight." Alisa ran her hand through her hair. "Ewww! I need a shower!"

Danny nodded. "That may not be all bad. A thicker layer of ice could possibly support the weight of the bikes. Then we could ride rather than push. We'd have to go slow so we don't slip, but it would be faster than pushing through two feet of snow."

They quickly drank their coffee after it was brewed, ate some granola bars and dug out the bikes. Once the tent was taken down and the gear loaded up, they headed out.

Steven turned for one last look at the igloo. "We did a good job building the shelter. I'm going to miss that little ice hut."

Alisa smirked. "If it had a Jacuzzi tub, I'd agree with you."

The next three hours were spent slowly trudging through the deep snow and crunching through the layer of ice on top. Danny marveled at the magnificence of the snow and ice coated vistas. The crystalline landscape, like a sculpture cut from a giant sugar cube and dipped in glass, glistened in the brilliant white light of the sun. It was a cumbersome and tiring journey, but oh so beautiful.

"I need a break!" Alisa called out.

"I think we could all use one." Danny was deeply discouraged by the slim distance they'd covered.

Steven pulled the map out. "I think that was Route 67 we just passed. We're about two miles outside of Greenwood. The road we're on now, US 178, cuts around town, but that adds two miles to our trip. At the rate we're moving, that equates to an extra hour."

Danny looked at him. "If it's a big enough town to have a bypass, it would be suicide to walk through it."

Steven laid the map at his side. "I didn't say go through town, I'm just stating the facts."

"An hour extra?" Alisa's face showed her displeasure.

"Do you think people are going to be outside in this mess? Maybe it would be safe to go through town." Dana let Puddin' out of the carrier on the paracord harness for a break.

Danny looked at her. "Maybe, but if we get that one wrong, the consequences are much greater than the extra time to go around."

Alisa stuck her hand in the air. "And with that little reminder, I vote we go around."

Steven chuckled and raised his hand. "I'm with Alisa."

Dana held one of Puddin's paws in the air. "So are we."

"Then it's unanimous." Danny took a couple swigs from the water jug and passed it to Alisa.

Steven picked the map back up. "But, once we hit Greenwood, we have to keep moving until we are well outside of town."

"Which is how far from here?" Dana asked.

Steven stared at the map for a moment. "About eight miles."

"Then we better get a move on. It will be close to dark by the time we get there." Alisa put the cap back on the water jug and slung it over the bike she was pushing.

"Will we have to build another shelter?" Dana put Puddin' back in the carrier.

Danny slowly stood up. "There's no wind right now. If it stays like this, we'll be okay in the tent."

The steady movement and the warmth of the sun kept them from getting cold. As they pressed forward, the ice became progressively thinner. They stopped again for a quick snack just outside of Greenwood.

Everyone made a conscious effort to hydrate, and stretch out before the next leg of the trip. For security purposes, they would minimize breaks for the remainder of the day.

Alisa got on her bike and tried riding for a few yards, but the crackling sheet of ice atop the snow made it all but impossible. She relented and got off to push alongside of the others. "I tried, but it ain't happening."

They moved as quickly as they could without wearing themselves out. The bypass section of US 178 was still a moderately populated area, but they saw no one else willing to navigate the ice covered snow.

They took one more short break when they hit a long wooded stretch of the road, then continued their trek.

They hit the intersection of the bypass and the business route of US 178 just after four o'clock, but had to keep going for another hour before they were well outside of town.

At 5:15, Danny stopped near a sign. "Greenwood Memorial Gardens. There's an office building in the middle of the cemetery. Might be better than sleeping in a tent."

"No way! I'm not sleeping in a cemetery!" Alisa sounded adamant.

Steven pointed toward the back. "Looks like a

maintenance building toward the back. Would you sleep at the edge of a cemetery?"

"And that's better, how?" Alisa held her bike with one hand and put the other on her hip.

"Let's take a vote." Danny held his hand up.

Dana shook her head. "Puddin' votes no also."

Steven also held up his hand. "The cat doesn't get a vote on where we sleep."

Dana furrowed her brow. "You counted her vote when we decided to take the bypass."

Steven huffed. "We didn't count her vote. It was already unanimous and . . ."

Danny cut him off. "Hold up. Ladies, if we stay in the maintenance building, we can probably build a fire in a barrel or something. I can boil a lot of water and we can cordon off an area for bathing."

"You can boil enough water for a bath?" Alisa was suddenly very excited.

Danny put his hand up. "Not a tub bath, but maybe a cat bath, with a wash rag, soap and a warm pan of water. We're all pushing four days without bathing. Who knows when we'll get to Nana's or if we'll get another chance."

"But, we have to sleep in a cemetery to get a bath," Dana clarified.

Alisa clarified further, "And not even a real bath."

Steven peered into the cat carrier. "What's that? I think Puddin' just voted to stay here."

Dana fought back a smile and looked at Alisa. "No she didn't."

Alisa squinted and glared at Danny. "If we stay, do you promise to heat enough water for us to wash our hair?"

"I'll see what I can do." He rolled his eyes.

"What do you think?" Alisa looked at Dana.

Dana winked at Alisa and shrugged, but said nothing.

Alisa began pushing her bike toward the entrance of the cemetery. "You owe us!"

Dana followed her. "And we better get to wash our hair!"

When they arrived at the maintenance building, the lock was already removed and the garage area looked as if it had been looted.

Danny leaned his bike against the wall and dropped his bag by the door. He went inside and surveyed the scene for usable items. "I don't see the metal trash can I was hoping to build a fire in, but there's some pallets in the corner. That will make for good firewood. I've only got two cans of Sterno left, so I'd like to conserve them if possible."

Steven looked in the doorway. "We've got a few cinder blocks outside. We can use those to build a fire pit."

Danny turned to follow Steven to the blocks. "I saw a video on how to build a rocket stove. I wish I'd written down the instructions or drawn a diagram. It would be really useful to know right now."

Steven grabbed two of the concrete blocks. "Yeah, if we still had YouTube, the apocalypse wouldn't be so bad."

Alisa and Dana came out of the building. Alisa held up a plastic storage bin. "We can use this to fill with water for our cat baths. And, we found an office that we can use to take turns bathing."

Danny looked at the eighteen-gallon plastic tote. "We'd have to melt a lot of snow to fill that tub."

"You don't have to fill it all the way. It's not like we can get in it for a soak any way. But, it's big enough to hold our head over so we can pour water over us to wash our hair," Dana said.

Steven continued stacking the blocks near the garage door of the maintenance building. "Let's get the fire going so we can start melting snow."

Danny gave him a hand. "The idea behind the rocket stove is for it to suck air from the bottom and feed it upward. I think I can incorporate the ideology into our fire pit. We keep the top opening fairly small and build a tunnel on the bottom for the air to get sucked into."

Steven brought out one of the pallets. "We don't want to be busting up wood all night, so the opening will have to be big enough to feed these boards into."

The fire pit didn't look much like the contraption Danny saw in the video, but it would have to do. They found a small amount of gasoline in an old weed eater and used it to jump start the fire.

"Now we need a grate, so we can put our pan over the fire." Danny looked around.

"There's a roll of chain-link fence." Steven looked in the direction of an old tractor.

"How will we cut it?" Danny asked.

"We don't. We'll just roll out the amount we need and weight it down with more concrete blocks. The rest can hang off the side."

"Sounds like a plan."

In minutes, they had a roaring fire with several containers melting snow. They used the large cooking pan, the tops and bottoms of both of the metal mess kits, plus a coffee pot and a metal trash can which the girls scavenged from the office.

Dana bathed first, then Alisa. Afterwards, the boys took turns in the make-shift bathroom. By the time they had eaten supper and cleaned up, it was after nine o'clock.

Steven stood up and pulled his shotgun out of his bag. "I'm going to check out the office building. If it has carpet, it will be a much better place to sleep than these hard floors."

"I'll go with you." Danny turned on his flashlight.

"It's more exposed to the road than this location." Alisa stood near the warm fire.

"We're going to have to take turns on night watch anyway. After you finally got cleaned up, wouldn't you rather sleep in a clean office than a grimy garage floor?" Steven asked.

Dana held Puddin'. "He's got a point."

"Yeah, I guess." Alisa ran her fingers through her hair near the heat of the fire to try get it to dry faster. "So, we should probably all head over there together, in case there's trouble."

"Let us check it out first, from a distance. If it's clear, we'll come right back for the bikes and the bags." Danny positioned his Glock so it would be easier to access if needed.

"Okay, we'll get everything ready to move." Dana placed Puddin' back in the carrier.

Danny and Steven soon returned with the all

clear and they hauled their belongings to the office building to sleep for the night.

Danny rolled out his sleeping bag, got in it and stretched out. It felt good to be on the soft carpet, and it felt even better to not be cramped up in a tent with three other people and a cat. He drifted off to sleep in seconds.

Morning came early as he awoke to Alisa's voice.

"Danny, get up. It's four o'clock. You've got fourth watch. I'm going back to sleep. See you in the morning."

"Okay, love you." He immediately got out of the sleeping bag because he knew he'd go back to sleep if he didn't.

Danny used the quiet time to pray and read a few chapters from his Bible with his flashlight held low. He was careful to stay away from the window when his light was on, so as not to alert any would-be marauders of their presence. At 6:00, he went outside to check the ground. Indeed, it had frozen solid overnight and now provided a very firm, yet slippery surface to travel on. He let the others sleep until 6:30, then woke them all. "Guys, the ice is frozen hard outside. We should get moving at first light. Once the sun starts shining on the ice, we'll probably have the same problem we had yesterday."

The others stirred slowly and Danny went back to the maintenance building to get another fire going for coffee and oatmeal.

By 7:30, they were on the road. It was slippery, and made it harder to ride the bikes. The morning sun rose and the icy countryside shined.

Even with the slippery roadway, they'd covered about twelve miles by lunch. They ate a few granola bars, drank some water and rushed to get back on the road before the road began to get slushy. The snow was still beneath the surface of the ice, so when it became too thin and started cracking, travel time would greatly increase.

The roads stayed firm until three o'clock. By 3:30, everyone was off of the bikes and pushing them along as they walked.

"Any chance we'll get there today?" Dana asked.

Steven shook his head. "Nope. We've done over twenty miles so far, but we'll be lucky if we make it another five before we have to make camp. We don't want to go through Anderson tonight anyway. We'll get as close as we can, then hit it first thing tomorrow morning. If all goes well, and provided we can ride the bikes in the morning, we should be at Nana's by this time tomorrow."

They limited their breaks and pressed on. At 5:30, Danny stopped. "We've got just enough light to pitch the tent. This section of forest will give us good visual cover for the night."

"Yeah, I don't think I can walk another step. My feet are killing me," Alisa said.

"Mine, too. And my back," Steven said.

"Can you imagine how hard this would be for people who aren't used to being on their feet all day? It's almost like we were being conditioned for this trip while we were waiting tables." Dana followed Danny as he walked toward the tree line.

Steven smiled at her. "Yeah, it's almost like it was part of some big plan. Like someone knew you would have to endure this. And he cared enough about you to put you with the right people, at the right time to get you to a safe place."

Dana nodded. "Yeah, maybe."

Danny just listened. It sounded like she might be coming around.

CHAPTER 24

Behold, God is my salvation; I will trust, and not be afraid: for the LORD JEHOVAH is my strength and my song; he also is become my salvation. Therefore with joy shall ye draw water out of the wells of salvation. And in that day shall ye say, Praise the LORD, call upon his name, declare his doings among the people, make mention that his name is exalted.

Isaiah 12:2-4

Wednesday morning, Danny woke up cold. The pile of sleeping bags and combined body heat helped, but with no other form of shelter besides the tent, the cold air found its way through to his bones.

He looked over to see that Steven was already awake and left the tent. He could hear him outside doing something. Danny put his shoes and coat on and went outside. "Good morning. How did you sleep?"

"Okay, the cold woke me up." Steven had a pan of water boiling.

"Me, too. I'm ready to get to Nana's. Our one-day road trip has turned into nearly a week."

"And we're still not there yet."

Danny inspected the ground by stomping it with his shoe. "Looks like everything is frozen solid. We should be able to ride the bikes. I think we'll get there today."

Steven sighed. "I ain't holding my breath. I'll celebrate when we're standing on her porch."

The girls were up shortly thereafter. Coffee, breakfast, and striking the camp happened in rapid succession as everyone was anxious for the long journey to be finished. The frozen roads were as slick as a peeled onion, but the group navigated them just fine. The maneuver that required the most adjustment to the icy surfaces was for the girls in mounting the handlebars. But, with each successful ascension, they got better at the operation.

Knowing they were getting close seemed to add a touch of wind to their collective sail. The four friends advanced along the path steadily.

As reliable as dots in a scatter plot, the increasing density in stranded vehicles was proof that they were approaching a town. Danny waved for the others to stop. "We've got about two miles 'til we hit Anderson, then Nana's is about seven miles from there. Everyone should take a quick break now so we don't have to stop in town. Once we're back on the road, stay behind me because we'll have to turn on Route 22. That's almost right through the center of town. Anderson is mostly nice folks, but as we've seen, an EMP can bring out the worst in people."

The others stated that they understood and agreed with Danny. After a short break they were back on the road.

They followed River Street, then turned left onto Route 22, just as Danny had said. The town was silent. No one was outdoors. As they passed by the two and three story brick buildings, the evidence of looters and scavengers was everywhere. Windows were broken, trash was strewn about the streets, and the inside of shops were in total disarray. They passed by several store fronts, and an old Methodist Church.

Then, Danny noticed something that really didn't fit. It was a little boy banging on the window from inside one of the abandoned cars. His heart sank like he'd seen a ghost. "Oh no," he said in a low voice only to himself. He kept pedaling as expeditiously as possible without risking a spill on the icy road.

"Danny! Wait up!" Dana's voice was not far behind him.

Danny slowed, but kept moving.

Dana rode up beside him with Alisa on the handlebars. "We have to stop! There's a little boy back there in an abandoned car."

Danny stayed focused on the ice covered path

beneath him. "We can't. We have to keep going. The EMP was last Thursday, today is Wednesday. It's been an entire week. There's no way that kid has been in that car for a week. He'd be dead."

Steven was riding close on the other side of Danny. "We don't know for sure. Maybe his mom or dad left him there and died before they could get back to him. Maybe he had water and a blanket. I think we need to go check it out."

Danny couldn't believe Steven was arguing for going back. "Seriously? Steven, it's a trap."

Steven stayed close to Danny's bike. "Maybe so. If that's the case, the kid could have been kidnapped by someone for the purpose of setting the trap. Who knows what they'll do to that little boy if we don't help him."

"Danny please. At least stop so we can talk about it," Dana pleaded.

Danny kept going. "We're in no position to help. Our job right now has to be to get home safely."

Steven scowled at him. "Then I'll go back by myself. Can you at least stop to give me directions to get to Nana's from here?"

Danny did not like where this was going. He kept going until he'd cleared the railroad tracks, some four blocks from where they'd seen the child in the car. He pulled his bike off to the side of the road and walked it back into the shrubs that followed the tree line.

Steven followed him. "I understand your reasoning, but I have to do this."

"You're going to get yourself killed Steven." Danny crossed his arms.

"Where's your faith?" Steven held out his arms.

"Faith? Am I supposed to trust God when I walk into a trap?" Danny was shocked at Steven's reasoning.

Dana jumped in. "I've heard all of you go on and on about how Jesus came to die for you and how you want to be like him. But when you get the chance to die for someone else, you run away. I'm going with Steven to get the little boy."

Danny protested. "Whoa. Jesus fulfilled a purpose by dying, he paid for our sins. It was an essential part of his mission. Walking into a trap and getting killed doesn't fulfill any mission unless your goal is feeding worms."

Steven shot back. "What about the apostles? All of them were killed for their faith, except John, who was boiled in oil and still didn't die. Do you think their death had a purpose other than martyrdom?"

Alisa chimed in next. "Yeah. A week or so after I got saved, I started questioning all of this stuff; whether or not it was real. Then I heard Pastor Earl talk about how all the apostles were killed. Most were beheaded or crucified; the same people who were cowering behind locked doors after Jesus was killed. Suddenly, they were willing to die horrific deaths because they wouldn't deny the fact that Jesus came back to life. For me, that was the deciding argument that his resurrection has to be real. Very few people will die for the truth, but who would be willing to die for a lie? Certainly not all of the apostles.

"I'm sorry, guys. I'm with Danny on this one. I hate to walk away as much as anyone, but he's right. This is a trap and whatever that kid's situation is, we can't help him."

Steven lowered his head. "I understand. Can you draw me a map?"

Danny exhaled deeply. "I wish I could change your mind about this. You don't need a map. Just keep following this road for about another five or six miles. You'll cross a creek, then there will be a middle school on your right. After that, it's the next farm on the right. Just stay on Route 22."

Dana looked at Alisa. "Can you take Puddin'?"

"Dana, you can't do this." Alisa stood with her arms crossed.

"I have too. I respect your decision. You have to respect mine."

Danny was disgusted with this situation. "You guys are going to need two bikes so the boy can ride the handlebars. If Alisa rides on mine, we can't carry the cat."

Steven dug some extra shotgun ammunition out of the bottom of his pack. "We'll be okay with one bike. We can walk six miles."

Alisa began crying and hugged Dana. "Be safe. If there's trouble, just run. I'll take Puddin' to Nana's."

Dana hugged her back. "Thank you. We'll be safe."

Steven soon had his gear positioned. "Dana, we'll ride up to the car where the boy is. Then we'll get off. You put the little boy on the handlebars and start riding and I'll be walking behind you with the shotgun to make sure no one gives us any trouble until we get back across the tracks."

Dana hopped on the handlebars. "Sounds good. Let's go get him."

Danny watched as his friends rode back toward town. "Come on, let's get everything stashed in the back of the woods beside the tracks."

Alisa followed him. "What are we going to do?"

"We're going to follow Steven at a distance. If he gets in trouble, we can at least lay down cover fire."

Alisa dropped her pack near her bike. "Wouldn't this have worked better if you'd told him beforehand?"

Danny pulled the AK out of the pack and unfolded the stock. "Maybe, but then it would be like I was agreeing with the mission in the first place. I kept hoping he'd back out. I am still with him. Here, take the Glock and the extra magazines. If people start shooting, just keep firing and changing the magazines. Don't worry about hitting anything. Just keep them from coming out in the open. That will give me a chance to see where they are. When they pop their heads up, I'll be able to take a shot with the rifle."

Alisa took the Glock and tucked the extra magazines in various pockets. "Ready when you are."

Danny led the way, sprinting with the rifle in his hands and being careful not to slip on the ice. He passed through the backyards of the houses on the right to stay out of view from the location of the abandoned car. St. Paul Street ran behind the houses and the businesses, parallel to Route 22. Danny and Alisa followed it to a narrow opening between the buildings nearest to the abandoned car with the child in it. Danny motioned for her to stay low.

Danny arrived at the position just in time to hear someone call out to Dana and Steven.

"Drop your bike, your bags and your weapons, and go back the way you came."

Danny shook his head. He turned to look at Alisa and whispered. "Are you ready?"

She held the gun with both hands. "Ready as I can be."

Steven called back to the voice that came from cover. "We can't do that. We're going to take the boy to a safe place and we'll be on our way. We don't want any trouble."

Danny watched as Dana opened the car door to get the child.

The small boy, who looked to be five or six screamed when she tried to take his hand. "Daddy! Help me! Daddy!"

A shot rang out and Steven dropped to the ground with a yelp.

Danny saw the head of the shooter on the roof across from them. He took a shot and the man dropped backwards.

Two other men ran out from behind the building, shooting toward the passage where Danny was crouched down.

"Back up! Back up!" Danny pushed Alisa out of the passage and around to the back of the building. He led the way around the building to Route 22 in an effort to flank the ambushers. Alisa was close behind him.

He looked around the corner in time to see

Steven lying in the road with Dana at his side. One of the attackers was going for Steven's shotgun which was laying on the road about ten feet away from him. Danny took aim and shot at the man. He missed and the man ducked. The attacker returned fire with a large revolver.

Danny took cover behind the wall of the building while the man fired three more shots in his direction. Danny peeped back around to see the man bent over the shotgun and picking it up. He had just enough time to take aim before the man raised back up. When he did, Danny fired three shots close together and the man folded over, on top of the shotgun.

The little boy was screaming, Steven was laying in the road with Dana over top of him crying. Still, he forced himself to turn and check to see that Alisa was okay. Once he confirmed she was still behind him, he quickly turned back around to locate the other gunman, who was now picking up Steven's bike and riding away. Danny hesitated to pull the trigger and cringed at shooting the fleeing man in the back.

Alisa noticed that he wasn't firing. "Danny, we really need that bike. It might be the difference in life and death."

Danny took a deep breath and fired. The shot missed as did the next three. The man rode farther and farther from Danny's range, but he couldn't help but wonder if he'd subconsciously missed on purpose. He knew they needed the bike, but he didn't know if he was willing to kill over it.

"Stay here. If you see anyone, start shooting. I'm

going to check on Steven."

"Okay." Alisa took Danny's place at the corner of the building.

Danny knelt beside his friend. "Where are you hit?"

"My shin and calf. I think it hit the bone. It hurts like heck."

The child was still screaming. Danny turned to Dana. "Take the boy around the corner with Alisa."

Dana complied.

Danny looked at the bloody mess on Steven's lower leg. "Think you can stand up?"

"No way."

Danny looked around. "We have to get you out of this area. We don't know if that other guy is coming back or if there are other people around."

"Sorry, man. You were right. We should have left it alone."

"I don't know. Obviously this kid's dad was a real piece of work if he was using his own son for bait. Maybe the boy will live because of what you did."

"Or because of what you did. Thanks for sticking around." Steven's face showed his immense pain.

"Hang on. I'll be right back." Danny ran back to the corner where Alisa, Dana and the screaming child were waiting. "Dana, grab the shotgun and take the kid back to the tracks. Alisa, I'll carry Steven by the arms. You try to hold his good leg and prop his bad leg on top of your shoulder. We have to move him before we all get killed."

Dana picked up the little boy, stopped to grab the shotgun, then began walking briskly back toward the tracks. Danny slung the rifle across his back and led Alisa over to Steven.

Danny removed Steven's backpack and put it on himself. They picked him up as planned and he let out a horrible yell.

"Sorry, buddy. We have to get you out of here." Danny moved backwards as smoothly as he could.

They made it one block and Alisa said, "I'm losing my grip. We need to reposition his leg."

They sat him down and Danny asked. "If we fireman carry you, can you hop on one leg?"

Alisa looked compassionately at Steven. "It will hurt you a lot less if you can."

Steven nodded, his face wrenched with agony.

Danny grabbed one arm and Alisa the other. They picked him up and he yelped again.

Danny felt his friend go limp just before they reached the tracks. "Just keep dragging him."

"He's not conscious, Danny. We have to stop and see if he's alright."

"Nope. We have to get him to cover first. Then we'll help him." Danny kept moving.

Finally, they reached the woods on the side of the tracks. Danny looked at Dana who was rocking the crying boy. "You have to find a way to shut him up. He's going to get us all killed."

Dana took the screaming child to the woods. "Hey! Hey! Do you want to see my kitty cat?"

Danny removed the pack and laid Steven out in the grass. Next, he retrieved his first aid kit from his pack. He took out the EMT shears and cut the material off Steven's pants and away from his leg. He opened the compression bandage and wrapped it tightly to keep pressure on the wound.

Alisa watched. "Is that going to stop the bleeding?"

"I don't know." Danny stuck his finger against Steven's throat to make sure he still had a pulse. It was weak, but it was a pulse.

"He's alive?"

"Yeah. He probably passed out from loss of blood or pain." Danny stood and peered around the corner of the shrubs to see if they were being pursued yet.

Alisa stayed by Steven. "Should we try to wake him?"

Danny turned back around. "It's probably better if we let him rest. We'll have to figure out a way to get him to Nana's"

Dana came back carrying the little boy who had stopped screaming long enough to eat a granola bar. "Is Steven going to be okay?"

"I hope so." Danny looked at the young child.

"This is James." Dana held the boy securely.

"Hi James. I'm Danny."

James turned away from him. "You killed my daddy. I hate you!"

Alisa walked around to look at the boy. "Where's your mommy?"

"On a boat with her boyfriend."

"They went to the lake? Does your mom's boyfriend have a boat? Have you seen it?"

"No. The big boat. She was going for one week on the big boat, but she never came home. She took me to daddy's house and said she would come back in one week to get me. Then daddy ran out of food and beer at his house."

Alisa looked at Danny. "She probably went on a cruise."

"Out of Charleston, most likely." Danny thought for a moment. "Did your mommy fly on a plane or go in the car?"

James buried his head in Dana's neck.

Alisa gave Danny a sympathetic look. "James, how did your mommy get to the big boat?"

"Michael's car."

"And Michael is mommy's boyfriend?" Alisa gently stroked his hair.

"Yeah." James tore open the granola bar wrapper in search of the crumbs which he meticulously picked out and ate.

"Are you still hungry?" Dana asked.

He nodded.

Dana put the boy down. "Want some potato soup and crackers?"

He nodded again.

Dana dug a pull-top can of potato soup from Steven's backpack and opened it. She found a spoon and handed it to James who made no fuss over the soup being cold.

Dana dug out a package of crackers. "When was the last time you ate?"

"Yesterday, when I woke up. After the lights got turned off at daddy's, him, Carl and Todd went to the store with their guns and got some beer and food. That didn't last very long. Monday, they went back to get more, but nothing was left."

Steven's eyes were open and he was listening to the little boy, but he didn't speak.

Dana smiled at Steven and put her hand on his cheek. "You going to be okay?"

A faint smile came across his face and he gave a slight nod.

"Good. I prayed that God would keep you alive." Dana's eyes welled up with tears.

"You want some water, buddy?" Danny poured a cup from the jug and held it to Steven's lips.

Steven sipped the water then looked at the can of soup in the child's hand.

Dana made the connection. "I think there's a can of beef stew in there. Would you like it warmed up?"

Steven gave another faint nod.

Danny retrieved the folding stove and a can of Sterno while Dana found the stew.

Alisa gave some water to James. "Do you have any other family that live around here? Grandma and grandpa maybe?"

He shook his head. "They live in Oklahoma. It's far."

Alisa looked at Danny. "Should we leave a note at his mother's in case she comes back?"

Danny stirred the stew. "Anyone could find that note, including Todd or Carl or whoever that was on Steven's bike. Besides, we have to get Steven to Nana's. We can't be running all over town looking for his mom's house."

"So, we'll take James to Nana's with us." She spoke low so James wouldn't hear the conversation.

Danny shrugged. "I guess so. Even if the ship was out of range of the EMP and it made it back to port, the odds of his mother making her way home are pretty slim."

Alisa held Danny's hand. "We probably saved his life, you know. His dad was well into the desperate phase. He would have either gotten James killed or he would have eventually starved to death."

Danny sighed. "Thanks. I wish I felt better about it. Right now, all I can think about is that I killed his dad, the one person that little boy had in the world."

After Steven ate his stew, he fell asleep for a while. The others ate some of the remaining cans of ready-to-eat food. While they were eating, they deliberated over a plan to get Steven home.

Dana scraped the sauce from the side of her can of ravioli with a spoon. "Maybe he'll be strong enough to ride the handlebars when he wakes up."

Danny finished chewing a bite of canned chicken and dumplings. "I'll be very surprised if he is."

Alisa was eating the final can of Spaghetti Os. "Could we build a stretcher out of something? It might take a while, but we could carry a stretcher for six miles if we have to."

Danny looked at the saplings lining the railroad tracks and considered what other materials could be used to fashion a stretcher. "Maybe, I don't know. We've only got a few more hours of daylight. I really wish we could get him home fast. We have to get his wounds cleaned up soon, or he's going to get a bad infection."

"Should you guys pray? Maybe God will help us." Dana's voice was somewhere between desperate and hopeful.

Danny knew it didn't really work like that, but he

wasn't about to admit that to Dana. "Sure. Let's all hold hands and go around and ask God to help us get Steven home. I'll start."

Alisa, Dana and Danny held hands and formed a small circle.

Danny bowed his head. "God, we could really use your help right now. I pray that you will give us the wisdom and the strength to figure out a way to get Steven home safely and that you'll help his leg heal and not get infected."

Alisa said a short prayer next. "Lord, you know that Steven was trying to help James when he got hurt. Please help him. Thank you for keeping us all alive and show us the way to get Steven home."

Dana looked up to heaven. "God, you probably don't know who I am; I mean I haven't really talked to you much before. I know I said that if you would keep Steven alive, I would believe in you. I'll keep my end of the bargain. You kept him alive so far. Thanks for that. But, he needs to get to Danny's grandmother's house so we can get his leg cleaned up. Otherwise, he's going to die and I really love him. We need a miracle right now. I know you don't owe me a thing . . ." Her voice cracked and she started crying. She sniffed and continued with the prayer. "But if you'll do this one thing for me, I'll never doubt you. I promise."

Danny quickly wiped the single tear from his own cheek before anyone saw it. He was surprised by the faith of Dana, an unbeliever, and at the same time, somewhat ashamed of his own lack of faith. He decided that he would do whatever he could to help get Steven home. "Amen."

The girls looked up and hugged each other.

Danny quickly found the wire saw from his pack and picked out two sturdy straight saplings along the tracks. He cut down the first one and instructed Alisa and Dana to start removing the limbs with a knife.

He had just begun sawing the second when he heard a vehicle approaching. He coiled the wire saw and dashed back to the others. "Get down! Someone is coming!"

Danny grabbed the AK and lay prone in the grass. Alisa pulled out the Glock and took cover behind a tree.

Dana grabbed James, put her hand over his mouth and softly said, "Shhhh."

The vehicle came closer from the same direction as the shootout. As it slowed to cross the railroad tracks, Danny could make out that it was an old pickup truck. He lay still, hoping that the driver would continue on and not look their way.

That didn't happen. The truck came to a complete stop and the driver rolled down the window.

Danny put his thumb on the safety to double check that the rifle was set to fire. He held his breath and took aim.

"Say Boy! Ain't you Miss Jennie's grandbaby?"

Alisa stuck her head out from behind the tree. "Catfish?"

"Yeah, come on out here. What y'all a doin' over there in them bushes? Don't you know Miss Jennie's been worried somethin' fierce over you?" Catfish crossed the tracks and pulled to the side of the road.

Danny slowly got up, pushed up the safety and slung the rifle over his shoulder. He ran his hand over his head as he processed what was happening. "Hey, Catfish. We got in a little trouble. My friend was shot in the leg."

Catfish opened the door of the truck. The oxidized hinges squeaked and the sound of bits of rust dropping inside the door could be heard when he slammed it shut. He tugged the front straps of his overalls and adjusted his cap. "Well let's get him in the truck and get him out to Miss Jennie 'fore his leg rots off."

"Yeah, okay." Danny couldn't believe what was happening. He looked at Dana who was beaming with a smile that stretched from one ear to the other. He wasn't sure if she'd really expected a miracle, but he could tell she knew one when she saw it.

They carefully loaded Steven into the back of the truck.

"Don't worry about getting' blood on the tarp. It's old anyhow. I got a load of field corn under the tarp. I swapped out one of my hogs for the corn, ya see. Might not be too comfortable to sit on, but we'll be to the farm in a jiff." Catfish smoothed out a place for Steven's leg. "Let's get the rest of your effects and get goin'. Miss Jennie'll be happy as pig in a peach orchard when she lays eyes on y'all."

Danny stacked the two remaining bikes on top of each other in the bed of the truck.

Dana pulled out the comforter and covered Steven. "I'll ride back here with him."

"You ride up front. I'll stay with him." Danny

arranged the packs in the truck bed.

Catfish smiled, revealing his less than perfect, tobacco stained teeth. "That purdy little girl can ride up front, next to me."

Dana rolled her eyes at Danny. "I insist."

Danny chuckled and shrugged at Catfish. "She wants to ride in the back."

"Suit yourself." Catfish got in and started the engine.

Danny and Alisa sat up front with James in her lap. Puddin' was in the carrier on the passenger's side floor board.

Danny silently thanked God for sending Catfish and asked him to forgive his lack of faith.

"I been keepin' an eye out for ya. Miss Jennie said y'all would be along directly. Course, that was four days ago."

Alisa looked over. "We can't tell you how grateful we are for the ride. It's been a long, tough trip."

"And she's okay? Nana, I mean?" Danny asked.

"She's finer than frog's hair. I don't believe Miss Jennie ever did get used to havin' a mess of wires runnin' all through the house. She'd just assumed there never was no 'lectricity to begin with." Catfish chuckled. "She'll miss watchin' her stories on the television though. Don't you tell her I said that. I'll deny it 'til I die."

Danny wasn't sure he knew what Catfish was refereeing to. "Your secret is safe with me."

Ten minutes later, they pulled up the long gravel driveway to the house that sat several hundred feet off of the road. Catfish tapped his horn twice and

Rusty came barking and wagging his tail.

Nana stepped out on the porch. "Where y'all been? Did ya stop by Flardy on the way here?"

Danny got out and went straight to helping Steven out of the truck. "It was a rough journey, but we made it."

Nana immediately saw his leg. "I'll put some blankets on the couch and draw some hot water. Get them nasty bandages off of him."

Soon, they were in the house and Nana was cleaning Steven's leg.

Steven yelped in pain.

Nana stood. "I'll be right back." She soon returned with a pint of whiskey. "Lisa, run out there on the back porch and get him a can of Coke. I don't know whether he'll be able to get this down."

Alisa looked surprised to see Nana holding a bottle of whiskey but she didn't address it. "Yes, ma'am."

Nana waited for the Coke, then fed a sip of whiskey followed by a sip of Coke to Steven. She repeated the operation several times until Steven seemed significantly more relaxed. Then, she proceeded to clean out his leg. "Looks like buckshot. Three holes going in, but only two coming out. I'm going to have to find that other piece." She poured a bit of the whiskey directly in the wound.

Steven winced, but was obviously feeling much less pain than before.

Everyone watched as Nana probed with a pair of tweezers until she'd found and extracted the last ball of buckshot. Next, she soaked the wound with iodine and wrapped it tightly with clean strips from an old white sheet. "We'll have to keep these changed out."

Danny saw Nana's open Bible laying on top of a pillow at the side of the couch. "It's good to be home, Nana."

Nana had followed Danny's eyes. "The Spirit told me to get on my knees and start praying about two hours ago. I figure y'all was in a heap of trouble."

Danny hugged her. "We were."

She kissed him on the head. "Ya'll get cleaned up. I'll take care of this mess and get some vittles goin'. You can tell me all about it over supper."

Nana boiled water, on her gas stove, for everyone to use in getting cleaned up. She made a big meal of homemade vegetable soup from her garden, cornbread and fried apple pies.

Danny introduced everyone and gave an abbreviated account of the journey, and a highly sanitized version of how they came to have James with them.

Nana picked at her food, but was more concerned that everyone else had enough to eat. "Now, Dena, you're Steven's little girlfriend ain't you?"

"It's Dana, and no, we're just friends."

Alisa winked and whispered to Dana. "You'll get used to it."

Nana sipped a cup of coffee. "The way y'all was a dancing at the weddin', it sure looked like you was purdy good friends."

Dana blushed and kept her head down.

Danny was embarrassed for her, but he also

enjoyed watching people squirm under Nana's sometimes, less-than-polished comments.

"Well, I'll tell y'all like I told these two before they got hitched. If I catch y'all messin' around in my house, one of yous will have to sleep in the barn from here on out."

Dana didn't have to look up for Danny to see her face was now blood red.

She let her hair hang in her face. "Yes, ma'am."

"And who's cat is that in there in the bag?"

Dana's voice became very soft. "Mine, ma'am."

"I thought I was done with havin' cats in the house after Howard died. He had cats in here eatin' off the table. Feeding them ice cream; had me fixin' eggs for 'em. My goodness!"

"She won't be any trouble. She can even stay in the barn if that would be better," Dana pleaded.

Nana walked into the living room and came back carrying Puddin' in her arms like a baby. "This cat wouldn't last five minutes out there in the barn. Sure ain't no account for catchin' a mouse. Look at her, she's spoiled. I recon you might as well keep her in the house."

Dana's face lit up with joy. "Thank you!"

Nana petted Puddin'. "You're spoiled rotten ain't you. Let's see if we can't find you some condensed milk."

Catfish laughed. "If that cat wasn't spoiled when she got here, she sure will be now."

Danny cleared the table and followed Nana into the kitchen. He sat the dishes in the sink. "I don't guess you've heard anything from Cami."

"She'll be along directly. That Nick is a smart

boy. He'll get them home safe." Nana found a dish for the cat and poured out some condensed milk from a can. "I see the girls are taking after that little boy in there."

"Yeah. I guess I ended up bringing more people out to the farm than I originally intended."

"They ain't no problem. There's going to be a lot to do around here. We can use every extra pair of hands we can get. But that little boy, you killed his pa. I know you did what you had to do. But he'll carry a vengeance in his heart and in his head. He might kill you when he gets old enough. Wouldn't do neither one of you no good to keep him around here. You best let Catfish carry him on over to some other folks that can care for him. There's some folks from church that have got a farm down Route 91. I'll ask him if he'll take the boy on out there."

"Okay." Danny knew Dana and Alisa would be disappointed, but Nana's reasoning was sound. He knew it would be tough for James to heal if he had to see the face of his father's killer every day.

After dinner, James left with Catfish. Danny checked on Steven who was sound asleep on the couch. Next, he brought in some more wood to place next to the old potbelly stove, then got ready for bed.

Nana finished getting Dana set up in the other guest room, then came to Danny and Alisa's bedroom to kiss Danny goodnight. "I know y'all have had a real bad time. I'll let everybody sleep in tomorrow, but just this once."

"Thanks Nana." Danny hugged her.

"Goodnight, Nana." Alisa hugged her, then

closed the door behind her.

She turned and smiled at Danny. "We made it! We're in a warm house with a comfortable bed, with food, and safety and . . ."

"Each other." Danny grabbed her and kissed her.

She gave him a long passionate kiss then pushed him back. "And each other. I love you Danny Walker."

He pulled her back close. "And I love you Lisa Walker."

"Ha ha." She pushed him back. "But seriously. Stay on your side of the bed tonight. I'm still traumatized about sleeping with you at Nana's"

He got in the bed and winked. "Okay. But just this once."

Soon they were sound asleep.

"Danny! Danny, wake up!" Alisa's voice grew sharper and more clear. "Danny. Are you awake? Danny!"

He felt her shaking him and opened his eyes. His heart was pounding, and he could taste the salt from his sweat running off of his head and into his mouth. He sat up and clamored for his flashlight on the night stand, knocking his watch onto the floor. He clicked on the flashlight. He took a deep breath and let it back out. "I'm awake."

The flashlight showed that her face was full of fear as she clasped his free hand in hers. "Another dream?"

He took off his damp tee-shirt and wiped the perspiration from his face. "Yeah."

Thank you for reading
***Seven Cows, Ugly and Gaunt, Book One:
Behold Darkness and Sorrow***

Amazon reviews are the best way to help get the book noticed. If you enjoyed reading it, please take a moment to leave a five-star review on Amazon. If you don't feel the book quite measured up, drop me an e-mail at **prepperrecon@gmail.com** and let me know how I can make future books better.

Keep watch for
***Seven Cows, Ugly and Gaunt, Book Two:
Ichabod***

You may also like my previous fiction series,
The Days of Noah

In ***Book One: Conspiracy***, The founding precepts of America have been destroyed by a conspiracy that dates back hundreds of years. The signs can no longer be ignored and Noah Parker is forced to prepare for the cataclysmic period of financial and political upheaval ahead.

Watch through the eyes of Noah as a global empire takes shape, ancient writings are fulfilled and the last days fall upon the once great, United States of America.

Stay tuned to **PrepperRecon.com** for the latest news about my upcoming books, and great interviews on the Prepper Recon Podcast.

33918541R00208

Made in the USA
Middletown, DE
01 August 2016